And Then He Pressed Play

Track One

Robert J. Halliwell

To everyone who was told their love was wrong.
It wasn't.

Content Warning

This book contains:

Violence and hate speech against 2SLGBTQIA+ characters
Hospital scenes
Drinking
Panic
Teens who swear like punctuation

I promise you, hate will never win in my books.

Hey everybody, it's A.J. here.

So, I made a lot of mistakes in the first few weeks of my exchange program (even after that if I'm being honest), but I thought I could pass along some of the things I learned so you don't make some of the same mistakes.

I love Ireland and so many of the people I met on my program, but believe me when I say, if you see an Irish word and think you know how it's pronounced, you're probably wrong. So, here's a little cheat sheet to help you out.

Orlaith: OR-lah

Aoife: EE-fa

Cian: KEE-an

Tadhg: TIE-g(like tiger with no er)

Niamh: NEEV

Niall: NILE(like the river)

Áine: AHN-ya(like in Buffy!)

Cathal: KA-hil/KA-hal but said quickly (isn't lenition fun?)

Sliotar: SHLIT-er (it's spelled like a Pokémon isn't it?)

Craic: CRACK(Can be used as a greeting, also means fun, a good time.)

One of the great things about most of the Irish people I met is, if you make a mistake they won't hold it against you as long as you learn from it. . . They will slag you for it, but that just means they like you. Usually.

I hope this helps! Have fun in Glenbridge.

1

Save me!

The chorus to "Bring Me to Life" rang in A.J.'s ears as he leaned against the damp, moss-covered wall at the far end of Glenbridge Secondary School. Even though the volume on his whirring Discman was cranked to the highest setting, it wasn't enough to drown out the absolute bedlam that roiled around him. He'd thought his eleven years of attending school had shown him all the shades of feral guys came in, but standing to face the churning sea of testosterone before him, those years of experience all but melted away.

He couldn't say for sure whether it was the fact Glenbridge had no girls to act as a buffer, or if his new classmates just didn't come with volume knobs. Whatever the reason, he was doubting the wisdom of signing up for the exchange program with each passing second.

The main attraction stood at the end of the yard farthest from his wall. At least twenty guys, ranging throughout all the grades by the looks of them, were playing some sort of game A.J. had never seen before. Everyone carried strips of wood that looked like a cross between stubby hockey sticks and baseball bats. As far as he could tell, the goal was to balance, hit, or otherwise carry the baseball-sized

1

ball from one end of the field to the other and get it past the goalie, all while being as loud as possible.

Separate from this unknown sport, groups of students stood in clusters throughout the yard. This wasn't much different from what he was used to at first glance, but on closer inspection, each group was in a state of constant motion. Guys were speaking with their hands, elbowing their friends or slapping each other on the back with every other word. They seemed to communicate exclusively by shouting, with accents that A.J. had trouble understanding—even without the music thudding in his skull.

There didn't seem to be another quiet person for him to approach. Not one other guy off on his own, reading a book, listening to music, or acting like they hadn't downed about five cans of Monster.

A.J. rolled his shoulders, and the fabric of his uniform bit into his neck. He'd thought by making sure his clothes were in pristine condition before setting out that morning, he was applying a layer of camouflage. A uniform made things easier—or at least it should have.

To his dismay, it looked like everyone else had shredded the handout without looking at it. Shirts were rumpled, sleeves were rolled up, and despite the leaflet's mention of neutral footwear, he spotted more than a few pairs of brightly coloured Nikes milling about.

In the brief lull between songs, his eyes fell on one of the worst offenders of this near-universal breach of dress code. Flame-bright hair stuck out at every angle across his head, like he'd rolled out of bed and walked straight out the door. His blue and silver striped tie was so loose the knot thudded against his sternum whenever he was in motion—which seemed to be his default setting.

He laughed as he peeled back the top of a yogurt lid and flung it with a casual flick towards one of his friends. It landed with a good stick on the boy's breast pocket—right over the school crest.

A.J. was wondering how hard the first boy was going to get punched when the second one's lip twitched. He grabbed hold of the lid and, with surprising dexterity considering the size of him, flung it back at the first boy. It landed between his eyes with a splat that A.J. thought he heard above his music. The rest of the group exploded with laughter as the redhead peeled the lid off, still wearing his crooked smile.

Without warning, the yogurt-covered boy turned from his group to toss the lid towards a nearby trash can. A.J.'s eyes darted away and came to rest on a patch of clover. Had the other boy seen him staring? Classes hadn't even started yet, and he was already acting like a friendless loser.

He *was* a friendless loser.

His fingers found the dial of his Discman again, yearning to crank the volume up past its limits.

He'd all but decided to cut his losses and head inside early when he heard it. The sound of a muffled voice, far too close to be there by accident.

Shit.

A.J. let his eyes linger on the clover before dragging his gaze upward. Sure enough, there stood the boy from before.

A stray streak of pinkish yogurt clung to his fire-spun eyebrows where the lid had landed. Tiny beads of moisture glistened on his pale skin, shining among the freckles spread across the bridge of his sharp nose. It was impossible to tell whether it was sweat or not. If A.J. had learned one thing about Ireland in the two weeks he'd been

3

there, it was that the humidity never dropped below chicken noodle soup.

A.J. fumbled with the dial while the other boy's head tilted to the side, like he was trying to figure out the plot of a show he'd dropped into mid-season. With his music humming instead of roaring, A.J. shifted his gaze to meet the boy's hazel eyes.

"What?"

The word came out sharp. He ducked his head.

To A.J.'s relief, the other boy didn't seem to mind being barked at, and turned back to his friends.

"Mickie, you langer! You owe me a Red Bull! He's not a feckin' mannequin!"

There was a whoop of laughter from the group as a boy with sandy blond hair threw his hands up in mock frustration.

"What . . . ?" A.J. repeated, his brow furrowed.

The other boy turned back, smiling wide enough to show off every one of his slightly crooked teeth.

"The lads thought you were a mannequin, but I knew you weren't. Saw you puttin' somethin' in your pocket," the boy said, his voice rising and falling in a lyrical way the voices back home didn't.

"Oh . . . my Discman," A.J. said, pulling the thing out.

The other boy let out a low whistle, leaning forward as if to get a better look.

"Bit of a relic, yeah? Sound, though. I've a SanDisk somewhere. Keep losin' the damn thing." The corner of his mouth twitched. "Wanna trade? Would be pretty hard to lose that beast, even for me."

A.J.'s eyes flicked up to meet the other boy's long enough to notice the flecks of blue among the hazel, then settled somewhere around his chin.

"Oh, I uh, n—"

The other boy let out a barking laugh and clapped him on the back so hard it almost knocked his earphones out. "I'm just slaggin' you!" The boy gave A.J.'s shoulder a shake before pulling away. "Dunno where mine is to trade you, anyway."

He looked back at his friends and, when he saw they'd gone back to talking among themselves, shrugged.

"First day, yeah? Haven't seen you 'round here before. Name's Bren."

A.J.'s shoulders tensed, still tingling where Bren had slapped him. He knew guys like this back home—loud, charming, and impossible to read. Bren had given him no reason to be suspicious, but A.J. couldn't bring himself to trust the smile beneath that mop of messy hair.

"I'm A.J. and yeah, it's uh, my first day."

Bren's eyes narrowed. "Not from around here are you? America?"

A.J. took a breath. "Canada, actually."

Bren's face lit up like a firework, his eyes gleaming. "Canada?! Go 'way! That's mad. Do you live off maple syrup and fight polar bears for fun?"

A.J. repressed the urge to take a step back from Bren. Loud as he'd been before, he was now near a full roar, lit up with delight over the novelty. A.J. blinked stupidly as his brain lurched into overdrive. Was Bren being serious? Or was he expecting him to just laugh it off?

"We don't—I mean they're up n—and I—" What little confidence he was managing evaporated as Bren tilted his head. A.J.'s mouth snapped shut as a squeak left his throat.

The silence stretched on, growing heavier with each second. A.J. willed himself to say something—anything—to make it go away. Bren's smile flickered as A.J.'s eyes found the patch of clover between them again.

"Somethin' down there?" Bren's voice came, sounding less genial than before.

Before he could attempt a reply, a ringing tenor burst out from the direction of Bren's friends.

"Hey, Bren! Robot's same as mannequin! If he's got an antenna, I don't owe you shite!"

A.J. was dimly aware of the snort of laughter that erupted from Bren as his thumb cranked the volume on his Discman back to max. A look at the bemused expression on Bren's face told A.J. he'd noticed the returning roar of music.

His stomach churned as Bren spared him a final confused look before heading back to his friends at a trot. A.J. didn't need to hear what they were saying to know what they were talking about now.

2

Everyone was too busy bellowing at each other after a summer apart to notice A.J.'s burning cheeks as he made his way across the room. It didn't bode well for his odds of finding a friend among the shouting, but it came with a perk nonetheless—all the good real estate was open. He picked out a desk three rows back, next to the windows. If it worked in Canada, he was sure it would work in Ireland.

A chorus of scraping metal rose from the back row as a trio slammed into their seats. One of them waved across the room and shouted something that sounded like "cock-jockey," which somehow no one paid any mind.

Woe to the shy boy naïve enough to think the back row was a good place to hide out.

A.J. took his time unpacking things in an effort to keep himself from looking too lost, sliding his notebook and pens around the surface of his desk for a while before tucking his backpack under the seat. He straightened up to face the whiteboard and his heart fell when he saw the teacher hadn't appeared in that time. Bren had though, volume still set to max as he jabbered on about licking a jellyfish to impress a girl he met at the beach over the summer.

"Couldn't feel me tongue for a week after. Swear to god, like."

Bren seemed too consumed with holding court to notice who was behind him as he sat on the edge of his desk. Thank goodness for minor miracles.

"And that was the only action your pasty arse saw all summer."

Everyone laughed again, though a moment later, Bren lunged forward and pulled Mickie into a headlock. Bren's desk scraped against the grubby linoleum as they grappled, Mickie's face getting redder despite the smile.

This at least felt familiar to A.J. It was comforting in a way. No matter the corner of the world, guys were weird and quick to beat each other up.

He was mulling over the idea of which one of them might win in an actual fight when a middle-aged man wearing a worn suit and an even more exhausted expression trudged into the classroom. He hadn't reached his desk before he brought his hand to his face, thumb and index finger pinching together like he was fighting off a migraine.

"What ye two get up to in your own time is your business, but hands off in class, so." Bren gave Mickie's head another twist and Mickie took a half-hearted swing at his kidneys before they separated, still grinning like idiots. "Right, now that O'Shea and Walsh have hold of their shared brain cell, sit your arses down."

His voice came out in a low rasp that might have sounded more intimidating if not for the lilt of his accent. He waited for everyone to sit before turning to the whiteboard, briefcase dropping beside him with the dull thud of habit.

"Unfortunately for me, a lot of ye know this already, but I'm Mr. Kelleher." He wrote his name on the board in long, lazy strokes. "Even worse, I know most of ye. Anyway, I've ye for form this year.

Just remember, lads, fifth year's your dry run for certs, at least try to take it serious, so."

He slid a piece of paper off his desk, his free hand rubbing at his salt and pepper stubble. A.J.'s shoulders tensed as Mr. Kelleher's eyebrows raised towards the end of the list.

Please don't, thought A.J. as Mr. Kelleher opened his mouth.

"O'Shea, necktie goes around your neck. It's right there in the name y'wee eejit."

A.J. breathed a sigh of relief and made a mental note to thank whoever the patron saint of socially aware teachers was. Bren grumbled but pulled his tie tight.

"Alright, since it's the first day, we're gonna do roll a little different. Gonna start over here"—he pointed to the guy sitting in front of Bren—"and go down the line. When it's your turn, stand up and say your name and one mad thing about yourself."

The look on his face told A.J. he was second-guessing that already.

"Remember where we are. This is school, not the GAA."

Sweat broke out across the back of A.J.'s neck so fast you'd think it'd started raining. Everyone had to know each other already. This could only be for his benefit.

He heard the first guy grunt out his name and something to do with his "scrambler" before his ears shut off. What was he going to say? Saying he was from Canada felt like putting a target on his back. But, if he didn't, people would find out sooner or later. Then he'd be that weirdo who tried to pass as Irish—instant mortal enemy.

To A.J.'s relief, Bren took his turn to launch into a long-winded story about how his great-great-granddad was related to someone important that A.J. had never heard of. He recognized the hallmarks of someone who was trying to waste the class's time so they wouldn't get to any actual work. Maybe extroverts had their uses after all.

When Bren's soliloquy was stretching to the point that people started murmuring, Mr. Kelleher let out an annoyed grunt and waved his hand. Bren sat down and twisted around in his chair. From the look on his face, A.J. was sure Bren hadn't realized who was sitting behind him before then.

A.J. took a deep breath and, after a pause that only stretched slightly too long, stood up.

"Hi, my name's A.J. Walker, I'm from Canada and . . ."

His mind went blank as he realized there wasn't anything interesting about him. Heart hammering out of his chest, his mouth opened before he could stop it.

"And I don't fight polar bears."

He stood rigid as snickers rippled through the room and heat bloomed in his cheeks for the second time that morning as he unstuck his frozen legs enough to sit down.

By the time his ears had stopped ringing Mickie was saying he'd jumped into the River Glen last winter after losing a bet. Judging by the snort from Bren, A.J. didn't have much trouble guessing who'd put him up to it.

He was thankful to the boy. It seemed like the class had moved on from his polar bear moment, even if he'd be seeing it in his nightmares for at least a month.

By the time they were rounding the last of his classmates, A.J. had names for the last two members of Bren's group. The lanky guy with close-cropped hair and a slightly baleful expression was Rory. His family had gone to the Louvre with some of his relatives from Nigeria over the summer, and said the Mona Lisa "looked right tiny" in person.

A few desks later, and the wall of a guy Bren had pelted with the yogurt lid introduced himself as Brick—which no one questioned.

He added that he got his deadlift up to 150 kilos, and a couple of guys wolf-whistled.

A.J. couldn't help but notice how different most of his classmates sounded from each other. Bren and Mickie had a tendency to rush their words and drop their H's. Brick spoke much more slowly, but his D's all came out soft, and his R's hard. Then there was Rory, who, for some reason, sounded like Brick if he were narrating a BBC documentary.

It was all very strange. Back home, outside of the occasional Francophone or Hutterite, everyone sounded more or less the same—vaguely Canadian.

A.J. was almost enjoying himself by the time the last guy stood up. He had buzzed hair, a square jaw, and a pronounced brow that made it look like he was stuck pre-scowl. When he stood up, his chest puffed out like he was getting ready for a fight.

"I'm Cian," he looked around the room, not smiling. "And I'm the reason there aren't any bears in Ireland."

Deadpan. Back to his seat.

A few people chuckled, but there was a glint in Cian's eyes that made A.J.'s shoulders tense. He'd caught the same look on guys back home. It was never a sign of good things.

"Alright, now we've all had a bit of a laugh, let's get the boring bits out of the way."

Mr. Kelleher listed off the flow for the school year, along with the rules they were expected to follow if they wanted to remain enrolled at Glenbridge.

Smoking at school was grounds for suspension on the first offence, yes, even if you were having a rough day. Classes followed a rotating schedule through the week: compulsory subjects mixed in with their electives. He made a point of repeating how important it was to treat this year as a test run for their certs. From what A.J. gathered from his exchange paperwork, the certs were like the SATs on steroids, but weren't until the end of next year—not his problem.

All in all, it wasn't so different from what he was used to.

"Right, you'll need your schedules then," Mr. Kelleher said and began rummaging around in his briefcase.

In the momentary distraction, Bren's hand appeared over his shoulder and dropped a piece of folded paper on A.J.'s desk without looking back. A.J. stared at the white triangle for a full ten seconds before he unfolded it.

A sigh left him before he could stop it. It was a doodle of a robot with gears for eyes, and an antenna sticking out of the top of its square head. The robot's body was shaped like a Discman, with the play button taking up most of its chest.

Beneath this doodle were the words "ROBOT LAD—PRESS PLAY TO ACTIVATE," while off in the corner was something that looked like a giant dog with a circle and a slash through it.

He was wondering why Bren thought he had a beef with dogs when it clicked. The dog was a bear, and Robot Lad didn't fight bears.

A.J. stared at the back of Bren's head. A muscle in his neck twitched like he was trying to resist the urge to look back. A.J. folded the paper into a neat square and slipped it into his bag. If Bren was looking for a big reaction, A.J. was determined to make sure he wound up disappointed.

Mr. Kelleher set a stack of papers on the desk at the front of A.J.'s row.

"Since I'm such a sound guy, I got your schedules all organized for ye. Take one and pass them back. If ye plan on losing them, at least try and memorize them first." He repeated this with the other rows until the room was full of the sound of shuffling papers.

A.J. had to wonder if Bren ever stopped grinning as he turned around to pass on the small stack of schedules. Their eyes met, and Bren winked before turning back around, his fingers drumming against the desk.

What the hell was that?

A.J. brushed the thought away. He'd save trying to figure Bren O'Shea out for a time when he wanted a headache.

***

A.J. stood with one foot still in the music prefab after everyone else had funneled out for lunch. The odds of Mrs. Doherty following the rest of the class out were looking slim as she pulled a lunch box from one of her desk drawers. Plunking out a song or two on the baby grand at the front of the room would have to wait.

Most of the class was still making its way towards the school. If he joined them, they'd probably lead him to the cafeteria, but then what? The only person he was even on a first-name basis with was Bren, and there was no way he'd be sitting *there*.

He could always ask if he was allowed to eat in here. He'd probably have more in common with Mrs. Doherty than most of his classmates. When she'd announced that most of the term would be spent on theory and composition, nearly everyone had groaned. But A.J. was actually looking forward to figuring out how to write an entire piece on his own. The jingles he'd noodled out here and there with his dad's help hardly seemed to count.

His stomach growled at the thought of the ham sandwich waiting in his lunchbox, and he took a couple of steps towards the school. What if he just forced himself to walk into the lunchroom and sit down? It wasn't like he'd never made a friend before.

His arm froze as he reached out to pull open the door that led back into the school. He was standing up in front of the class again, trying to be normal and blurting out that he didn't punch bears in his free time. He let the door ease back into place and turned on his heel.

Oh well. At least he'd have plenty of time to work on that assignment.

***

"Christ above, how many days 'til the hols?"

Bren shouldered his way into the last empty seat at the dodgy plastic table. He ripped his tie up over his head and crammed it into his bookbag with deliberate force.

"Maths, politics, and history all in one morning. Say hi to Monday for the next eighteen weeks, lad," Mickie groaned, taking a bite of cold sausage roll.

"Eighteen weeks? Christ."

Bren unwrapped his sandwich and shoved a handful of crisps between the slices of white bread.

"Halloween before that," Rory said.

"Thank fuck for that. Already sick of this place."

He popped a stray crisp into his mouth then wiped his fingers on his trousers.

"Anyone seen Canada since history?"

Mickie shrugged. "Hell if I know. Why?"

Bren mirrored him, "I'm wonderin' what Canadian lads eat for lunch."

"Maple syrup?" Brick offered.

"Well, yeah, but, like, on what?"

A chuckle rippled through the group.

"He's in my music class," Rory said, as if there hadn't been an interruption.

"He play giant fuckin' violin, too?"

It had been years since Rory had reacted to Bren referring to his cello like that, but he still enjoyed doing it anyway.

"Don't think so. Saw him staring over at the piano."

"Makes sense. He seemed a bit fancy, like."

Bren had been trying to find the right word for the lad all morning, and that was the closest he'd been able to get to a satisfying answer.

"You mean weird," Mickie said, picking at a spot on his chin. "He's off. Doesn't talk, hardly moves—like somethin' out of Doctor Who. And what the hell was up with that polar bear bit?"

"I think he was trying to be funny," Rory said.

"He was bein' weird."

"Lay off," Bren said, grabbing the Red Bull from what remained of Mickie's lunch. "Give the lad a couple days to adjust. He's probably just confused livin' somewhere that isn't a big block of ice."

"I still think he might be a robot," Mickie muttered, eyes narrowing as Bren chugged half the Red Bull.

Bren snorted and punched Mickie's shoulder.

"Your tears just make it taste better. Keep it up."

A new round of chuckles rippled through the group. Even Mickie joined in. Bren laughed right along with them—but he couldn't help wondering what Robot Lad actually ate for lunch.

16

3

A.J. found himself alone when he wandered into the Home Ec room five minutes before the bell. The ghost of warm bread filled his lungs as he slung his bag around one of the blue plastic chairs that sat four apiece along a series of rectangular tables. His heart lightened at the thought of a class where he'd be able to keep his hands busy—even if it meant talking more.

He didn't have time to take his things out of his backpack before others started drifting in from the hallway. He wasn't sure if it was because Home Ec appealed to a specific crowd, or that lunch was weighing everyone down, but the guys in this class seemed more subdued.

By the time the class was half full, only one of the newcomers had opted to sit at A.J.'s table. He had short black hair gelled into a crunchy-looking fauxhawk above an expression that didn't seem too intimidating.

Might as well give it a shot.

"Hey, I'm A—"

"Liam! Didn't know y'were takin' Home Ec, you muppet!"

A.J. would have slid under the table and through the floor if he could have. There was Bren, face alight with its latest smirk, striding across the room toward the seat between him and Liam.

He plunked down between them and let his bag fall to the floor. Before Liam could reply, Bren nodded in A.J.'s direction.

"Thought it might've been a typo or somethin' when I saw Home Ec on your timetable. Guess even Robolad needs food, too."

A.J.'s eye twitched in an echo of memory. So that was what the wink had been about. When Bren homed in on something, he didn't let it go. A.J. hoped his focus would shift somewhere else before the day was over.

The bell had barely finished chiming when in walked their teacher. He was a big bear of a man, already clad in a flour-stained apron. The lights gleamed against the top of his bald head as he took his place behind his desk.

"Right lads, good to see so many of you back this year." He ran a hand through his gingery beard with an expression that put A.J. in mind of a classmate more than a teacher. "Looks like we got some newcomers, too. I'm Mr. Twomey, and it's my job to make sure you don't live off sausage rolls and spaghetti hoops once you're done with school."

He consulted the sheet of paper he'd pulled off his desk and ran a finger through the air across the rows of tables.

"Here's what we're gonna do since you're already in groups."

A.J.'s eyes darted around the room. Sure enough, every table held three or four guys, which meant . . .

"We're gonna start off with a little team bake. We're just shy of two hours, so get to know your brothers in flour, and come up with something together."

With no further instruction, Mr. Twomey unlocked the pantry and sat down at his desk.

Bren wasted no time in launching into his ideas, which included battered and fried Jaffa Cakes and "bread pudding but with Tayto on top."

"I could fry some Jaffa Cakes," Liam said, his voice deeper than A.J. had expected. "But crisps on bread pudding sounds fuckin' rotten."

A grunt came from behind Mr. Twomey's desk.

"Sorry, feckin'."

"That's the lad."

Bren jostled Liam by the shoulder before ploughing on. "It could work. Sweet and salty, balanced like."

The two bickered back and forth, not paying A.J. any mind. Between the chatter around them and the thickness of their accents, A.J. wasn't sure he understood more than every third word. He was pretty sure Bren had doubled down on his crisp angle when he stopped mid-sentence, and perked up like a dog that had caught scent of something interesting.

"Sorry, Robolad. Almost forgot about you. What do y'reckon we should do?"

A.J.'s stomach lurched at the casual way Bren used the demeaning nickname, but he forced himself to keep his face neutral.

"Whatever's good with me."

Bren's expression fell. "Come on! You're from Canada. You've gotta have some mad desserts over there."

Sure that refusing would only add fuel to Bren's fire, A.J. racked his brain.

"What about Nanaimo Bars?"

"Told you, didn't I? Sounds mad already."

"What are they?" Liam asked.

A.J. balked. They were so ubiquitous back home, he'd never considered they weren't a thing over here.

"It's a sort of . . . dessert bar, usually a Christmas thing, in my family anyway," A.J. said, picking at the seam of his slacks. "It's uh, coconut chocolate cookie—I mean biscuit, with custard frosting and then melted chocolate on top?"

Liam made a face like A.J. had uttered some kind of unholy edict, but Bren was grinning.

"That's the most words I heard y'say since I met you, and they sound feckin' delicious! That's what we're makin'!"

A.J. didn't have time to protest before Bren leapt up and made a beeline towards the pantry.

"Gobshite don't even know what he's lookin' for," Liam sighed, sounding resigned. "You know all the ingredients?"

"Yeah . . ." A.J. said, nodding, "But I don't know the measurements by heart."

"Nanaimo Bars, yeah? You keep that one from grabbing anything too mad, and I'll go print off a recipe."

And just like that, A.J. was on babysitting duty. From across the room, Bren exited the pantry holding a can of Bird's in one hand and a bag of powdered sugar in the other. He stared at the two ingredients for a moment before laughing and, to A.J.'s dismay, waved him over with a casual "What else?".

After a few awkward minutes of enduring Bren's stream-of-consciousness solo, the rest of the bake went better than A.J. had expected.

He'd been sure he and Liam would be spending the majority of their energy keeping Bren in check. To his surprise, Bren got quieter than A.J. had ever seen him once they got going. And while he scorched the first batch of chocolate, Bren had double-checked, more than once, whether they were making the silly little dessert right.

When the last layer of chocolate had turned mirror smooth, Bren handed A.J. a knife and waited as he cut squares. Bren was the first to dive for a piece and looked at the treat in his hand like it was a precious gift.

"Right, in we go!"

Before A.J. could stop him, Bren crammed the entire thing into his mouth, cheeks puffed out like a ginger chipmunk. He watched as Bren's expression went from wide-eyed excitement to . . . something less pleased. He swallowed with an exaggerated gulp and thumped his chest with his fist.

"Christ on a bike, Robolad! You tryin' to knock me teeth out?"

"Did we feck it up?" Liam asked, eyeing the tray.

A.J. took a bite of his own square. Coconut, sweet custard icing, and thick, snappy chocolate. It tasted like home.

"They taste fine to me."

"Christ, lad, you eat these to keep warm, like? Can already feel the sugar. Heart's goin' a mile a minute." A.J. didn't have time to respond before Bren grabbed the tray and rushed over to one of the other workstations, Liam following in his wake. "Conor! Jordo! Try these and tell me they're not the sweetest thing y'ever put in your feckin' mouth."

A.J. turned away as a guy with close-cropped hair made a comment about Bren putting things in his mouth. A second later, dual cries erupted from that side of the room.

He should have known. He was just the punchline to another of Bren's jokes. Weird Canadian guy likes weird Canadian food.

A.J. set to washing the dishes, doing his best to focus on the sound of clattering measuring cups in the frothy sea. Another burst of laughter rang out from behind him. A.J. clenched his jaw and scrubbed harder, the warmth of the water not quite reaching his hands.

22

4

By the time school let out, the clouds had parted enough for bits of blue sky to break through the grey. Bren brought his arms over his head and popped his neck, doing his best to shake the day from his shoulders.

"We doin' anythin'?" he asked the group at large, Mickie, Brick, and Rory walking in lazy strides beside him.

"Can't, GAA," Brick said, patting the duffle slung across his shoulder.

Mickie rolled his eyes.

"Gotta get Cara from juniors."

"Gonna stop by the chipper, you can come."

Bren laughed, cuffing Rory's shoulder. "Unless you plan on payin' and tellin' me I'm pretty, I'll pass."

They reached the end of the schoolyard amid the sound of shuffling shoes.

"See ya."

"Alright."

Gravel crunched beneath Bren's feet as he strolled along the road that would take him to the outskirts of town. The smell of diesel made his nose wrinkle as he passed a crooked row of cars on his left. He slipped off his tie and slid the damp fabric through his fingers as he walked. As far as first days went, this one had been pretty entertaining. The usual crew had all been there—familiar faces he'd known since primary school. Then there was the new lad.

Bren turned at the next corner, thinking hard. How many times was he supposed to talk to the guy before he warmed up? He couldn't help but wonder if that wasn't how they built them in Canada. Cold country, cold people.

As if the thought had summoned him, Bren saw Robolad wandering halfway up the street with his hands hidden in his pockets, shoulders slumped. Nobody he knew walked like that. At least not anymore.

He thought back to the first day Rory had shown up at school. Barely ten years old and looking like he might blow away if a stiff breeze came by. It hadn't been until they'd been sent to get the telly for one of the rare class movie days that Rory even said enough for Bren to clock that he was English.

Maybe that was it. Robolad didn't get on with crowds.

One more try then.

If he was still bristling in a crowd of two—well, that was his answer.

Bren broke into a jog, making it through the crosswalk between them as the light turned red. A.J. let out a yelp and twitched away from the hand Bren had used to clap him on the back.

He was only a couple centimeters shorter than Bren, but it felt like a stiff breeze might do him in too.

"Hey, Robolad. Live this way too? Small world."

His eyes narrowed as the music ringing off his headphones grew quieter. "Yeah, up there."

He gestured vaguely down the street before he started walking again.

Christ, lad. Give me something to work with.

They walked in silence past another four shops before Bren decided A.J. wasn't going to say anything else.

"It's A.J., yeah? What's that short for?"

A.J. eyed him like he didn't know what to make of the question.

"Uh, is it private or something?"

A.J. shook his head. "It's not short for anything. It's just my name."

Bren nodded. Better not push the lad.

"So, any craic lined up?" he asked once he'd confirmed the music hadn't made a return.

A.J. stopped again, brow furrowed like Bren had shoved one of his gym socks under his nose.

"Crack?"

Now it was Bren's turn to frown. "Yeah, y'know—like—anythin' mad? Fun? You know what fun is, right?"

"Oh . . . I thought you were asking if I had drugs."

Bren laughed, short and barking. The confused expression reappeared on A.J.'s face.

Wait. That wasn't a joke?

"Nah, no drugs, lad . . . Just, anythin' fun?"

He shrugged.

"Not really."

No smile, not even eye contact.

"Cop on. First day in Ireland and you're not doin' anythin' with it?" Bren asked, trying hard not to sound too offended.

"I've been here for two weeks."

"Oh." Bren laughed at himself. "Yeah, it'd be mad if you got off the plane first day of term."

"I'd have pretty bad jet lag."

25

Bren's lip twitched.

Ok, that one had to be a joke.

They walked on. The street was silent apart from their footsteps and the sounds of another group chattering off in the distance.

"Like Ireland so far?"

There was a good lag before he replied.

"It's beautiful. Wet, though."

Bren was glad he didn't shrug this time. He didn't think whatever this was could survive a swift kick to the arse.

"Yeah, that's Ireland. Sorry, you're not gonna be proper dry 'til you're back in Canada."

Bren thought he heard A.J. start to reply as a trio of girls strolled out from a side street. One of them was sipping from a large red and yellow coffee cup, while the other two gobbed on at full volume like they weren't standing two feet apart.

He didn't recognize any of them, but their maroon jumpers told him they went to Crossgroves. To be a fly on the wall over there on sports day . . .

They didn't pay them any mind as they passed, but Robolad's head turned to follow them.

Not a glance. Not a peek. A proper gawk.

The corner of Bren's mouth rose. "Ah, so which one caught your eye?"

"What?" A.J. asked, snapping away from the gaggle.

Bren jerked his head back at them.

"Come on, lad, I saw that look. So which one? The blonde? Can't say I blame you." He raised his hands in front of his chest, like he was trying to manage a pair of overlarge water balloons.

"It looked like she had Timmies for a second."

"Had what?" Bren asked, his hands falling back to his sides.

"Tim Hortons. It's coffee back home."

Bren's brain short-circuited. "So you were staring at her . . . cups?" he offered, trying to bring the conversation back to a place that made sense.

"I guess."

A.J. looked back down the street even though the girls were long gone.

"They're the first girls I've seen all day. It's weird."

Something clicked into place in Bren's mind.

"Oh, Canada's big on mixed schools, right?"

A.J. nodded.

"How do you get anythin' done?"

He shrugged.

Bren sighed.

The two of them walked in silence for the longest time yet. They stopped at the fork in the road at the very edge of town. Not much but fields and farms if they kept going. Despite himself, Bren gave a half-smile.

"Gonna be mad if you're going right, too. Might know the folks you're stayin' with."

Robolad shook his head and nodded to the left.

"I'm over there."

Bren's smile vanished.

"Oh, right—well, see ya tomorrow," Bren said, heading right.

There was a soft grunt, then the faint murmur of music as they parted ways. Bren thrust his hands into his pockets and let out a low whistle. He could imagine the lad strolling up to one of those beasts on the hill—the kind that could hold his entire house in its living room.

27

He shrugged as he let the gate clatter shut behind him, grabbing a couple of stray raspberries from the bush that bordered the bungalow's walls. At least he had his answer. Robolad wasn't shy—he was posh. Probably upset his exchange sent him to Glenbridge instead of Dublin.

He pushed the door open and popped a raspberry in his mouth as the smell of turf smoke hit him.

No sense in thinking about it anymore.

5

Even though it wasn't raining, A.J.'s shirt clung to his chest the moment he stepped outside. The morning sun was struggling to peek from behind a veil of hazy clouds that drooped down too close to the earth for his liking. It looked like Bren was right. He'd have to make peace with being soggy around the edges until he got back to Canada.

Canada . . . a strange feeling bloomed in his chest at the thought of home.

It wasn't that he was ready to throw in the towel after less than a month abroad, but what he wouldn't give to be walking towards Peacock Collegiate rather than Glenbridge Secondary.

He turned up the volume on his Discman as "The Wizard and I" reached its crescendo—Elphaba belting her heart out while his own rested somewhere in the pit of his stomach. Inspiring as the song was, it just wasn't him. He'd tried to rise to the challenge of the exchange program, and so far, he'd done nothing but fail.

"Just be normal today, ok?" he mumbled to himself as he pulled open the wrought iron gate at the edge of the front lawn.

He tugged at the sleeve of his uniform, hoping it looked casually disheveled now—even though he'd spent the last ten minutes rumpling it up. The clean lines of his crisp uniform had put a target on his back yesterday, he knew that now. He hoped that it wasn't too late to take it down.

A.J. paused towards the end of the block and forced himself to take in a deep breath. The scent of rain and something green mingled with the faintest trace of smoke coming from down the hill. It was strange, the view of the town from up here. To his left were shockingly green fields and rolling hills stretching as far as the eye could see. To his right, clusters of houses and stores grew denser as they got closer to the center of town. He couldn't put his finger on it, but something about the scene made the tightness in his chest loosen.

He turned away from the view and headed down the gentle slope with as much bounce as he could manage.

Today was going to be different.

When he rounded the last curve before the fork in the road, A.J.'s breath caught.

Bren was strolling up from the opposite end with the kind of easy-going stride he'd been working so hard to emulate. With the second deep breath of the morning, A.J. quickened his pace and caught up.

"Good morning."

His voice came out stiffer than he'd intended, but it was a definite improvement from yesterday. Bren nodded without looking over.

"Mornin'."

The tone caught A.J. off guard. It wasn't cold, but compared to the other day . . . maybe he was a slow riser? Well, if things were going to be different today, then he should be the one to start a conversation.

It was much easier said than done.

Anxious knot in his stomach aside, what did he know about Bren? He didn't think "Hey, you're the loudest person I've met on two continents" would go over all that well. There had to be something else—

"So, you like baking?"

A.J.'s insides withered as Bren first looked offended, then like he might laugh, and not in his usual way.

"It's an easy pass for certs."

"Oh. Those are a really big deal, right? Teachers keep on mentioning them."

"Whole life leads up to 'em over here, so yeah, big deal."

A.J. recognized the dismissal in Bren's tone and thought of the headphones hung around his neck.

Maybe they just needed a new topic.

"Hey, have you ever seen the view from up on the hill?"

Bren raised an eyebrow but didn't say anything.

"I guess you probably have. It's just—I never really looked until this morning. It's crazy how green everything is. Like something out of a postcard."

A sneer played at the corner of Bren's mouth as he shook his head.

"That why you came here? Rollin' hills and thatched cottages?" He gestured to the drab grey buildings that rose on either side of them. "Bit of a letdown, like?"

A.J. couldn't tell if he was imagining the edge in Bren's voice or not, but his heart sped up anyway.

"What? No. I mean, I knew you had normal buildings and stuff, too. It would be like . . . thinking Canada is all igloos and cabins."

"Isn't it?" Bren replied, a trace of humour in his words.

A.J. snorted, then blushed a second later.

"I mean, we have them, but no one lives full-time in igloos. They're for hunting trips and stuff."

He knew he was talking too much, that it was probably making Bren uncomfortable, but he couldn't stop.

"My family has a cabin at a lake, but it's just for summers."

Bren's smile twitched again, though A.J. was sure he saw him roll his eyes.

They were in the town proper now, so at least there were other sounds to fill the uneasy silence between them, but A.J.'s hand twitched towards his Discman nonetheless. Maybe something on low?

The chorus of "Every Time We Touch" was on its third repeat when Bren spoke up next.

"What's with the uniform today? Butler take the day off?"

A.J. furrowed his brow. The family he was staying with was pretty well off, but they weren't butler-rich or anything.

"What? I don't have a—"

A.J.'s sentence was cut short when Bren lurched to the right and slammed his shoulder into A.J.'s. It hadn't been forceful, but caught off guard, A.J. stumbled and had to flail his arms to stop from falling over.

There was a lurching tug as his headphones were yanked out of his ears, then the sound of plastic clattering against concrete. He looked down in time to see his Discman bounce once against the pavement; the cover popping open and the mixed CD flying out in a flash of silver. It skidded and bounced across the sidewalk, coming to rest label side up.

A.J. shuffled forward like a sleepwalker, a dull ringing in his ears now. The gaudy Sharpie doodles left by his friends looked woefully out of place against the speckled grey of the concrete. "Good luck,

A.J.!", "We'll miss you!", "Bring me back a leprechaun!" Stupid little signatures that vied for space with the "A.J.'s Big Ass Exchange Mix" plastered across the top half.

He could still see Nat when she handed him the thing, clad in its jewel-bright case. She'd tried to play it off as casual, but between gathering everyone's songs—likely giving her computer at least three kinds of malware in the process—and passing it around for everyone to sign, the effort hadn't been lost on anyone.

A.J. scooped up the CD like it was a wounded animal. He turned the shining disc over in his hands and stifled a cry. An angry scratch ran about a quarter of the way towards the center of the disc.

To A.J.'s horror, a lump rose in his throat.

"Shit, it get scratched?"

A.J. turned around to take the Discman off the ground, his eyes low to hide the burning wetness that was forming despite his best efforts.

"Wha—oh, come on. I didn't hit you that hard."

The ringing in A.J.'s ears grew louder. He had enough time to close the silver player around the disc before something broke.

He snapped his head up, eyes fixed on Bren.

"What the hell is wrong with you?!"

Bren looked like A.J. had slapped him but recovered in an instant.

"What? It was an accident. Calm down."

A sound that was caught somewhere between a snort and a scoff forced its way out of A.J.

"Seriously?! Was it a fucking accident that you've been on my case the second you saw me?!"

Bren's face was burning now, too, though his eyes were free of tears. He opened his mouth to argue back, but A.J. beat him to it.

"Like, holy shit, dude—I'm weird! I get it! But I didn't ask for any of this! You could have just left me the fuck alone!"

A.J.'s voice cracked from the force behind the words. His head spun. Everything was too sharp, too real—from the scratch of his clothes against his skin to the damp, urban scent invading his nose. He spared one last burning look at Bren before turning on his heel and storming off, so far beyond caring where he was going.

6

The jagged stub of Bren's pencil smacked against his desk with a dull thunk. A sigh escaped him as he brushed the snapped graphite onto the floor. He crossed the room and jammed the splintered end into the sharpener.

Three periods in, and he couldn't get the look on A.J.'s face out of his head. He'd been crying—full on crying like someone told him his mam had died. Bren didn't know if it was about the CD or the shoulder check, but either way, it had been a hell of an overreaction. The lad had a right to his feelings, but that didn't mean he had to go tearing up over something so stupid.

Bren flopped back into his chair and pulled himself close to the desk with a loud screech. Miss Murphy paused long enough to throw him a dirty look, then plowed right on with her monologue about the term's syllabus.

Who the fuck cries over a CD player?

It would be a lot easier to get A.J. out of his head if they didn't have near-identical timetables. Turns out, when the weird new kid misses his second day of class, people talk. Every whisper added an extra layer to the iron ball rooted in the pit of Bren's stomach.

The lad was right. He should have just left him the fuck alone.

***

It was a relief to get out of the quiet of class and settle into the rowdy energy of the canteen. Mickie had already finished the first half of his sandwich, while Brick was gnawing away at a drumstick like a Great Dane in trousers. Cian sat beside Mickie but was leaning in towards his own group.

Bren thudded down next to Rory and fished the Red Bull out of his backpack. A crack of the can and the taste of taurine later, and he was ready to put the morning behind him.

"Fuckin' hell, I was prayin' Miss Murphy was gonna retire over the summer. You see that look she gave me?"

A series of half-hearted groans rippled through the group.

"I think you need to be human to retire," Rory said, though his eyes were bright.

A round of laughter this time.

Bren took a bite of sandwich and let his thoughts relax.

"Speakin' of non-humans, where do y'think Canada's run off to?" Mickie asked through a mouthful of apple.

"Mitching?" Brick asked.

Mickie snorted, "Not with that stick up his arse."

"Why are you thinking about his arse?" Rory asked, his voice neutral.

"Oh, fuck off!" Mickie said, the tips of his ears going red as he threw his crumpled sandwich wrapper at Rory. "You know what I fuckin' meant."

Cian, who had apparently been eavesdropping, leaned in.

"Thinking you might wanna pull the stick out for him there, Micko? Bet he'd give you a little kiss if you do it right."

Cian's table snorted with laughter as Mickie punched Cian in the arm with a hasty "Piss off."

Bren joined in with the laughter because Mickie looked so cross, but he couldn't ignore the way his chest tensed. Even if A.J. were gay, what did it matter? The lad kept to himself, and it wasn't like him being that way would hurt anyone.

He thought about telling Cian to ease up, but pushed the idea aside. He barely knew A.J. and wasn't about to go fighting his battles.

So why did part of him want to?

7

Bren didn't see A.J. again until first period the next day. He walked in seconds before the bell rang, his eyes fixed on his trainers. He'd swapped his bulky headphones for a pair of earbuds that stayed in even after Mr. Regan told everyone to shut up. It didn't last long.

When his name was called for roll, Mr. Regan tapped one ear. A. J., who'd kept his eyes down and muttered "here," missed it entirely.

"Walker, I don't know how it is in Canada, but this is maths, not a study period. Earphones out or you're going to lose them."

Snickers rippled through the class, and properly scarlet, A.J . shoved the earphones down the front of his shirt. Without another word, Mr. Regan turned round and started scribbling equations on the board.

For once, Bren gave maths his full attention.

***

"Whoa, rough mornin', darlin'?" Mickie asked, face done up in an over-the-top pout as Bren flung himself into the seat beside him.

"Fuck off."

38

"What's wrong with this one today?" Mickie asked as Rory took the space opposite them.

Rory looked Bren over and shrugged. "No one likes Wednesdays."

"Don't remind me," Mickie said, pulling out a crumpled square of tinfoil. "Three more days of shite before the weekend."

Bren was too busy with his own thoughts to follow the conversation from there. It was beyond stupid how much of his attention the whole A.J. thing was taking. Worse, it was obvious enough that *Mickie* had picked up on it.

"Gotta hit the jacks."

Mickie and Brick were too busy chewing to notice or care. Rory tilted his head, but didn't say anything. Hands thrust into his pockets, Bren stormed out of the canteen. It was time to put this shite to bed.

***

Bren swore under his breath as he skulked off the ramp that led to the music prefab. After twenty minutes of looking everywhere else, he'd been sure he'd find A.J. there. Something about the locked door and darkened windows told him he was wrong.

He brushed the scattered droplets from his shoulder with a huff. In typical soft day fashion, it had been drizzling on and off since classes started, so it didn't seem likely A.J. would be outside. But Bren was running out of places to check. He'd make one loop around the school, and if he didn't find him, he'd have to give up and try to catch him after class.

He rounded the corner towards the back, where an old storage shed stood next to one of the more interesting features of the school—a foundation of bricks beneath wooden beams and dingy glass that needed washing about five years ago. Bren always wondered why the school didn't take better care of the greenhouse; the thing had been half-falling apart since before his first year. Shoddy as it was, the biology unit they'd spent growing plants in it had been one of his favourites overall.

He was about to pass it by when he noticed one of the windows hanging open by about an inch. Sometimes lads snuck smokes in there to avoid getting spotted by the few teachers who could be bothered to enforce the rule. It was worth a look at least.

The sweetish scent of decaying plants filled Bren's nose the second he stepped inside. He ran his fingers along an empty planter bed as he walked toward the farthest of the two aisles.

Fucking finally.

A.J. was lying on the floor between the planters with his head propped on his backpack and earbuds ringing. Bren watched as, eyes shut, A.J. brought a lone sandwich-half to his mouth. Even though he'd spent the better part of lunch tracking him down, Bren wondered if maybe he shouldn't leave the lad alone. He wasn't smiling, but he looked way more relaxed than Bren had ever seen him. The first class after lunch was Home Ec, though, and the thought of sitting next to him with this stupid misunderstanding hanging between them was making his neck sweat.

Taking no special care to keep quiet, Bren strode over to A.J. and tapped his foot with the tip of his trainer. A.J. let out a strangled gasp that might have contained words as he sat bolt upright. Bren jumped back, holding his hands up.

"Shit, didn't mean to—Fuck! Sorry, that was stupid."

A.J.'s brows knit together, and he leaned to the side, like he was trying to check if someone was hiding in the aisle. Bren looked over his shoulder to double check. No one else was there. When he turned back, A.J.'s expression had softened.

"Bit of a weird place to eat lunch, yeah?" He sniffed at the air. "Smells better than the canteen, I guess."

A.J. didn't crack a smile, just raised an eyebrow like he wasn't sure if Bren was being serious or not.

Bren sighed, then kicked at one of the dirt-caked floorboards.

"So look, it's like . . ." His words hung in the air. He'd been so caught up in making sure this got settled that he hadn't given any thought on how they were going to do it. At least A.J. had turned down his music—that was a start. "I was just tryin' to be friendly like. Y'get that, right?"

A.J.'s lips narrowed to a fine line as his eyes fixed somewhere around Bren's sternum. This time, it looked like he was trying to look through him.

"You were . . . weren't you? Fuck."

Now it was Bren's turn to frown. "Why'd you think I wasn't? Christ, I was bein' proper friendly, like."

"You and your friends were . . ." A.J. sat up straighter, his eyes fixed off to the side of where Bren was standing. "Laughing."

"And laughing's a hate crime in Canada or somethin'?"

"You weren't laughing . . . at me?"

And just like that, it clicked. Every failed joke. Every time A.J. had started to say something but looked away. Fuck, he'd thought it was weird that he didn't come over to hand out the rest of the Nanaimo Bars.

"What? You barely said enough to laugh at."

"I don't fight polar bears," A.J. countered.

Bren suppressed a snort. "Fair enough. That was funny."

Some of the tension seemed to leave the air, though the knot was still coiled in Bren's chest. He stared down at the Discman beside A.J.

"Still works?"

A.J. shrugged. "Only lost tracks one and two. I'll survive."

"Fuck, I'm sorry. I was just messin' around. Didn't mean to hit you that hard."

A.J. shook his head. "I shouldn't have blown up. That wasn't about you."

A.J. looked up at Bren, who had felt his eyebrows raise despite himself.

"It wasn't *all* about you."

Bren let out a sigh and slid to the ground opposite A.J., hands coming to rest on the damp earth.

A handful of raindrops burst against the roof in a scattered chorus to break the silence. Bren was about to speak when something bounced off his chest and landed in his lap. He pulled up a snack-sized candy bar, bright yellow with red lettering that read "Coffee Crisp."

"This payback for the shoulder check? Coulda bruised me. Arm like that and all."

A.J.'s expression quivered, but he pressed on.

"I'm sorry. I'm not usually so—I mean, I AM, but, it's," A.J. laughed and gave his head a shake. "It's just, this is a lot. Everyone I know is literally an ocean away and it's like, everything here is kind of the same but different. Like, everyone speaks English, but when you guys get going, I can hardly understand you some of the time." A.J. forced out a long exhale like he was literally letting off steam. "And it doesn't help that like, half of you are just, stupid hot."

Bren hoped it didn't show, but the knot had reappeared in his chest, and with a few extra twists at that. So there it was, right out in the open. He didn't want to think what some of the other lads might do if they got word of that.

Bren let out a low whistle.

"Whoa, when you talk, you really do it proper like."

For the first time, A.J.'s eyes locked onto Bren's. He held his gaze with his eyes narrowed like he was checking for something. Bren wasn't sure if he found what he was looking for, but his face relaxed and he looked away. "Sorry I—"

Bren shook his head. "Nah, better than tryin' to guess what you're thinkin' at least." A smile pulled at the corners of his mouth before reality pulled it back down. "So you fancy . . ."

"Guys?" A.J. finished, sounding almost bored. "Despite my best efforts to reprogram myself? Yup, gay as they come."

The uneven pitter-patter above filled the latest silence that stretched between them.

"So, us Irish lads are 'stupid hot', huh?" Bren asked, trying hard not to sound too amused.

"I think it might be the uniforms."

"Yeah? Like a lad in a tie, do you?"

A.J. turned pink but didn't reply.

"So, who d'you got your eye on? Fuck, I'll light meself on fire if you say Mickie. He's got ears like feckin' satellite dishes."

A.J. let out a squeak and stared down at his sandwich.

"Wait . . . which half am I in?" Bren asked, giving a wink that A.J. couldn't see. "You got a thing for pasty gingers with crooked teeth?"

He pretended not to notice that A.J. wouldn't have looked out of place in a lobster tank and got to his feet. He slapped on his best attempt at a pouty smile and loosened his tie as he ran a hand through his hair, batting his lashes. "You might be onto somethin'. Reckon I could be a model if I had a mind to."

He bit one end of the Coffee Crisp wrapper and tore it in half, with a shake of his imaginary curls. Holding the bar between his thumb and index finger, he took a bite, his free hand resting on his chest.

A laugh rang through the greenhouse, so different from the huffs Bren was used to A.J. making.

"You're ridiculous."

Bren looked down and inhaled the remnants of the Coffee Crisp. A.J. was wearing the first proper smile Bren had seen on him. Wide and unbothered, it brought the laughter all the way to his eyes.

Bren sputtered as he tried to hack the shards of chocolate out of his lungs.

"Hey, you ok?" A.J. asked, getting to his feet.

Bren gave a thumbs up and continued to cough through streaming eyes. Choking to death on weird Canadian chocolate hadn't been a part of the plan, but he had to admit, he'd still take it over how he'd been feeling all morning.

The warning bell rang out over the grounds, and Bren forced himself to find his voice.

"R-right, H-home Ec, then?"

"Are you gonna make it?" A.J. asked like he was trying not to laugh.

"Not if you keep giving me danger disguised as sweets," Bren said, airway finally clear.

"No promises, man. I've got a whole box back home."

Bren let out a raspy laugh as they left the greenhouse. He was glad A.J. still looked pleased, but was thankful his smile had ebbed. The way his eyes had lit up . . . Bren wondered if that was something he could draw out of him again. Even if he couldn't, he thought he'd have a lot of fun trying.

8

The house was silent save for the strings of music pouring from the speakers that sat on either side of the monitor in the McCarthys' computer room. A.J. sat cross-legged in the plush wheelie chair as his foot bobbed along to Pink's "U + Ur hand." He was glad that Meredith and Niall's friends had invited them out for the night. He hadn't been able to let his music loose outside of his headphones since he'd got to Ireland.

At the pop of orange at the bottom of his screen, A.J. pulled up his conversation with Nat. They'd spent the last half hour discussing the merits of a Glenbridge to Moose Jaw super-subway system when she'd changed her status to AFK.

LittleMoshpitKid46: "Alright, back"

AJWalker90: "WB. Everything ok?"

LittleMoshpitKid46: "Yeah, rents wanted something. My mom says hi. Or, more accurately HIIIIIIIIIII AJJJJJJJJ!!!!"

AJWalker90: "Lol. Tell her HIIIIIIIII TAMMMYYYY!!!! back."

A.J. scrolled through his contacts as he waited for Nat's reply. The usual ones were all there, a familiar line of friends, family, and a few people he'd met online and never talked to anymore. It was the new addition to the list that kept pulling at his attention, though—Red-BullBren69.

Even though Bren had added him about an hour after school let out, they hadn't done much more than say hello. A.J. was still working up the nerve to try starting up an actual conversation when Bren said he was headed over to Mickie's to play the new FIFA game.

He hadn't told Nat about the scene in the greenhouse yet, and he wasn't sure why. He'd wasted no time in raging to her about him after the whole shoulder-checking incident, after all.

LittleMoshpitKid46: "She laughed"

The Bren-shaped bubble popped, and A.J. landed back in reality.

AJWalker90: "You just screamed that at her didn't you?"

LittleMoshpitKid46: "She was in the other room"

AJWalker90: "Some people would use their feet."

LittleMoshpitKid46: "Those people and I can't be friends"

The bubble rallied. Less than twenty-four hours ago, he had been sure that Nat and Bren would have gotten along like a pair of cats in a sack. Now, he was starting to wonder if Nat might wind up liking Bren better than him if she got the chance.

LittleMoshpitKid46: "Oh hey! I almost forgot!"

"I ran into your dad and Rudy down at Crescent Park the other day."

"His new cane's looking slick. Still hate that I can't pet Rudy when he's working though"

AJWalker90: "Dogs with jobs, gotta show them respect."

It was nice to know things were still chugging along back home. Dad going for walks whenever he was stuck on a song, Nat wanting to pet every dog she saw. Without meaning to, A.J. found himself wondering if Bren liked dogs, and then what breed he might be if he were one.

AJWalker90: "Hey so, jarring segue but . . . you remember that guy Bren?"

LittleMoshpitKid46: "The testosterone twat waffle who's been giving you shit? I'm familiar"

AJWalker90: "Yeah so . . . I guess he was actually being friendly the whole time. I think I was the dick, lol."

LittleMoshpitKid46: "This is the same guy that fucked up your CD right?"

AJWalker90: "Yeah, but he apologized, mostly. I think he's actually really nice."

"I told him I'm gay, and he was ok with it. Only like a 5% chance it's a Carrie at the prom kind of thing."

There was a significant lull before Nat's next message.

LittleMoshpitKid46: "Shit, well just be careful, ok? I don't want to fly across an ocean to throw hands, but I will if I need to"

AJWalker90: "Plane or broom?"

LittleMoshpitKid46: "Depends on what he does"

AJWalker90: "Lol. I don't think you'll have to bust out the broom."

A.J. held back a yawn and uncrossed his legs.

AJWalker90: "I gotta get to bed. I've got maths tomorrow. That damn S makes things a lot harder than regular math."

LittleMoshpitKid46: "<3 <3 <3 <3"

AJWalker90: "zzzzzz"

A.J. popped his CD out of the computer and shut it down. He stopped by the kitchen on the way to his room to dig a spoonful of cottage pie out of the casserole dish in the fridge. There was still enough left from dinner that he was going to have to take some for lunch. A hopeful thought bubbled up in A.J. as he made his way upstairs—maybe he wouldn't be eating alone tomorrow.

9

A.J. fiddled with the earphones in his pocket as he made his way down the hill. He already half-regretted his decision to leave them out of his ears as much as possible today. But he was determined to actually talk to people, and that wouldn't happen if he kept running to music.

A smile forced its way onto his face when he rounded the bend. Bren was leaning against the low stone wall by the fork in the road, like this was something they'd been doing for years.

When he saw A.J. his face broke into a grin, and he waved him over.

"There he is. Thought I was gonna have to go 'round the hill lookin' for you."

A.J. felt his brow furrow but caught himself.

"Sorry, didn't know you needed help walking to school."

His gut gave a funny lurch halfway through his reply. Bren's eyes grew wide as he let out a short, barking laugh.

"He's got jokes! Fuckin' love it!"

A smile crept across A.J.'s face. "Thanks for waiting, though. You didn't have to."

Bren laughed again. "Christ, givin' me whiplash. Don't need to get all formal."

A.J.'s cheeks grew warm, but he forced himself to nod and head down the path towards school. Bren followed at his side and A.J. let his shoulders relax. This was a lot easier than yesterday's walk.

"So you gonna talk once we get to school?"

A.J. took in a deep breath. "I'm gonna try."

"Talkin's good. Don't be afraid to throw whatever shite the lads give you right back, especially Mickie." He looked thoughtful, then added, "And stop runnin' off at lunch. Just sit down and say hi."

Despite his best efforts, a snort escaped A.J.

"What?" Bren asked, stopping to look at him.

"It's just, this is very Elphie and Glinda."

"Who?"

"Wicked?" A.J. asked, and when Bren stared back at him, pressed on. "Stephen Schwartz . . . ? I'm gonna make you pop-u-ler . . . lar?"

"This like, some kind of Canada thing?"

A.J. let out a sigh. "How the hell am I going to be friends with you?"

"You could start by telling me what the fuck you're talkin' about."

A.J. rummaged in his backpack and pulled out his CD binder. After flipping around, he found his copy of *Wicked* and swapped it into his Discman. Bren gave it an apprehensive look but took it all the same.

A.J. smiled when the opening strings of music burst out from the earphone dangling by Bren's chin. From the look on his face, A.J. guessed it was the first piece of Broadway to cross his path.

"Right," he said, "who's the wan tryin' to shatter glass?"

"That would be Miss Glinda Upland, and careful—I don't know how to throw a punch, but I'm sure I can figure it out."

Bren looked surprised but laughed anyway.

Five minutes and several high notes later, Bren handed A.J. back his Discman, looking like he was trying to work out a riddle.

"So that's the kind of music you're into?"

"Just be glad I didn't make you listen to *Cats*." Judging by the look he gave him, Bren thought he was talking about a recording of actual cats. "But I like lots of normal stuff, too. Cascada, Evanescence, Green Day."

"American Idiot!" Bren cried, sounding relieved to latch on to a world he understood.

"That's the one."

They kept talking music over the next ten minutes. A.J. made a mental note that if he was going to connect with Bren then starting with punk or rock was the way to go. Not his strong suit, but he was enough of a fan to hold his own.

He was having such an easy time talking now that he'd gotten going, he didn't notice at first when Bren slowed his pace.

"Hey, so, about the . . . likin' lads stuff."

It was clear that he'd been sitting on the words for a while. A.J. matched Bren's pace but didn't say anything.

"It doesn't bug me one bit, like. But some of the other lads can be real pricks about stuff like that. So maybe just keep it under your hat, yeah?"

A.J. pulled his leg back mid-step, rocking in place. He'd been pretty sure Bren was going to be the kind of guy who'd pretend that part of their conversation hadn't happened. Quiet acceptance, with maybe a touch of denial. This was something different. It sent a jolt through his stomach that chilled and warmed as one.

"I do have *some* self-preservation skills, man. I mean, I'm not going to deny it if anyone asks." He watched Bren's face for some kind of grimace, and found a smirk instead. "But it's not like I'm going to go around waving rainbow flags everywhere."

He allowed himself a smirk of his own.

"I left those in Canada anyway."

"Sound," Bren replied, though he didn't seem convinced.

By the time they reached school, Bren had reverted to his usual self and was chatting away about what he hoped they'd make in Home Ec this term. When they passed the gates, A.J.'s eyes did their usual sweep across the yard. It was the same as it had been all week. Guys, noise, and—

"Oh, come the fuck on!"

Bren's face scrunched up in mock offence. "You got something against éclairs?"

A.J. waved a hand towards the school. There was Rory, at one of the shoddy benches that bordered the field. He was just sitting there, reading by himself. Bren squinted like he was trying for extra credit on an eye exam.

"What am I lookin' at?"

"Rory," A.J. said, and when that didn't seem to cut it, he waved his hand again. "Do you know how hard I looked for like one quiet guy my first day?"

"Aww, look at ickle Rory, sittin' there all sensitive like," Bren replied, his accent morphing into a horrible London parody.

He bounded forward without another word, and after running his thumb along the Discman in his pocket, A.J. followed.

Bren sat down opposite Rory and snapped his book shut before tugging it out of his hands. "Oi! Watcha doin' being all gloomy and shite?"

A.J. hung back a few paces, suddenly aware of his arms and how stupid they looked dangling at his sides.

"Well, I *was* reading," Rory sighed and then nodded towards a group of guys kicking around a soccer ball. "Brick and Mickie are over there if you need to let off some steam."

"Can't, stopped 'round your place before I picked up this one," he said, jerking his thumb over his shoulder. "Your mam really wore me out."

A.J. was thinking about reaching for his earphones when Bren grinned back at him. "Crack on, Robolad," Bren said, sounding English again, "hurry up and say how do you do to the other quiet one."

A.J. forced himself to give something that he hoped resembled a smile and closed the distance between them.

"Hi, uh, I'm A.J.—oh, shit. I guess you already knew that." He let out a nervous laugh, then nodded towards the book in Rory's hand. "Is that any good?"

Rory's eyes met his, but for some reason, it didn't make him want to phase through to the earth's molten core.

With the usual impulse averted, A.J. wondered if Rory hadn't slept well last night, or if the bags were a permanent feature.

"Yeah, it's pretty good. Vampires, but it asks some big questions about morality and what makes up a society."

Bren let out a groan, head flopping to the side like he'd lost all the bones in his neck. "Why'd you gotta go and ruin vampires with philosophy? You know Buffy's right there on the telly, right?"

"You know there's moral questions in Buffy, too, right?" Rory asked.

"You're lookin' too deep. It's girls in leather kickin' monster arse."

"I'm with Rory, man. You're missing a lot of subtext," A.J. said, shaking his head as he shared a smug look with Rory.

Bren looked between them, eyes wide. "Aw shit, now there's two of 'em."

"No there's not. He's Rory, I'm A.J."

Bren groaned and let his head thud against the table.

"Do you wanna borrow this when I'm done?" Rory asked, ignoring the latest groan that left Bren.

"Sure! I won't dog-ear it or anything, either. I hate that."

Bren turned his head so that his cheek was smushed against the concrete table, not lifting it when he spoke. "Alright, can book club be done now? We got six hours of school for that shite."

Rory shrugged and put his book away. In the silence that followed, A.J.'s eyes fell on the group messing around with a soccer ball.

"Hey, what was that game those guys were playing on the first day? It was like, if field hockey and lacrosse had a baby."

Bren's head snapped up off the table, eyes gleaming. "That, Robolad, is the greatest feckin' sport on God's green earth. Sit down, shut your gob, and let me tell you about hurlin'."

10

A.J.'s stomach churned as he stood frozen in front of the canteen. Talking with Rory had been easy. He was quiet, sharp, and a little weird in a way that felt familiar to A.J. Brick and Mickie seemed like different beasts entirely—and not just because Brick looked like he could knock out a bull with one well-placed punch.

His thoughts wandered to the cool quiet of the greenhouse he'd come to call home over the past week. It took a great deal of effort to remind himself that he'd been excited about not eating lunch alone less than twelve hours ago. More than that, not showing up might upset Bren.

Without meaning to, his hand slipped into his pocket and tugged out one of his earphones. A comforting thought, but out of the question for now, at least.

Just be normal.

***

"I swear to God, Miss Murphy's out to get me. How come everyone else gets to write four thousand words and I've gotta do five?"

Mickie interrupted himself by downing half of his Club Lemon in one, wiping his mouth with the back of his hand as he slammed the bottle down.

"Miserable cow."

"Maybe try staying awake next time," Rory said before taking a bite of his granola bar.

"I wasn't sleepin'! I was prayin'. In Religion, no less! Should count for extra credit."

Bren laughed, but was distracted by the sight of A.J. shuffling into the canteen. Not only was the lad earphone-free, but he was actually smiling—sort of. It wasn't the same one Bren had seen in the greenhouse, but it was an improvement on his usual look for sure. He looked like he was having trouble spotting them, though.

Bren jumped to his feet and waved. "Oi, Robolad! Over here."

A few people broke from their conversations to look at A.J. standing in the doorway. His cheeks turned red, but he headed over anyway.

When Bren sat back down, Mickie was glaring at him.

"The hell you call Canada over for?"

"Ah, fuck off, he's sound enough," Bren said, taking a swipe at Mickie, who dodged the half-hearted attempt. "'Sides, he made mates with our ickle Rorls. Started a proper little book club and everything."

If Rory was annoyed by this, he didn't show it.

"Seriously, do we gotta go adoptin' the lad? He's fuckin' weird," Mickie said, still looking like he'd taken a bite of bread and Tayto pudding.

Bren didn't have time to reply before A.J. was at their table holding a packed lunch and looking like he was a hair away from sweating.

"Hey, uh, thanks for letting me sit with you guys."

Bren had to work not to sigh. The lad sounded like he was talking to the Queen of England or something. The accent wasn't doing him any favours either.

"You gonna sit, or just stare?" Mickie asked, not sounding like he wanted A.J. to sit at all.

Was he thinking about what Cian had said the other day?

"Oh, right!"

A.J. hesitated as he looked between the empty seats. Before Bren could say anything, he took the spot to his right, instead of the one beside Brick.

Bren couldn't be sure, but he thought that A.J.'s hands were trembling as he hurried to unpack his lunch, which contained a violently red bag of crisps that Bren swore said "Ketchup" across the front.

"S-so, uh . . ." he let his sentence trail off as he shifted his lunch around, "what's the craic?"

The Red Bull in Bren's throat threatened to return as he stifled a snort. God bless him—the words were right, but he sounded like someone's nan trying to be cool.

"Christ, lad, how long you practice that one?" Bren said, once he'd forced down the Red Bull.

"In my head or out loud?" A.J. said, looking like he was having trouble not laughing at himself. "Did I say it wrong or something?"

"Delivery was off," Rory said, "like you were trying to sell us dictionaries."

Bren snatched the crisps from A.J.'s lunch for a better look.

"Accent was cute, though. It might make me take a run at you." He popped the bag open and chucked a couple of crisps into his mouth. "If y'weren't a bloke."

57

A.J. looked like he was thinking about hopping on the next plane back to Canada, but rolled his eyes and snatched the bag back.

"Ok, no craic. But, is anyone doing anything this weekend then?"

The question hung in the air, and when it didn't seem like anyone else was going to, Bren picked it up.

"Nah, just gonna try and forget about this place until Monday. How 'bout you?"

A.J. had chosen that moment to take a bite of his lunch and rushed to swallow it.

"Talk with some friends back home. Maybe try and catch a hurling match on TV. It sounds really cool now that I know it's not just chaos with sticks."

Brick, who'd looked like he hadn't noticed that A.J. had sat down before this, perked up.

"You've never seen a match?" he asked, setting down the chicken roll he'd been about to bite into.

"He didn't even know what it was before this mornin'!"

"What?!" Brick asked, his voice booming out like a small bomb. "You've been in Ireland since Monday and didn't know what hurling was?"

"That's what I said!" Bren cried, glad, but not surprised that Brick was on his side about this.

"Sorry! I'm not really a sports guy unless it's on ice," A.J. said, his face not reddening for once.

"Wait, wait, say that again!" Bren replied, trying hard not to laugh.

"The thing about sports?"

"No! Sorry. Soor-ry."

A.J.'s shoulders pulled forward, his gaze falling to the food on the end of his fork. Then his eyes snapped up and rolled as he raised his middle finger.

"Sorry, you guys all say it wrong."

"Who the fuck's this lad now?" Bren cried, trying hard not to laugh again.

A.J. waved him off and took a bite of shepherd's pie.

"Ok, but you serious? You interested in hurling?" Brick asked.

"Yeah, I mean. Bren made it sound pretty cool, like lacrosse on steroids."

"You mean lacrosse is hurling with the fun taken outta it," Brick said. "Hurling's the oldest field sport in the world."

"Wait, really? Lacrosse is, like, a thousand years old."

Brick grunted, though he was wearing a smile that only ever came out when he got to talk GAA.

"Hurling's got two thousand years on that—ancient Celts."

"Ok, now I want to see it even more."

"There's a club match in Cork on Friday."

A.J. took another bite of his lunch and tilted his head.

"Ok, but I don't have a car, or know where the hell Cork is."

"Sounds like we just got somethin' to do tomorrow," Bren said and gestured around the table. "How 'bout it? Head over to Cork, drag Robolad along?"

Rory shrugged like it was a long-standing plan, and Brick gave an excited "Fuck yeah!"

Bren looked to Mickie, who was eyeing A.J. like someone who hadn't ruled out that he was something out of Doctor Who.

"I got that religion essay."

"Oh, fuck off, we all got that," Bren said.

"Yeah, but I got a thousand more words than you lot."

"Only 'cuz you're dumb enough to fall asleep in front of Miss Murphy."

"You should have said you were praying," A.J. said, "extra credit."

Mickie's face scrunched up into something close to confusion before he cracked a smile.

"Fuck, that's what I tried to tell her, didn't believe me."

Bren breathed a silent sigh of relief.

They launched into planning the trip, A.J. cutting in here and there with a smile fixed on his face. Bren wasn't sure if he was imagining it or not, but he thought it looked different from the one he'd seen in the greenhouse—or at least, he felt differently about it.

11

AJWalker90: "I did a thing!"

A.J. typed out his message milliseconds after the sphere next to Nat's name went from grey to green. Nat's reply came through about a second later.

LittleMoshpitKid46: "Hello to you too, school was fine, thanks for asking"

AJWalker90: "Lol, sorry, just excited."

A.J. drummed his fingers along the keyboard to the beat of "Basket Case." Since Bren had mentioned liking Green Day, it felt like a good idea to study up.

LittleMoshpitKid46: "Just busting your balls. What's up?"

AJWalker90: "So I, uh, made friends, I think. A bunch of guys are going to a hurling match on Friday and asked me to come."

He took a bite of one of the cookies laid out beside the computer while he waited for Nat's reply.

LittleMoshpitKid46: "They have curling in Ireland?"

AJWalker90: "I mean, maybe? This is hurling though. It's older than lacrosse and actually pretty cool. I think. I haven't seen a real match yet."

LittleMoshpitKid46: "Ok, proud of you, but how the hell did you get the invite?"

AJWalker90: "They're all friends with Bren and I sort of got folded in because I'm friends with Bren. I think."

LittleMoshpitKid46: "So you're friends with the jocks? That's . . . different"

AJWalker90: "They're not jocks. I mean, Brick is for sure, but the others are just sort of . . . normal. Rory's actually really smart."

LittleMoshpitKid46: "One of them's named BRICK? How haven't we talked about this before?"

AJWalker90: "I'm like 99% sure it's a nickname. It has to be."

LittleMoshpitKid46: "Ok, you HAVE to find out for sure. That shit's going to keep me up at night"

A laugh forced its way out of A.J. He lifted a headphone and checked over his shoulder. The McCarthys were still watching TV upstairs by the sounds of it.

LittleMoshpitKid46: "You gonna be ok? That's what like four guys you barely know and a stadium full of screaming people"

If A.J. was being honest with himself, that had been the first question to cross his mind since he'd had an entire road trip built around him.

AJWalker90: "I'm gonna try."

He stared down at the crumbs left on his plate.

AJWalker90: "So I sort of spiraled a bit after school and wanted to do something to not think about stuff and I made some Jam Jams . . . do you think I should bring some? As a thank you?"

LittleMoshpitKid46: "Ok, I love you to death, but under no circumstances should you give homemade cookies to a group where one of them is named BRICK"

A.J.'s heart fell, but it was the answer he'd been expecting.

AJWalker90: "But what if they're really good cookies?"

The chat shook as a blaring chime rose up over the music. Nat had Nudged the conversation several times in a row.

AJWalker90: "Alright alright, I get the message."

A.J. breathed a sigh of relief when the Nudges stopped. Nat was right, of course, there was every chance the gesture would have burned up what meager social credit he'd built over lunch. He wasn't sure when he'd started caring about that sort of thing, but he thought it was probably safe to blame Bren. Blame him or thank him. He wasn't sure which yet—he'd worry about it later.

***

A.J. wasn't sure what happened to Friday. One second he was sitting down in maths, and the next thing he knew he was standing in front of the school, trying not to look too nervous. He'd had a study period for his last class and hadn't seen any of the others when he'd made his way out to the front of the school.

He was thankful Bren had texted him about bringing a change of clothes that morning—though he was still wondering why he'd specifically mentioned blue. Even though school had only let out five minutes ago, at least a third of the guys had already changed into street clothes. The uniform didn't bother him much at all, but then again, he'd only been subjected to them for a week instead of eleven years.

The longer he waited by the gates, the deeper the gnawing grew. What if it had all been a joke and he wound up watching the crowd thin to nothing without ever seeing a trace of his new "friends"?

No, he reminded himself, *Bren's not like that. He's a good guy . . . right?*

He was starting to wonder how pathetic it would be if he texted Bren to make sure the trip was still on, when a hand fell on his shoulder.

After his heart fell back through the top of his head, A.J. saw it was Rory who'd nearly killed him. He was dressed in a sky-blue shirt with a small green crest pinned over his heart.

"Survived your first week?" he asked, looking somehow less tired than usual.

A.J. felt some of the ease he had been faking wash over him for real.

"Barely," he said, managing a smile. "Think it'll get any easier?"

Rory's gaze softened like he was looking through A.J.

"Being mates with Bren will help," he paused to pull out the copy of *I Am Legend* that he'd been reading the other day and handed it over. "He's sound. As long as you don't mind loud."

A snort escaped A.J. He wasn't sure which words he'd use to describe Bren, but loud was high on the list. The thought latched on, and he blurted out, "How are the two of you even friends?"

Of all the guys he'd met since coming to Glenbridge, Rory felt the least compatible with Bren.

Rory shrugged. "I moved here when I was ten. Talked to Bren one time in my first week and he just sort of . . . never stopped talking back."

A.J.'s reply was drowned out by a blaring car horn as a beat-up Toyota rolled up on their right. One of Brick's powerful arms was dangling out the window as it groaned to a stop. He spared the two of them a look before slamming his palm against the door with a thud.

"Get in, ladies, it's time to make a man out of Canada."

Bren and Mickie hollered from their seats, Brick's baritone joining with a blast of the car horn. After a look towards Rory, A.J. shuffled forward, unsure if he'd bitten off a bit more than he could chew. There was no going back now, though. All he could do was thank his lucky stars that he'd talked to Nat—he didn't want to think about the kind of noises those three would make if he'd brought along homemade cookies.

A.J.'s shoulder brushed against Bren's for the dozenth time in the twenty minutes since he'd crammed himself into the backseat. He'd long since stopped apologizing and instead tried to sit himself more evenly between Bren and Rory.

Up front, Mickie and Brick were bellowing along to some song A.J. had never heard before.

"Shit, I'm kinda jealous!" Bren said, his voice raised so that he could be heard above the singing. "First time seeing hurlin's gonna be in a proper stadium, like."

Brick scoffed mid-verse. "We're not taking him to The Páirc. *That's* a proper stadium."

Bren reached across A.J. and shoved the back of Brick's seat. "No shit, The Páirc's proper, dumbass. I mean, he's not gonna be watching it on telly, or some shite school match. That's all I saw till I was ten. Fuckin' ten!"

"Yeah, yeah, we all know the sob story," Brick replied, jerking the wheel and Bren fell back into his seat.

With Bren's face lit up above his blue and green striped jumper, A.J. had little trouble imagining Bren cheering his tiny heart out at his first match.

"At least you knew what the fuck it was," Brick added. "Poor Canada thought it was lacrosse until yesterday."

65

"You gonna be ok, Canada?" Mickie interjected. "Gonna be loud as fuck."

A.J. shook his head, pointless considering Mickie couldn't see him. He ran his thumb along the edge of the Discman in his pocket. He didn't plan on using it, but the idea of leaving it behind that morning had made the back of his neck sweat.

"I don't mind loud."

That was only true as long as it was music, but Mickie didn't need to know that.

"Just worried I won't know what the hell's going on."

"It's pretty easy to follow," Rory said. "Sliotar past the goalkeeper is three points, through the posts is one."

"Way more to it than that!" Brick barked.

"Yeah, but we don't wanna go overwhelming the lad. He already looks like he's gonna pass out," Bren said, nudging A.J. in the ribs. "Brick'll make sure you know what the fuck's happenin'. Might have to pop those earphones in if you wanna watch the match in peace, though."

"The hell you always listening to anyway?" Mickie asked.

"Oh, uh, a bunch of different stuff, I guess. I like all kinds of musi—"

"Hey! Show the lads that one song!"

A.J. frowned, not having a clue which song he meant.

Bren elbowed him again. "With the wan who was tryin' to break me eardrums."

It clicked. "Oh! Uh, I don't think they'd like it."

A.J. could think of any number of songs he had that this group might like, but nothing from *Wicked* was on that list.

"Come on! It's mad. Like ten minutes long, horns and opera and people talkin' instead of singin'." By the time he'd finished talking,

Bren had already helped himself to A.J.'s book bag, digging around like there might be a prize at the bottom.

"It's—ok, fine, let me do it."

He pulled the bag away and handed over the black and green CD to Mickie.

A.J.'s apology was lost when the opening notes exploded out of the car's speakers.

"Is this fuckin' Disney?" Mickie asked over Glinda's first set of lines.

A.J. couldn't pinpoint the tone, but it didn't sound like enjoyment.

"Uh, no, it's Broadway."

"Shut up and let her sing," Bren said, looking over to A.J. "What was her name? Glimma?"

"Glinda!" A.J. corrected. "Seriously, man, have you never seen *The Wizard of Oz*?"

Bren tilted his head. "Yeah? What's that got to do with this?"

A.J. burst out laughing.

"I say somethin' funny?"

A.J. pulled himself together enough to throw an elbow back at Bren. "No, just, I'll explain later. Shut up and let 'Glimma' sing."

Bren opened his mouth, like he was about to ask a serious question, but did as he was told.

A.J. closed his eyes and let the music wash over him. He'd wanted to be as normal as possible on this trip, and Bren had wasted no time in making that impossible. To his surprise, A.J. found he didn't mind. He wasn't about to go erasing who he was to be liked, so they were bound to hear something from Broadway sooner or later. Better it come from Bren's meddling than his own awkward insistence.

Even though there was some embarrassment bubbling beneath the sudden spurt of confidence, it felt well worth it—if only for the odd expression on Bren's face.

12

The stadium was already buzzing by the time they made their way to their seats. The smell of grass fought against the heat of too many bodies pressed in together. Bren took his seat with A.J. on his right, who was adjusting the lumpy green hat he'd bought from an old bird out front.

His stomach gurgled as the curry chips they'd polished off on the drive over fought for space with the latest addition. They'd barely gotten out of the car when Mickie pulled out a two-litre Tanora, took a swig, and handed it over. The fact that Mickie had brought it hadn't surprised him. What had made him do a double-take was how quickly A.J. had gone along with it.

After Bren had taken his own glug and passed it on, he'd expected A.J. to stammer and refuse. Instead, after a sniff, he took a pull like a man dying of thirst and wiped his mouth without batting an eye. It was double-impressive, seeing as the dodgy vodka Mickie always got a hold of tasted like hand sanitizer.

"So, who are we cheering for again?" A.J. asked, even though he'd sat through Brick rattling on about the Harps for the last thirty minutes.

Brick leaned towards A.J. with the back of his hand raised.

"Ok, ok!" he said, shifting away from Brick before crying out, "Let's go Harps!"

The cry was echoed on their side of the stadium, and A.J. called back with a loud whoop.

Bren didn't know how to sync this version of A.J. with the one he'd met on Monday, but he wasn't about to question it. He cupped his hands on either side of his mouth and joined in.

Next thing, he was on his feet cheering as the fifteen blue and green players made their way onto the pitch. A.J. rose a second late, but cheered as loud as anyone. He even joined in on the spattering of boos when the grey and purple Giants appeared on the opposite end.

"Ok, so how does it start? Do they jus—"

A.J. was cut off as the ball was thrown in and everything went crazy. Haleford got possession—just barely—and sped the sliotar a good thirty meters down the pitch. A simmering roar built from their side of the stadium as their forward drove the sliotar to the goal—where it was stopped by the keeper.

A collective groan rose around them.

"Holy hell, that was fast!" A.J. cried, while three seats down, Brick yelled something Bren couldn't quite make out.

"That's hurling! Greatest sport on earth for a feckin' reason!" Bren said, leaning in so A.J. could hear him.

The keeper pucked the sliotar down midfield as the other side of the stadium cheered.

"Couldn't he have gone for a point? The goalie can't block up there. It would have been free, right?"

"Keeper!" Bren corrected, "And it's still early. He was just showin' off."

70

The sliotar moved back towards the goal, a handpass by the Harps. The Giants tried to block, but the ball made its way back to the forwards. Then, from just past midfield, number fifteen sent the ball sailing down the field and through the posts.

Their side of the stadium cheered, though none louder than A.J., who had leapt to his feet. Watching A.J. act like they'd just won the cup over a single point made his heart pound like he was seeing it for the first time, too.

"Fuck, we need more of this lad!" He cried, shaking A.J. by the shoulder after he'd sat down.

A.J. turned at Bren's touch. He was wearing the same kind of smile that Bren had seen back in the greenhouse.

"You should see me beer-drunk during hockey season!"

Bren could picture it. A.J. bundled up in a jacket and jersey, red-faced and screaming like a lunatic while guys with bad mullets beat the crap out of each other on ice.

His churning stomach broke him away from the thought. The vodka definitely wasn't sitting well with the chips.

By the time the teams had jogged off for halftime, Bren's throat was sore from shouting. Brick had swapped seats with Rory at some point so he could bellow hurling facts at A.J. more easily. Bren had wondered if he'd have to tell the big guy to ease up, but A.J. had leaned in to yell back questions without a hint of a stammer.

"Right, I'm gonna go get a drink. Anyone comin' with?" Mickie said, slapping his hands on his knees.

Rory shook his head, while Brick rumbled out, "Driving."

A.J. looked thoughtful, then stood up with a whoop. By the look on Mickie's face, he hadn't expected that.

"Come on, I amn't tryin' to shag Canada here. You comin', Bren?"

A.J. looked Mickie up and down and shook his head.

"Don't worry, man, I'm not trying to get with Dumbo."

Mickie's mouth fell open. He looked like he couldn't tell if A.J. was being serious or not. In the end, he laughed about it.

"Better luck next time, mate," Bren said, rising to his feet. "Let's go."

A.J. wasted no time and began talking full stream about some of the more exciting plays they'd seen so far. It was obvious he still didn't fully understand what he was talking about, but he sounded like a lifelong fan—if a drunk one.

They were briefly separated when a group of whooping blokes pushed past them. When the mass of painted faces cleared, a single earphone had worked its way into A.J.'s ear.

"Oi! Don't go fadin' on us! Got another half to go!" Bren cried, slapping A.J. on the back.

"I'm taking them out after halftime. Promise."

"Good lad!"

Bren nodded Mickie along. "Come on, let's down that shite you brought and get back. Don't want the new super fan to miss a second."

**

"From halfway down the field! Christ above, they keep playing like that, and we might make it out of county for once!"

Even though they'd been in the car for the last half hour, Brick was still shouting like he was fighting to be heard over a crowd.

"They'll find a way to fuckitup. Always do!" Mickie slurred from the front seat.

"Maybe we just needed a Canadian fan. Never seen them play like that before," Rory said.

"Guess he's gotta stick around 'til January at least," Bren said, sounding slurry as he wrapped an arm around A.J.'s shoulders.

A.J.'s heart lurched.

Too close.

He could feel the heat pouring off of Bren's side. He did his best to shrug him off, and wound up close enough to smell the unholy combination of curry and orange-y vodka on his breath. It made his head spin, and not just because he'd had his fair share to drink.

"I'm here until June," A.J. said, forcing himself to sound annoyed. "Now get off me, you reek."

Bren didn't resist the shove and fell back laughing. He raised an arm and gave himself a sniff.

"I even put on Lynx this mornin'."

Then, to A.J.'s horror, he wiped his armpit and reached across to shove his hand under Rory's nose.

"What d'you reckon?"

Rory, for all his usual restraint, punched Bren in the arm hard enough that A.J. heard the thud above the music. "I reckon we need to get you some water."

Bren laughed again despite the punch and settled back into his seat.

"It was your breath," A.J. blurted. "Sorry, vodka-curry is a lot up close."

In the resulting laughter, A.J. wiped his hands on the insides of his pockets, wishing his heart would slow down.

"Well, there goes my plan to kiss you, like," Bren said, puckering up.

It was lucky Brick had been listening and swooped in—though A.J. doubted he knew the favour he'd just done him.

"Can we stop talking about how Bren smells and get back to hurling? That was so fucking good for a club match!"

"What's wrong with a club match?" A.J. asked, clinging to the life raft Brick had thrown him.

"Nothin'! All hurlin's grand!" Bren said, which got a drunken whoop from Mickie.

"He's right," Brick said, "but league matches are on a whole different level."

"Damn, I hope I get to see one. That was so much fun."

"Well, fuck, let's keep it goin'! Mam's with a patient all night!" Bren said, kicking the back of Brick's seat. "Xtra-vision then, my place!"

Brick let out a booming laugh. "Alright! Drunk Bren's payin'!"

"I amn't drunk, you muppet, just havin' a good time, like. Mickie hogged the booze."

Mickie flipped Bren off without looking back.

"I guess we don't really get a say, huh?" A.J. asked, leaning towards Rory.

"Easier to just go with it."

"Guess so." He'd tried to match Rory's delivery, but wasn't sure he'd managed it.

For once, he found it easy to shut off the part of his brain that wanted to spiral. Instead, he leaned back in his seat and smiled like an idiot.

***

74

A.J. swore under his breath as he stumbled over a pothole on the road that wound towards Bren's house. He didn't understand how he was wobbling more now that he'd sobered up. He was glad Mickie had suggested Brick drop them off at their houses. The sleepover sounded fun, but less so if he'd have to sleep in his jeans. Stripping to his boxers in a room full of aggressively straight Irish guys was not on his bucket list.

He peered at the outline of the bungalow on the other side of a low wooden fence that looked like it needed painting about three years ago. The entire thing could probably fit in the McCarthys' living room, but the sight of it brought a smile to A.J.'s face.

Green rose on either side of him as he pushed open the crooked gate. There were a few flowering plants A.J. couldn't identify, their buds long since asleep. A few near-ripe raspberries clung to a scruffy bush that ran the length of one of the house's walls.

He paused with his hand raised in front of the door. Brick had dropped Bren off at the movie store a few blocks away at his insistence. He'd told them to just come on in if he wasn't back before they got there—still, A.J. had lingered at the McCarthys' so he wouldn't be the first one over.

The tin of cookies he'd shoved into his backpack at the last second rattled as he tested the doorknob. It turned, and after a step forward, he was peering into Bren's living room.

"Hello?" he called, trying to keep the nerves out of his voice.

Bren appeared out of the lone hallway, still dressed in his Harps shirt—though he had swapped his pants for a pair of checkered pajama bottoms.

"I said come in, not lurk in the doorway."

A.J. jumped forward and hurried to close the door behind him. He knew Bren would probably slap him if he said it out loud, but he

75

was immediately struck by how cozy the house felt. The McCarthys' place was warm, of course, but it was a clammy sort of warmth depending on which room you were in. Unfortunately, his bedroom was one of those rooms.

Something in Bren's place seemed able to keep the soup-level humidity outside at bay. He tried to figure out what the difference was as he slipped his shoes off.

"Shoes off and all," Bren said, shaking his head. "That from livin' up the hill or a Canada thing?"

A.J. paused. It was such an ingrained habit that he hadn't realized he'd done it.

"Canada thing."

"Fair enough. Well, if you couldn't tell, we're not fancy 'round here, so just put your shite wherever and relax, like" Bren said, then disappeared back into the hallway without another word.

A.J. stepped out of the entryway and into the house proper. To his left was a cramped kitchen with a circular table off to one side. Directly in front was the living room—a beat-up beige recliner, a boxy TV, and a couch that looked like it might have been white at one point.

On the side of the room farthest from the door stood a wood-burning stove in a weathered hearth. A single blackened log was smouldering behind the soot-covered glass. It was radiating a gentle heat, along with a scent A.J. couldn't quite put his finger on. It smelled like a campfire, but with a faint, sweetish smell and just a dash of something green.

Puzzled, A.J. dropped his bag in front of the couch and sat down. It groaned under his weight, but was surprisingly comfortable once he'd settled in. Not wanting to help himself to the TV, he contented himself with looking around the room. The paint on the walls was chipped in places, and there was a water stain on one corner of the ceiling that looked like a horse with three legs—if he squinted. More interesting were the handful of framed photos lining the walls.

One showed a woman with flaming red hair standing with a younger, gap-toothed Bren in a white suit. It looked like it might have been taken in a church. Bren's posture was stiff, but he was wearing a smile that told A.J. he'd just achieved some kind of milestone. The picture next to it showed a version of Bren that looked more familiar. His hair was shorter, and his face looked younger than the one he'd met on Monday. A.J. guessed he was twelve, maybe thirteen, at most.

He was standing in the kitchen with an elderly woman, her auburn hair grey in places. They were each wearing flour-stained aprons and near-matching smiles, his oversized and goofy, hers firmer at the edges, though her eyes shone with warmth.

A clatter followed by an annoyed "Fuck!" made its way from down the hall Bren had disappeared into.

"Need some help?" A.J. asked, already getting to his feet.

Bren didn't reply, but the clattering got louder.

He followed the sound down the hall, intent on seeing what the hell Bren was doing, but pulled up short at another picture. This one showed a chubby baby in an orange knitted onesie, his arms thrust forward like he was trying to reach through the picture.

A.J. had to work hard to shut down the urge to coo at baby Bren. When he pulled himself away, he nearly ran into teenage Bren, who was struggling to waddle through the doorway while holding a battered Xbox piled high with pillows and a stack of DVDs.

"You lookin' at me baby pictures?" he asked, peeking out from behind the tower. "Shoulda taken that shite down."

A.J.'s cheeks turned so red he was surprised they didn't ignite.

"Sorry, I wasn't snooping. It sounded like you needed help."

He took the stack from on top of the Xbox before Bren could object, and was surprised to see he looked a little pink, too. It could have been from anything, but A.J. decided to push his luck.

"So you were kind of extra squishy as a baby, huh?"

Bren didn't turn any redder, but for some stupid reason, A.J. did.

"You callin' little me fat?" Bren asked, eyes narrowing before his expression brightened. "Yeah, I was a fat fuckin' baby. Feel kinda bad for me mam if I'm bein' honest."

A.J. laughed harder than he'd meant to, but didn't feel the immediate stab of embarrassment that usually followed.

"Hey, same here. My mom always talks about what a beautiful baby I was." He dropped the pillows onto the couch. "All I can think when I see pictures is, Holy hell, was my head huge.

It was Bren's turn to laugh now.

"Maybe you're part Irish. We got some big aul heads."

A.J. took a step back and framed Bren's face with his thumb and index fingers.

"You know, I think I see what you mean."

Bren balanced the Xbox in one hand and flipped A.J. off before pushing past to mess with the TV.

"Need help with anything else?" A.J. asked as Bren lined up the RCA cables.

"Nah, I'm good at stickin' things in holes. Just sit down."

A.J. did as he was told, even if that line was going to haunt his dreams for the rest of the week. He kept his eyes focused on the weird horse-shaped stain on the ceiling so he didn't stare at Bren bent by the TV.

"Think Mickie's gonna bring over more vodka?"

Bren let out a short, humourless laugh. "Only if he wants to get fuckin' murdered."

"What?"

Bren nodded towards the picture of the red-haired woman. "Mam would kill every last one of us if she found out we were drinkin' in the house."

By the way Bren acted, A.J. had assumed his parents would be easy going. He looked back at the picture of Bren in his white suit—at a church.

"Is she really religious?"

The question made A.J.'s insides squirm. If the answer was yes, he couldn't imagine she'd be thrilled about her son having a friend like him.

"Nah, that's all on me da I think. Don't want me turnin' out like him," Bren replied, as if A.J. had asked about the weather.

"Oh, is he . . . ?"

Bren powered on the TV and leaned back on crossed legs.

"A drunk? Yeah."

"Ah. I'm sorry," A.J. said, his voice softer.

Bren shook his head.

"Don't be. Prick ran off before I could hold me own head up, like."

A.J. felt like he should say something more, even if Bren didn't seem bothered. Before he could figure out what that was, Bren picked up the stack of movies and tossed one at A.J.

"That one any good?"

A.J. turned the case over to look at the spine. It was *Little Shop of Horrors*. He tried to stifle his groan, but didn't quite manage it.

"Please tell me this isn't all you got."

Bren shook his head.

"Got Resident Evil and Happy Gilmore, too. Cop on, though, that one good? Anythin' like *Wicked*?"

A.J. couldn't help but laugh.

"Not even a little. Did you seriously think it would be?"

Bren snatched the case back and squinted at the title.

"I don't fuckin' know. Never rented a musical before, have I?"

A.J. was saved the necessity of figuring out whether he wanted to laugh or cry as the door swung open. Rory strolled in with a wave, backpack slung over his shoulder.

"Oi, Rory, we got zombies, Sandler, and a singin' plant. Whaddya reckon?"

13

Sunlight had long since crept into the O'Sheas' living room by the time A.J.'s eyes brought the world into bleary focus. He was dimly aware of the sound of Mickie's muffled snores coming from the lumpy mass on the cot a few feet away. The weight behind his eyes told him that, even though the sun had been up for at least an hour, he hadn't gotten enough sleep. It had been worth it, though.

They'd made it through all three movies in the end—or at least, the movies had been played through, even if they didn't get the group's full attention. Mickie had complained more than once that *Little Shop* was "gay as fuck", but even he shut up during the finale. A.J. guessed singing mutant flytraps tearing New York City apart were enough to hold anyone's attention.

As predicted, he had to endure some shit-talk when he'd brought out the Jam Jams, but it hadn't made him want to curl up and die like it might have on Monday. It didn't hurt that the tin was almost empty by the end of the night.

He wondered what had woken him up as Bren came storming into the room. His hair was plastered into a flattened swoop on one side of his head, and judging by the Rory-level circles under his eyes, he wasn't satisfied with how much sleep he'd gotten either.

"Oi! Get up."

He hopped on one leg as he pulled on a worn black sock to join the frayed grey one on the other foot.

There was a series of groans from the lumpy masses around A.J. as everyone stirred. Brick reached for the nearest couch cushion and threw it blindly towards Bren's voice.

"Fuckin' forgot I got a shift today!" He hurried into the kitchen where there was a series of bangs and another loud "Fuck!" from Bren.

"Kettle's on. Have a cuppa then clear out."

A.J. had long enough to catch a glimpse of Bren taking a bite of what he thought might have been a Jam Jam before he was out the door.

"Fuckin' Muppet. . ." Mickie grumbled, sitting up to reveal bloodshot eyes and a very grumpy expression. "How come we gotta pay cuz he's got shit for brains?"

Brick yawned and rolled onto his side, a beefy arm rising from the blankets to scratch the back of his head. "Better clear out though, unless you wanna have tea with Maura."

"Fuck no. She's still pissed at me from last time I was over."

"What did you do?" A.J. asked, wanting to avoid whatever it was.

Mickie shrugged, "Said I'd shag Carmen Elektra inta next week if she ever came to Glenbridge. Like Bren hasn't said ten times worse."

A.J. thought he could avoid that pitfall somehow.

"Yeah, but not to his mam, dumbass." Brick chimed in.

A faint gurgling drifted in from the kitchen, and Brick leapt to his feet with surprising grace considering the size of him. He trotted across them with his boxers flapping, taking care to step over Rory.

Mickie groaned as he got to his feet, jeans rumpled with sleep. A.J. had done his best not to pay too much attention to it, but while everyone else had lost some of their clothes before it had been time to turn in, Mickie had lied down and pulled a blanket halfway over himself. A.J. couldn't help but wonder if he was the cause of that.

"Where'd Bren head off to?" A.J. asked, reaching for the shirt he'd peeled off last night.

"Got a job sellin' cream puffs. Has a hairnet and everything, proper gas," Mickie said.

A.J. furrowed his brow. "Like, at a bakery or something?"

"Yup," Mickie said, heading to the kitchen. "Get Rory up would you? Lad sleeps like a fuckin' corpse."

A.J. finished pulling his shirt on and gave the pile of blankets closest to him a shake. There was a low groan, but nothing else.

"Hey, Rory. We've gotta get up."

A louder groan this time, but nothing in the way of movement. Not knowing what else to do, A.J. pulled back the blanket. Rory rolled over with a grunt and buried his face in his pillow.

"Come on Rorls! Tea's on!" Brick said, voice louder than any alarm clock.

Rory swore into his pillow before pulling himself up, the bags under his eyes matched only by the scowl across his face.

"Morning sunshine," Brick said, prodding him with his foot before taking a sip from his mug. "Gotta clear out, Bren went and forgot he's working today."

Rory flopped down onto his bedding with a muffled thud.

"Bellend."

A.J. couldn't help laughing. Rory's usual deadpan was gone. Instead, the singular word wished Bren a slow and painful death.

"Too true," Brick replied, slurping his tea. "Think we oughta pay him a visit?"

Rory pushed himself up again, a cruel grin spreading across his face. "Yeah, if I'm up, he's gotta suffer too."

***

Bren wiped a bead of sweat from his forehead as the last customer left the store with their pastries in hand. Now that the rush was over, he was hopeful the rest of the shift would be a doss—even if Niamh was still fuming. It was a good sign she'd only chewed him out for a couple of minutes before sending him up front considering how late he'd been.

He was grateful she'd given him a job and everything, but sometimes he felt like she forgot he had other things in his life. She was always spouting off about applying himself more when this was just an easy way to make some cash. He forced a smile on his face as Niamh called him to bring up another tray of blackberry and ginger tarts, a fall specialty of hers.

"So, are you gonna tell me what's so important you forgot you were on for nine today?"

He should have known he hadn't heard the last of it. She was just like Nan in that way.

"Sorry ma'am," he said, laying on the charm thicker than he usually would. "I had some mates over and forgot I was supposed to visit me best bird today."

Niamh threw the stained tea towel she'd been using to wipe her hands at his head. "I outta have Callum throw your bony ass out the door for that one." Her eyes were blazing, but Bren was sure he saw the corner of her wrinkled mouth twitch.

Bren pulled the towel off his shoulder and tossed it towards the basket to join the others. "Why you always gotta bring Nan into this? I thought we were mates."

Bren sensed real danger in the way her eyes narrowed at him next. He was glad there wasn't a spoon in grabbing distance, at least.

"I am sorry though, honest. Had some of the lads over last night like, and just sorta forgot, like."

Niamh tossed a fresh towel over her shoulder.

"Not doing anything that'd make your mam scarlet I hope."

"Just movies and CoD," Bren said, heaving up the tray of tarts. "Shoulda seen what I got up to last weekend though."

He left the kitchen in time to avoid Niamh throwing anything else at him and got to setting the tarts out. He'd just cleared the tray when the bell over the door chimed.

"Afternoon! What can I get y—" he looked up as the door clattered shut behind the last of the group. "No. Get right the fuck out, the lot of you."

Rory, A.J., Brick and Mickie were standing in front of the counter. They were all grinning at him like idiots, though there was something dark in Rory's expression.

"Awww, look at him!" Mickie cooed like a mam at a christening. "Lil' hairnet and all."

Bren checked over his shoulder. "Look, Niamh's already pissed at me for bein' late, I don't need you lot fuckin' around."

He turned to A.J., hoping his nervousness might come in handy here. Unbidden, the last time he looked at the lad flashed in his memory. He'd been splayed on his back, gob open with a trickle of drool dribbling down his chin. Bren's usual instinct would have been to reach for a Sharpie. Instead, after watching long enough that he felt creepy about it, he'd let the lad lie.

"Payin' customers only." He said, folding his arms over his chest.

Rory stepped up to the counter and fished a crisp tenner out of his pocket.

"Just need to decide what to get," he crouched to get a better look at the case. "You got any. . .Cornish hens?" he asked like that wasn't completely mad.

Bren guessed he was still pissed about being woken up.

"You see any birds?"

Predictably, Mickie flipped Bren off and laughed like it was the cleverest thing he'd ever done.

"Got any lunch specials that come with coffee? I didn't get much sleep last night," he said, his voice dripping.

"It's a bakery, either order a pastry or fuck off."

"Hey, get me a sausage roll while Rory's lookin'." Mickie said, slapping his money on the counter.

Bren grumbled, but bent to get one.

"Nah, not that one," Mickie said, shaking his head, "Third from the left, second row back. No, you muppet, my left."

Bren grabbed the closest roll and squeezed while picturing Mickie's throat. He threw it in a bag and tossed it at him.

"Some customer service," Mickie snorted, already tucking in. "Oi, where's my change then?"

Bren shoved Mickie's note into the till and handed him the change, after dropping a euro into the tip jar.

Mickie made a sound through his mouthful of roll but didn't push it further. Even though he'd been laughing like an idiot along with the rest of them, A.J. sounded closer to how he had on his first day when he stepped up to order.

"What's like, the most Irish thing I guess?"

Bren scowled, trying to decide if he was taking the piss or not. Something in the way his eyes shone told him he was really asking.

"We do a good apple tart," he said, jerking his thumb to the small assortment in the display case. They never seemed to go as fast as some of the other stuff Niamh put up, but they always trickled out.

"I'll get that then, please."

"Please? Whose side are you on?" Mickie asked.

A.J.'s ears turned pink, but he pushed past it.

"Sor-ry for having manners, dick."

Brick oohed behind Mickie's back, which earned him a shove that didn't budge him one inch.

Laughing, Bren went to grab a tart.

"No, not that one. The one to the right of the one with the sort of lopsided top. . .please."

Bren groaned as the others laughed, but did as he'd been asked—feeling prouder than he had any right to.

By the time October rolled around, Bren could hardly believe A.J. had only been in Glenbridge for a month. There were still times when he'd stammer and go quiet, or keep an earphone in during lunch, but that didn't stop him from joining in. He'd started asking questions about Glenbridge and Ireland at large, and always seemed fascinated, no matter how dull the answer was. Even stupid things like finding out he could ask for curry sauce on his chips—which he said was almost as good as poutine—was enough to make him light up.

It took some prodding to get him going, but once he did, he seemed to take great pleasure in explaining Canada to them. How to pronounce Saskatchewan, the fact his town was home to the world's tallest moose, and how winter sometimes started in October and didn't let up until May. It had taken him the better part of an hour to convince Mickie that he and his family actually dragged a shack that slept six onto the ice and sat around fishing for days at a time.

There was no denying he was still a bit weird, but there was something about the way he was weird now that made it impossible for Bren to look away. Bold as he was getting, Bren found he kept wanting more and urged him on whenever he got the chance. That was, until Religion two days ago.

They'd gotten on the subject of the sanctity of marriage, and A.J. had, without a hint of hesitation, said that he didn't think religion should be used to keep consenting adults from being together.

Cian had wasted no time in chiming in by saying he didn't think people should get special privileges just because they chose to be gay. It had been an awkward moment, no doubt. Instead of shrinking, A.J. had kept his eyes locked on Cian and said if he believed people chose to be gay, then there wasn't a point in talking about it with him.

The look Cian gave A.J. after that had made the back of Bren's neck prickle. Miss Murphy had swooped in to move things along, but the class had already gotten around to murmuring.

Bren was on A.J.'s side about it, of course. He couldn't see who in their right mind would choose to be gay. But, he couldn't help but wonder what A.J. might have chosen for himself by standing up to Cian.

***

The sky was the same uniform sea of grey it had been all week when A.J. stepped out of Catch Of The Day. They'd been out of forks, so he was trying to pick at his snack without getting his hands covered in sauce.

He'd been skeptical of the combination of vinegar, curry sauce, and cheese all in one. But, it had become his go-to order ever since Bren had convinced him to try a bite of his a couple weeks ago.

The walk home felt strange without Bren's running commentary, but there wasn't anything to be done about it. Bren had landed himself in detention by shouting the punchline of a very off-colour joke when Miss Murphy happened to be around the corner. Still, A.J. felt Bren's presence through the mess of carbs he was working his way through. He shook his head at the thought as he bit into a curry-soaked chip.

Over the past week, he'd noticed more and more things were making him think of that freckled face. It wasn't like stuff around town didn't make him think of the other guys he'd come to call friends—but Bren was for sure getting more than his fair share of screen time.

It hadn't reached a tipping point yet, and A.J. was determined to keep it that way.

Bren was just his friend.

His loud, funny, and painfully straight friend.

Straight or not, he had a nice smile, and the way his eyes lit up whenever he laughed—

A.J. forced the idea from his head. Better to not let that particular train of thought get to the station.

The sharp, slightly spicy taste of the chips, the misty chill on his cheeks, and the angelic high notes of Miss Joni Mitchell flooding his ears. Life in Ireland was good. Why ask for more?

He'd made precious little progress towards home by the time he'd finished his chips. They'd been such a hassle to eat without a fork that he'd had to stop by the Centra. He brought a bottle of Club Lemon to his lips with a freshly washed hand as he turned the corner.

He heard them before he saw them. Cian and another guy A.J. thought might be named Tadhg were walking up from the other end of the street. Like him, they still wore their uniforms, though Cian had pulled a puffer jacket over his shoulders.

A.J. paused at the memory of Cian's face in Religion a couple days ago. A voice in the back of his head told him to duck back into the store until they passed. He thought of what Bren might say if he did that, though. He couldn't keep shrinking away from everything that made him nervous.

He forced himself not to stare at his feet, and instead did his best to seem interested in a store across the street as he made his way towards Cian. The forced bravery wasn't enough to keep his palms from growing clammy as he fiddled with the pouch of his bunnyhug. He caught a trace of chattering voices as they passed each other, but kept his eyes focused on the distance and his feet moving.

With the group behind him, A.J. breathed a sigh of relief, just in time to have his earphones yanked out.

"Hey, gay boy, I was talking to you!"

A.J.'s nails dug into his palms—he had misjudged the kind of bigot Cian was. Though his heart had begun to hammer in his chest, he forced out an even breath.

There was still a chance this wouldn't be as bad as he thought.

"Sorry," he said, doing his best to control his accent. He didn't feel like Cian needed any more ammo. "I had my music cranked up pretty high."

His eyes roved over Cian. He was a good three inches taller and must have had at least thirty pounds on him. Tadhg was much closer to his size, but at the end of the day, he tipped the scales into two on one.

"Think you're too good to talk back now?" Cian asked, his brow more pronounced than usual.

"What?" A.J. asked, a nervous chuckle coming to his defense, "I-I had music on."

"The fuck you always listening to anyway?" Cian asked, like he hadn't heard him.

"Oh, just regular music, I guess . . ."

For some reason, this made Cian laugh.

"Come on, let's see then," Cian said, holding out his hand.

A.J. stared at the hand like it might offer some way out of this. When all it did was wave for him to hurry up, A.J. sighed and handed his Discman over.

Of all the CDs he could have been listening to, why did it have to be that one?

When Cian opened the Discman, a round of cruel laughter broke out between him and his friend. The CD in question had once been a blank, but now housed a collection of his favourite female singers. He'd gone a bit bonkers with Nat's neon Sharpies when he'd decorated it. And the "Girl Power Mega Mix" title wasn't doing him any favours either.

"Christ, he really is a fuckin' fairy, isn't he?"

There was a fresh round of laughter as A.J.'s face burned. He wanted to snap back at Cian, but had enough self-control to hold the urge at bay.

"You know, I've been thinking about what you said a couple days back." He gave his shoulders a shrug. "Figure people like you do deserve some special treatment after all."

Cian gripped the top of the Discman and ripped it back.

"Wha—stop!"

Before the words had left him, a sickening crack rang out, and the Discman snapped in half. The lid dangled from a cluster of wires as Cian let it fall to the ground with a clatter.

"There you go, nice and special, so."

Tadhg let out a cruel laugh as A.J. suppressed the urge to reach for the broken halves. He wasn't going to bow to him.

Before he knew what he was doing, he'd locked eyes with Cian.

"Are you done trying to impress your boyfriend, loser?"

The air rang in the wake of his words, then pain exploded across the left side of his face. He stumbled back, but managed to catch himself before he hit the ground.

"The fuck you say to me?"

Cian shoved A.J. hard in the chest, his back slamming into the wall he'd used to catch himself. A.J. closed his eyes, bracing for another punch.

"Hey!" The cry broke through the silence like a firecracker. "The fuck you doin'?"

A.J.'s left eye had already started to swell, but he could still make out Mickie jogging up the street, Brick close behind him.

"This one was running his mouth," Cian said, hands turned upwards as if to say he hadn't been left a choice.

"Yeah? An' I'm sure you weren't running your gob first. Clear the fuck out."

Cian glared at Mickie before his eyes darted to Brick. As intimidating as Cian might have been in his own right, the nickname said it all.

"Didn't take you for a fag lover," Cian spat.

It was hard to tell through his still-watering eyes, but A.J. thought Mickie's angry expression faltered.

"He's sound. Now fuck off y'cunt," Mickie said, his scowl fixed back in place. "Unless you wanna see what happens when it isn't two on one."

Cian considered Mickie again and took a step back.

"Tell your boyfriend to keep his gob shut, or I'll fuckin' break it next time."

Cian spared A.J. a disgusted look, then headed down the street. By the sound of crunching plastic, he'd made sure to tread over the Discman.

Once Cian had walked out of earshot, Mickie turned back to A.J. "The hell did you say to him?"

A.J. wiped the wetness from his eye, hating that he couldn't stop it from streaming.

". . . Nothing," he replied, and when Mickie didn't look convinced. "At first. Then it just sort of came out."

"What'd you say?" Brick asked.

A.J.'s eyes fell to what used to be his Discman, and his chest tightened. He dropped to one knee and gathered up the pieces as gently as he could. Apart from being split in two, save for the small tangle of wires holding it together, the pause button was stuck pressed down, and the knob that held the disc in place rattled in the case.

"Asked him if he was done showing off for his boyfriend."

Mickie groaned.

"Christ, thought you're meant to be clever. Shoulda kept your mouth shut."

"Would you?" A.J. asked, placing the shards of his Discman in his bookbag.

Mickie opened his mouth as if he were going to object, but wound up shaking his head. "Guess not, but I know how to throw a punch, don't I?"

Brick scoffed. "Cian'd lay you out."

"Whose side are you on?"

A.J. let out another sigh.

"I should probably go. Put some ice on this or something." His head was throbbing, and the bickering wasn't helping. All he wanted to do was get somewhere where he could let whatever emotion he wanted cross his face.

Mickie nodded as Brick raised an eyebrow. "You good?"

A.J. tried to force a laugh, but it came out scratchy.

"I'm not made of glass."

There was an awkward moment where they all looked at each other, unsure of how to part ways. In the end, A.J. turned back towards the hills.

He hadn't taken a full step away before he pulled up short. He knew his voice was going to fail him, but he needed to get it out.

"Hey, just . . . thanks for c-caring."

He was gone before they had a chance to reply.

***

A.J.'s head gave a throb of protest as he stared at the glowing computer screen. Even though he knew it was barely noon in Canada, a part of him had hoped to see someone from back home online. He wasn't sure why, though; he had no intention of telling anyone what had happened. What good could it possibly do?

Nat could rage and storm all she wanted, but her scope for inflicting pain from across the Atlantic was limited. Then there was the fact that if his mom found out, she'd probably try to take it up with the school—or worse—bring him home.

He didn't know if the McCarthys had bought his lie about getting hit by the sliotar when he and Brick were messing around after school, but they didn't seem in a rush to rat him out at least.

He brushed the pieces of what used to be his Discman off to the side. After an hour of trying to fix it himself, he had to admit defeat. With the memory of tearing it out of its wrapping on his twelfth birthday fresh behind his throbbing eye, he couldn't bring himself to throw it away.

The vise tightening on either side of his temples made him wonder if he shouldn't take another dose of Panadol. Meredith said she was sure it was the same as Tylenol, but on the off chance it wasn't, it made sense to tread lightly. As a compromise, he decided to treat himself to a Magnum Bar.

Maybe this was a blessing in disguise? A month on and he'd made exactly zero progress on his composition project. Something in F minor felt fitting right now.

When he got back to the computer, a tab was blinking away at the bottom of the screen. His stomach gave a funny spasm when he got close enough to read the name—RedBullBren69.

A.J. eased himself into the chair with his heart hammering and opened the tab.

RedBullBren69: "Right, how come I'm finding out u got jumped by Cian from fucking Mickie?!"

A.J.'s eye throbbed with the memory of the punch as heat flushed across his face. Was he actually upset he'd been left out of the loop?

He thought about just changing his status to "away," but found he couldn't do it.

AJWalker90: "Are you mad I didn't tell you?"

He leaned back in his chair and took a bite of his ice cream to give himself something to do.

RedBullBren69: "The fuck? I'm pissed Cian fucked with my mate"

A smile pulled at the corners of A.J.'s mouth. *My mate*. He had been 90 percent sure they were friends for real, but seeing it stated so plainly made a tiny part of A.J.'s brain relax in a way it almost never did.

AJWalker90: "It sucked, but I'm fine. Really, I've gotten way worse from street hockey."

There was a much longer delay before Bren's reply this time.

RedBullBren69: "Cop on. Mickie told me about the Discman"

A.J. made a mental note to punch Mickie the next time he saw him.

AJWalker90: "Didn't you call it a relic on my first day? I needed a new one anyway."

RedBullBren69: "U lose the CD too?"

The question threw A.J. Why was he thinking about that?

AJWalker90: "My Girl Power Mega Mix is fine. Just need something to play it on now."

RedBullBren69: "That thing was a fucking legend. Sure u can't fix it?"

For some stupid reason, A.J.'s smile grew. It cost him something to type his next message.

AJWalker90: "Here lies Discman, 2001-2006."

RedBullBren69: "Aw shit. We'll find u a new one"

A.J. started to reply, but Bren beat him to it.

RedBullBren69: "Hey, if ur not too beat up, u should come round 4 dinner Sunday. Mam's been on my arse about it"

If A.J. hadn't already finished his ice cream, he would have choked. He knew Bren was just being nice, but that didn't stop his thoughts from wandering.

AJWalker90: "Your mom wants to have dinner with me . . . ? Lol."

RedBullBren69: "Lmao, it's not gonna be candlelight or anything. I think she just wants to make sure ur not another Mickie"

A.J. felt like he'd been punched all over again, but in a way that made him . . . happy? He was glad, in any case, that Bren wasn't there to see his hands tremble as he typed.

AJWalker90: "Oh, sure. Thanks. Should I bring anything?"

15

A.J. bit the side of his cheek as he made his way down the crooked road towards Bren's house. With no music to drown out the quiet, his mind refused to settle on a single thought, and instead hopped around like he'd been downing shots of espresso all day.

It's just dinner, he told himself for the hundredth time.

But that was a lie. From what Bren had said, the whole thing was an excuse for his mom to make sure he wasn't a horrible person. Somehow, he didn't feel like the bruise stamped across his eye was going to win him any points on that front.

Then there was that picture of Bren and his mom at church. How fire and brimstone was she likely to be? It was obvious Catholics reigned supreme in Glenbridge, but he was hanging on to the hope she might be a casual churchgoer, or else Ireland was less obsessed with quoting Leviticus.

He shifted the foil-wrapped tart he'd been cradling on the walk and reached for the door. Bren had said to let himself in, but every inch of A.J.'s upbringing was screaming that he needed to knock and wait. As a compromise, he knocked twice and, with his stomach clenched, turned the handle.

The delicious smell of meat and spices washed over A.J. the second he stepped in from the damp evening outside. Some of the tension left his shoulders as he took in the now familiar sight of the O'Sheas' bungalow. The air was warm as it had been the night he'd stayed over. He'd been there a handful of times since, but Maura had always been off at work. For all Bren said he saw her all the time, her job seemed to keep her away more often than not.

He now knew the cozy warmth of the house was thanks to the turf stove that smouldered in the living room. A.J. had blushed when Bren had first explained it to him—it answered the question of why Bren always smelled like he'd just come from a bonfire.

A.J. took in all this in the split second between stepping inside and a woman's voice piping up from the kitchen.

"Bren, he's here!"

A.J. stood in the silence that followed as Mrs. O'Shea turned around, her face wrinkled in vague annoyance. He could see how bits of her had made their way to Bren. He had her nose and the same wave to his hair, though hers had more of an auburn undertone compared to Bren's gingery red.

"You must be A.J.," she said, waving her hand. "Don't linger in the doorway, come on in."

She sounded tired, but there was a warmth to her words that put A.J. in mind of a crackling fire. He kicked off his shoes on instinct and stepped inside.

"Nice to meet you." His voice cracked on the first word, but he rushed on anyway. "Thanks a lot for having me over."

Mrs. O'Shea looked him up and down. "You sure you're in the right house?"

A.J.'s mind went into overdrive. As sure as he was this was Bren's place, he was forced to consider that maybe he'd made a mistake. "I, uh, what? I mean, uh, yes?"

Mrs. O'Shea looked at him like she didn't quite know what to make of him, but laughed right after.

"You're a polite one. Bren brings home shiteheads most times." Her eyes fell to the mound of tinfoil he'd forgotten he was clutching. "You bring somethin' too?"

A.J.'s mind latched onto the question with alarming speed. It was something he could answer at least. "Oh yeah, I uh—it's a tart."

"Guess we'll be having two then." Mrs. O'Shea said as she took the tart.

"Two?" A.J. asked, his brain still playing catch-up.

"Bren made a mess of me kitchen makin' some mad thing this mornin'." She peeled back the foil and smiled, "You in Home Ec with him?"

"Yes, ma'am," A.J. said before he could stop himself. "We're in the same group."

"Good, boys should know how to cook for themselves." She set the tart on the stove next to a much larger pie. "And no need to be formal. Just call me Maura."

He thought he saw something that looked like a smile on her face before she turned towards the hall again. "You go deaf? Get your bony arse in here!"

Footsteps tramped up the hall, and Bren wandered out looking like he'd just rolled out of bed.

"Was in the middle of a match. Shoulda just sent him back," Bren said, yawning as he scratched at the rumpled jumper he was wearing.

He barely reacted when Mrs. O'Shea cuffed him upside the head.

"I look like your maid? Now act like I raised you with some manners."

A.J. was surprised when Bren laughed and, rubbing the back of his head, nodded towards his mom. "This is me mam, Maura."

101

A.J. thought he saw something flare in Bren's eyes as they landed on his bruise, but it flickered out the next second. "And, Mam, yer man who looks like he came from MMA is A.J."

A.J.'s hand twitched in an attempt at a handshake, but Mrs. O'Shea tilted her head.

"How'd you get the shiner? You don't look the type to get into fights."

A.J. brought a hand to his bruise like he'd forgotten it was there.

"Oh, Brick was trying to teach me hurling and I kind of caught the sliotar with my face."

A.J. thought he saw Maura purse her lips before Bren came to the rescue.

"Right, proper intro an' all," Bren said, taking a step back towards his room. "Can we go now?"

"You can help set the table. Dinner's almost done," Mrs. O'Shea said, the appraising expression gone from her face.

Bren sighed and, slumped-shouldered, trudged into the kitchen.

"Oh, I can help with that," A.J. said, trailing behind Bren.

Mrs. O'Shea waved him off. "Bren'll manage on his own. You can take a seat."

A.J. did as he was told, and before he could form a reply, Mrs. O'Shea had bustled over with a mug of steaming tea.

"Bren didn't tell me what you fancy, so I had to guess. You like stew?"

A.J. nodded, "Yeah, that sounds great—stew, I mean."

She fixed him with another look he couldn't quite read, but he thought there was something like approval in it. He was saved the necessity of thinking of what to say next when Bren popped up at his mom's side and started setting down bowls.

102

"A.J.'s stayin' up the hill. Probably takes his stew with caviar by now."

A.J. laughed louder than he meant to.

"It's been mostly frozen stuff. The McCarthys don't really cook much."

Bren paused with a spoon halfway to the table, and his face fell. A.J. couldn't see why, it wasn't like the McCarthys were starving him or anything.

"Well, we're nice and simple around here," Mrs. O'Shea said, setting down a large Dutch oven with a muffled thud. "But at least it's from scratch on Sundays."

"Mam's a good feckin' cook, you're gonna like it," Bren said, back to his usual self.

A.J. smiled as the O'Sheas headed back to the kitchen. He'd been fed every day since he'd gotten here, but this felt like the first real meal he'd had since leaving Canada behind.

***

Bren was feeling better by the time he'd shoveled in his second mouthful of stew. Going off the baby carrots, it looked like Mam hadn't had time to go to the shops yesterday, but it still tasted good. Even though the lad looked happy, Bren couldn't help but focus on the purple crater around A.J.'s eye.

He'd been pissed when he'd heard about it from Mickie, but seeing it in person made him want to storm out the door right then and get Cian twice as good. Then there was the fact the lad hadn't bothered to tell him what had happened.

Weren't they meant to be mates?

103

"Wow. This is really good, Mrs. O'Shea."

Bren stopped himself from laughing just in time. If anyone else had said it like that, he'd be sure they were up to something, but he knew better by now—A.J. was polite, but he didn't suck up.

From the look on Mam's face, Bren thought she was having trouble figuring that out.

"That's how they are in Canada, Mam. Real polite, like."

She watched A.J. a while longer, then turned to him.

"You could take notes then," she gestured at the spoon clenched in his hand. "You're not supposed to eat like that once you're out of nappies, love."

Bren rolled his eyes and shoveled another spoonful into his mouth. Mam spared him a sigh before moving on.

"So, what made you come all the way from Canada?"

To Bren's surprise, A.J. didn't hesitate.

"I've wanted to do the exchange program since grade nine, but it's only open for eleven and twelve." He paused to take a sip of his tea, which Bren noticed he didn't take with sugar. "When I heard one of the spots was for Ireland, it sort of fit."

He left it at that, even though it seemed like there was more to the story.

Bren managed to make a "huh" sound through his bulging cheeks.

"I guess because it was far away, and I actually spoke the language," he said with a meaningful look to Bren. "I'm bad enough at talking in English. I didn't want to try it in German or something."

Bren laughed the second he'd swallowed the stew. "Found out the hard way we don't talk the same as Canada?"

A.J. perked up at that, pointing at Bren like he'd said something brilliant. "You kind of do, though! So is like eh. I think? Mr. Kelleher

104

uses it like that anyway." He looked thoughtful, adding, "It is kind of hard to understand the accents sometimes, but I've liked learning."

This made Bren smile for some reason. He hadn't realized the lad had been listening like that.

"Right, then next time you see Miss Murphy make sure you tell her Is breá liom tits móra. She'll love it."

Maura's dinner roll bounced off the side of Bren's head before A.J. had a chance to stammer. Bren rubbed the spot where it had hit him, then scooped the roll off the floor and took a bite. Mam groaned but looked back to A.J. like she hadn't just assaulted her son.

"Don't feel bad if it's givin' you trouble. We can't understand each other half the time," Mam said.

Bren couldn't tell what she thought of A.J. yet, but he was pretty sure she'd placed him closer to Rory than Mickie in her mind. It was a good start. He didn't want to have to have another mate that was banned from the house more often than not.

By the time dinner was over, Bren was sure Mam had warmed up to A.J. She'd refilled his bowl when he'd cleared it the first time, anyway. He'd been worried A.J. would turn down the second helping, but he'd reached for another roll and tucked in.

"Proper stew, Mam," Bren said, pushing back from the table and belching.

Mam looked satisfyingly cross before A.J. cut in.

"It was really good. Seriously, I think that's the best thing I've had since I came here."

There wasn't a hint of flattery in his words, only that bluntly earnest quality he sometimes had.

"Ta," Mam said, with a smile. That was one of the better things about Mam—she didn't smile unless she meant it.

He made to get up, eager to see how his pie turned out. A.J. had liked the tart from Niamh's so much he thought he'd put his own spin on it.

"Bring over A.J.'s while you're up."

"His what?" Bren asked, wondering if he'd heard her wrong.

"On the stove, right next to whatever was worth destroyin' me kitchen over."

Bren grinned. "I cleaned it up, didn't I?"

He pulled a stack of saucers from the cabinet and set them next to the pie while he dug around for forks.

"Watcha bring? More mad stuff from Canada?" Bren asked, thinking of how lethal the Jam Jams would be with a cuppa.

For some reason, A.J. turned pink and didn't reply.

By the time he'd set everything on the table, Mam had peeled off the foil to cut slices of the tart underneath. He recognized the golden shortcrust from Home Ec last week.

Guess he wanted another crack at it.

Mam didn't ask permission, just handed everyone a slice of each and poured more tea. He could taste the filling before he tucked in. His mind went to the bushes Nan had planted at the front of the house. Had A.J. picked raspberries because of that? The lad really did notice everything.

Something in him melted. The pastry was too thick, but the filling was a proper sweet-sour balance, with a hint of spice and a warmth Bren thought he recognized. He tried not to smile too wide as he went for his second bite. It tasted like something Nan might have made for Christmas.

"You put whiskey in this?" Mam asked.

"Oh, yeah. We soaked fruit in whiskey for Barmbrack, and I thought it might be good in a tart." The more A.J. talked, the more nervous he sounded. He looked like he remembered something and blanched. "Is that ok?"

Mam nodded. "Me mam put enough whiskey in her fruit cake to knock a horse on its arse. You're grand."

Bren watched as A.J. took his first mouthful of apple pie. He'd gone on instinct with this one, so he had no idea how it'd actually turned out. A.J.'s relaxed expression morphed into something more serious as he chewed.

"Is there . . . cheese in this?"

Bren's face broke into a grin.

"Yup. Cheddar in the crust and a bit of gouda grated in with the apples. Threw in some ginger and a bit of white pepper, too, for some kick. Extra sugar on balance, like." He watched as A.J.'s chewing slowed. "Good?"

A.J. swallowed.

"You didn't try it first?"

Bren shrugged.

"Didn't wanna ruin the presentation, did I?"

A.J. glared down at his pie. "It's . . . good."

Bren waited for A.J.'s face to relax before he took another bite of tart, his pie still waiting its turn.

"Seriously. I'm so angry about it, but this is really good."

Heat rose in Bren's cheeks as he swallowed—it was getting harder to tell himself it was just from the whiskey.

16

A.J. let his hand fall to his side as blood splattered across the bottom of his screen. He leaned back against the edge of the bed, Bren's legs dangling by his shoulders from his spot above.

"You're playin' extra shite tonight, Robolad."

He was right of course. He was crap at CoD even when his heart was in the game. The way he was playing now, he was little more than a training dummy that sometimes shot back. His mind kept working over the details of dinner despite his efforts to keep focused on gunfire. Had he made a good impression on Bren's mom? She'd refilled his bowl and seemed to have liked the tart, but she'd also given him a weird look when he offered to help her clear the table.

Then there was the unwelcome fluttering in his chest. It had started when they'd got to eating their stew. He'd sat watching Bren shovel in his food, fist clenched around the spoon like it might fly away if he loosened his grip. It was such a stupid detail. If anything, it should have been gross, or else have made him laugh. But, A.J. couldn't stop replaying it in his mind.

He took a couple of shots at Bren before ducking behind a pixelated oil barrel, not wanting to make it too easy for him.

"Movie after this, yeah?" he said, all smiles as he clipped a piece of A.J.'s leg that hadn't gotten behind cover in time.

"As long as it's not anything with guns," A.J. said, which got a whoop from Bren as he made A.J.'s screen go red again.

"I'd be runnin' if I had to play me too."

That's it, thought A.J. *you're not in love with your best friend over here. You're just intimidated by his button pressing skills.*

The delusion lasted all of five seconds as Bren shifted so his leg brushed against A.J.'s shoulder—last he checked, CoD envy didn't come with goosebumps.

Way to go brainless . . .

***

"Can't believe you haven't heard of Simon Pegg before," Bren said, nudging A.J. in the ribs.

He'd slid off his bed about halfway through the movie—A.J. had been weird about coming up even though the view was better.

"I don't think we get him as much back home," A.J. said, stretching his arms over his head as he stood.

Bren grinned, but he couldn't put his finger on why. He'd done the whole dinner, movie and CoD yoke with the lads more times than he could count, but his cheeks had never hurt from smiling like this. Maybe it was the tart. It was fuckin' good.

"Poor sods," he popped a shoulder then let himself fall to the side. "Havin' to laugh at, I dunno, beavers or somethin'."

"Hey! I was a Beaver Scout, dick."

Bren burst out laughing, "No way that's a real thing."

"It's real," A.J. said, his scowl not reaching his eyes. "I think I have to fight you now. For honour."

"Think you can take all this?" Bren asked, leaping to his feet, heart racing. If the lad went for it, he wasn't going to hold back.

A.J. looked like he was going to meet the challenge but took a step back. "Never thrown a punch in my life."

Bren's smile faded as his eyes fell on A.J.'s bruise. He opened his mouth to ask the question he'd been sitting on since Friday, but changed his mind at the last second. "Settle it in CoD? Canada Ireland grudge match?"

A.J. glanced at the clock. "It's getting late. Should probably get going."

"Ah, come on, it's half ten! I've seen yourself online past two."

"Yeah, online, not in your house. Don't wanna overstay."

Bren frowned. A.J. wasn't stammering or anything, but he'd taken on some of the twitchy energy he'd had that first day. "Who said you're overstayin'?"

"I-I mean, your mom's home and stuff, I guess," he said, picking at his sleeve now.

So much for not stammering.

"Ah, don't worry, mam likes you. Gave you seconds, didn't she? Actually, y'could kip over here and she wouldn't mind. Want me to ask?"

He made to yell to Mam and A.J. dove forward, clapping a hand over his mouth. A.J.'s palm pressed against his lips long enough for Bren to notice how clammy it was before he jerked away like he'd been bitten.

"Sorry!"

A.J.'s face was redder than Bren had ever seen it, and he was wiping his hand on his trousers like he was trying to start a fire. "I can't stay over. I've got uh, homework for Music."

"Ah, fair enough," he managed, scratching the back of his head. It was one of the only classes they didn't have together, so he couldn't be sure—but something told him A.J. wasn't off to write an essay on trombones.

He didn't get to say anything else before A.J. thanked him for having him over and was gone. He heard the front door click shut and with it, Bren flopped down on the edge of his bed. What the hell had that been about? The lad had acted like he'd asked him to cut off his arm or something. And why had his hand been so clammy?

As light as it had felt before, his stomach had dropped to somewhere around his trainers. A.J. was the one with the shiner—so why did he feel like he was the one who'd been decked.

17

A muffled cry forced its way out of Bren as the over-bright dream world collapsed around him. He kicked away the tangle of blankets wrapped around his legs and rolled onto his side. The faint glow from the stereo on the other side of the room told him it was half two.

He turned again, groaning as he buried his face into the flattened pillows beneath his head. Why the hell was he awake?

He'd barely finished forming the question in his mind before the answer broke through.

A.J.

He'd been having one of his usual mad dreams at first. He and Rory had been talking about whether or not Buffy Summers could kill a vampire with a sliotar—only Rory had Mickie's voice for some reason. Next second, he'd been walking around a graveyard in a hurling kit, and then he'd been back in his room watching Dawn of the Dead with A.J., who'd been a zombie for some reason.

A.J. had moved off his spot on the floor, so they sat shoulder to shoulder on the bed. Bren couldn't remember exactly what they were talking about, but his cheeks had hurt in that numb, dream-pain way from smiling.

The floor chilled Bren's feet as he pulled himself out of bed. A snack and something to drink, and he'd head right back.

He adjusted the front of his boxers, not paying the lingering tightness much mind. He woke up like that more often than not these days. It'd go away in a minute.

The fridge was full of its usual offerings. Cheese, some pineapple Mam had cut up a couple of days ago, a bit of chopped ham if he wanted. He grabbed the lone slice of raspberry tart without conscious thought and poured himself a glass of milk for good measure.

He sat in the living room instead of the kitchen, curling up on the couch and staring up at Maurice's horse-shaped outline on the ceiling.

The tart tasted just as good cold.

He couldn't understand why his chest felt so heavy. Hadn't he been happy in the dream? His stomach was in knots, too.

Something tugged at the edge of Bren's mind. He tried to push it away, but the thought pushed harder.

Collin.

It had been a night like this almost two years ago. He'd woken up after some mad dream about Collin with his face wet and his heart racing.

Bren couldn't see why his mind was trying to link A.J. and Collin together. They were about as different as you could get.

Bren had run into the guy on his first day of third year—literally. He'd been looking over his shoulder to yell something at Mickie as he turned a corner and walked straight into the bloke. Since Collin was nearly four years older and was training for a spot at Munster Academy, Bren had bounced off his chest and landed right on his arse.

Collin had pulled him off the ground like he weighed no more than a puppy and dusted him off with a laugh.

After that, they'd sometimes stop in the hall to chat between classes. Bren would have died before he'd admit it to anyone, but he'd always gotten a bit of a thrill out of that. Athletic, funny, popular with everyone—especially the ladies—he was what Bren wanted to be by the time he got to sixth year. He'd even had cool hair.

After Collin finished school, he disappeared to Cork before the first week of summer ended. Or at least that's what he'd overheard Niamh say to some old bloke who'd come into the bakery.

Bren shoveled a chunk of the tart into his mouth and exhaled through his nose.

He was way too tired to be thinking about this.

18

A.J. ran his thumb along the curve of the weather-worn rock in his pocket as he made his way towards the usual spot. As it was still cool from last night's drizzle, some part of his brain must have been hoping the stone might siphon off some of the heat that had been carving lines across his chest for the last twelve hours.

Bren had invited him over thinking it was just dinner with a mate, and it had made A.J. happier than he could put into words. And what had he done to repay him? Groped Bren's mouth, then ran out of the house and into the night like an absolute sociopath. Bren was chill as they came, but A.J. was sure he must have spent the rest of the night rethinking their friendship. That wasn't taking into account the thoughts that had been forcing their way into A.J.'s mind over the past few weeks, despite his best efforts. If Bren could see into his head for even one second, A.J. was sure Bren would vanish from his life—right after blacking his other eye.

He made himself sit with that reality. Bren at school, turning away every time he saw him coming. No more talking music with Rory, or hurling with Brick. Back to eating in the greenhouse for sure.

Just. Be. Normal.

He forced the words into his chest as he rounded the corner to find Bren waiting at the fork.

"Morning! How'd you sleep?"

A.J. flinched at his own brightness.

They turned in unison to make their way towards town.

"Slept alright," he said, glancing at A.J. before fixing his eyes back to the path. "You're lookin' a bit shite. Homework keep y'up?"

Right. That was the lie he'd fed Bren before he'd bailed.

"Oh yeah," he said, aware the bags under his eyes made him look like he was in competition with Rory. "Took a while to finish, then I sort of just slept like shit, I guess."

Bren nodded, eyes still fixed on where they were going.

An unfamiliar silence stretched out between them as they walked, raindrops falling in uneven bursts from clouds that refused to rain properly.

"Think we'll make anything good in Home Ec today?" A.J. offered, desperate for some of Bren's usual banter.

It took Bren longer than normal to answer, and when he did, his words came out flat.

"Hope so. Forgot lunch."

If it were anyone else, A.J. would have backed off, but Bren wasn't just anyone else. He was sure Bren would perk up if they found the right topic.

Food hadn't worked, so should he find a way to bring up the Harps? Or maybe try a joke? He didn't know how Bren navigated these waters so effortlessly.

A joke was probably safest.

Before he knew what he was doing, A.J. turned on his heel and cut across the path.

He reached his hand out and poked Bren in the chest—right where the play button had been on the doodle that had earned A.J. his nickname.

116

"Beep boop, who's being Robolad now?"

He forced himself to look Bren in the eyes, then froze.

He'd expected him to crack a smile and laugh, or else roll his eyes and brush him off. Instead, Bren's eyes were fixed on his with such intensity that A.J. couldn't help but stare back.

A muscle in Bren's jaw twitched, and unless A.J. was imagining it, he could see the rise and fall of his chest beneath his jumper.

A.J.'s hand pressed forward as if pulled by invisible strings, fingers flattening against Bren's chest so he could feel each beat of his heart.

Bren took in a shuddering breath as a fat raindrop burst on the end of his nose.

He didn't wipe it away.

It was this detail, for whatever reason, that snapped A.J. out of his stupor. He pulled his hand away—or at least, he tried to. Bren caught him at the wrist and held him there, his hazel eyes still burning.

A.J. tried to say something, but he may as well have left his voice back in Moose Jaw. He was sure he was wrong. He had to be.

This was a mistake.

The alarm bells blared louder as he leaned forward.

He was going to ruin everything.

There was warmth on his lips now. His breathing slowed, and his fingers curled against Bren's chest.

There was a single, terrifying moment where Bren made a choked noise in his throat—and then he returned the pressure.

Their lips parted, and Bren's tongue pressed forward to meet A.J.'s—tea, toast, and the faintest hint of spearmint.

A.J.'s hand trembled as it slid to Bren's hip, desperate to hold on to some part of him more substantial than his jumper. When A.J.'s

117

fingers brushed against the top of Bren's hip, he pulled away. His lips were still parted, chest heaving like they'd come from gym class.

A.J. leaned back in, and Bren jerked away like he'd been burned. He shot a panicked look up the road, and A.J. mirrored him. The stone wall was the only witness.

"B-Bren, sorry—I didn't mea—"

Bren let out a ragged grunt and shook his head. His hand clamped down on A.J.'s wrist again and pulled them back the way they'd come. A.J. forced himself to follow, his legs wobbling like they were made of Jell-O. He knew now wasn't the time to speak, and he was glad of that—he could still taste tea and toast.

118

19

The door to Bren's house clattered shut behind A.J. as the rain began to fall in earnest. He barely had enough time to notice how damp his shoulders were when Bren spun around to face him. They stared at each other, Bren's hand clenched so hard his arm was trembling.

"B-ren, wh—"

A.J. was cut off again as Bren collided with him. They met in a frenzied tangle, and A.J. had to throw an arm back against the doorframe to keep from falling over. Bren's tongue pressed against his lips, and A.J. let them part as the flame Bren kindled on the side of the road roared into an inferno.

He pulled Bren closer, desperate to close what little space remained between them. Bren's hand found his hair, and a moan forced its way out of A.J.

A sound bubbled out from the corner of Bren's mouth that he couldn't place at first. Then sense broke through the cloud of euphoria—he was laughing.

They broke away, A.J.'s heart pounding so fast he felt like he might pass out.

"F-fuckin-n' . . . f-uck!" Bren shouted, his words broken by bits of insane laughter.

A.J. was starting to worry now. He forced himself to look Bren in the eyes, and was surprised to see them shining— not with tears, but with a desperate burning that looked like it might spill over at any second.

An explanation for it all formed in A.J.'s mind. He'd kissed Bren, and Bren, being the amazing person he was, didn't know how to tell him he was out of line. Then he had pushed things too far with that stupid fucking moan, and now Bren was short-circuiting.

"Bren—are you? I'm so sorry, I thought—I mean. I didn't mean to—"

Bren laughed again, his fist coming down to land with a muffled thud on A.J.'s chest.

"Why y'always do that?"

A.J. stared down at the fist over his heart.

"D-do what?"

"Apologize like I'm gonna get mad at you for existin'."

"I-I don't . . . you mean, you're not mad?"

Another laugh, closer to his usual this time. "You think I put me tongue in your mouth 'cuz I'm pissed, like?"

The world swayed. "Put my tongue in your mouth" was not a sentence A.J. ever thought he'd hear Bren say.

"You . . . liked kissing me? I thought you were—"

Bren kissed him into silence, and A.J.'s hand found the small of Bren's back as a groan rumbled in his throat. He didn't understand how this could be happening. Things like this didn't just happen—not to him.

"Can you shut off that big feckin' brain of yours for ten minutes? Just give me ten minutes to—fuck!" Bren growled out the last word, as though he had interrupted himself. They kissed again, and Bren's tongue flicked into A.J.'s mouth for a blissfully agonizing second.

"If we're mitchin', I'm not wearin' this fuckin' uniform."

He hitched on the first Bren-like smile A.J. had seen all day and pulled at his hand. Fighting every instinct he had, A.J. kept his mouth shut and let himself be led to wherever this was going.

Bren's tie was off before he'd made it to his bedroom. He flung it to join the clutter of manky clothes at the foot of his bed. His jumper joined right after, and even though there was a chill in the air, his chest still burned.

His trousers had joined the pile when A.J. gave a muffled cry. Bren turned to find him standing in the doorway, so pale he could have blended in with the walls.

"What's wrong?"

A.J. made another strangled noise, his eyes flicking down before he turned red as he'd been pale. Bren looked down and was almost surprised to find himself stripped down to his boxers.

He pulled a pair of trackies off the floor and hopped on one foot to tug them on. "What? You've seen me jocks before."

It was true, gym class had made sure of that. Even if A.J. always looked like he was counting floor tiles in the minutes between him rushing in and out of the changing room.

A.J.'s Adam's apple bobbed, his eyes still fixed off to the side.

"N-not like this!"

Bren laughed. Somehow, A.J. being A.J. helped his panic even out.

"What? You put your tongue in me mouth, but you draw the line at starin' at me pasty ass thighs?"

"Y-you're the one who added tongue!"

Hearing it out loud like that sent a jolt through Bren's spine.

"Fuck, guess I did . . ." he said, then pulled on a faded T-shirt that used to have the Green Day logo on it.

He ran his hands over his arms. He didn't know when it happened, but he'd broken out in goose pimples, and his sack felt like it'd shrunk to the size of a coin purse.

"Gonna throw on some turf."

His eyes fixed on A.J.'s uniform—it looked like he'd gotten the worst of the rain somehow. "Get out of that and pick out somethin' dry, like." He waved his hand and left the room before A.J. could start stammering. "Just do it, lad, don't wanna kiss a wet rag."

Bren's heart pounded as he stoked the embers until a flame caught at the edge of a fresh chunk of turf. Kiss a wet rag . . . he had kissed A.J.

He tried to think about the last time he'd gotten up close and personal with Orlaith Murphy. The smell of her perfume, the curve of her hip against his hand. It had been grand, but it hadn't made his heart pound like this—nothing else ever had.

He was fourteen again, pulled off the ground by Collin's muscular arm. He'd put it up to embarrassment at the time, but the hammering in his chest back then was a perfect match for what he'd felt when A.J. had laid his hand over his heart.

"Fuckin' nervous Canadian lad . . ."

The smell of smouldering turf followed Bren into the kitchen as he did the only thing that made sense right now. Scalding tea, a splash of milk, and a plate of biscuits. Hopefully, A.J. would have spiraled himself out by the time he got back. He gripped either side of the water-stained tray like a lifeline and headed back to his room.

"Right, done malfunctionin' in here, Robolad?"

Bren had half expected to find A.J. still frozen in the doorway, or else fiddling with whatever he'd been turning over in his hand all morning. Instead, A.J. was lying on the bed, arm draped over his eyes like he was winding down for a nap. He'd put on a sky blue T-shirt and the pair of checkered pyjama bottoms Bren had worn two nights ago.

His mind flashed back to the morning after the hurling match. He'd wandered into the kitchen for a glass of water and noticed A.J. tangled in his covers on the floor. He'd chalked it up to being half asleep back then, but seeing him so relaxed like that had made something in Bren stir.

That was nothing compared to the sight of A.J. now. A.J. on his bed, wearing his clothes. His usual instinct would have been to say something. To take the piss and get the lad all flustered in the way he did. Instead, he walked with quiet steps, set the tray next to a pile of discarded socks, and sat down.

A.J. lifted his arm as the bed jostled, a sheen of sweat glistening across his forehead. Bren ran his thumb across A.J.'s eyebrow. Could fevers burn cold?

"Everythin' ok?"

"Just . . . breathing," A.J. said.

The tremble in A.J.'s voice told Bren there was more to it, but all he could think was how cute A.J. looked in his shirt.

"You sure you wanna do that in here?" Bren asked, gesturing to the room at large. "Smells like turf and pits."

A.J. shook his head. "It smells like you and . . ." He looked down at the shirt he was wearing and picked at the sleeve. "I like the way you smell."

Bren crawled over and pressed his lips against A.J.'s. Where the other kisses had built towards a frenzy, this one grew deeper. He needed the lad to feel some of what that sentence did to him.

The hunger that had been growing since they'd come crashing through the door morphed into something Bren didn't have a name for. Half of everything he was wanted to tear off their clothes and burn through the roll of condoms under his mattress. The other half wanted nothing more than this moment, to feel A.J.'s heart beating against his until the world stopped turning—or at least until Mam came home.

He was settling down to do the latter when A.J. pulled away.

"C-can we put on some music? Please?"

That second thing stirred at the pleading look in A.J.'s eyes.

"Ok."

He got off the bed and rummaged through the stack of CDs next to his relic of a stereo. Green Day, Offspring, an old copy of B*Witched he'd won in a raffle back in fourth class—he kept meaning to burn that one before Mickie found it.

"What kind of music?"

"Literally anything."

Bren popped in American Idiot and got back onto the bed. Once the song got going, A.J.'s face relaxed.

"What is it with you and music anyway?"

It was something he'd been wondering for a while now. He liked a good beat as much as the next guy, but it seemed like a lot more than that to A.J.

A.J. half rolled his eyes, but a smile spread over his face.

"Oh, that's my parents' fault. One hundred percent."

Bren waited for him to keep going, and when he didn't, raised an eyebrow.

"My dad's a composer, and my mom teaches music at Riverview. So there's pretty much music playing every second back home."

"A composer? Like?" Bren said, waving an imaginary baton.

"How am I attracted to you . . . ?"

A.J. laughed and leaned in for a kiss, but Bren pushed him down.

"Oi. What's that about then?"

"That's a conductor," A.J. said, shoving Bren's hip. "They help people play what a composer, you know, composes. It's right there in the name, man."

"That's cheeky comin' from the lad who didn't know what hurlin' was till I told him. It's right there in the name, lad."

Bren crawled back on top of A.J. and kissed away his comeback. From the sound he made, Bren was sure he didn't mind. The hunger rumbled, and Bren brought his hand to cup the side of A.J.'s face.

A pained hiss left A.J. and he flinched away.

"Wasswrong?"

Bren blinked his eyes open to see what had happened.

"Sorry, it just hur-"

Bren brought his hand to the border of A.J.'s angry, yellow-tinted bruise and traced it with the barest tips of his fingers. A.J. refused to hold his gaze.

"How come you didn't tell me?"

It took an entire verse of track three for A.J. to answer.

"I didn't want you to be . . . mad at me."

Whatever Bren thought the reason might be, that wasn't it.

"The fuck would I be mad at you for? Cian's the piece of shit that punched you."

A.J. sighed. "Ok, maybe not mad but . . . disappointed? I could have handled it a lot better. Kept my mouth shut."

"Wait, Mickie made it sound like Cian went after you for nothin'. What happened?"

A.J.'s voice was soft as he told the story. When he got around to the part about calling Tadhg Cian's boyfriend, he sounded like a kid telling his mam he'd pocketed some change from the collection plate.

"You think I'd be pissed you stood up to that fucker?" He didn't wait for A.J. to reply and instead kissed his bruise. "I'm feckin' proud. We just need to teach you to throw a punch. Bring the backbone home, like."

A.J. snorted. "Oh yeah, Cian better watch out next time."

Bren shook his head.

"If there's ever a next time, Cian's going home with his teeth in a fuckin' bag."

The fury in his chest rippled as he looked down at A.J. It met with the ache that had been smouldering all morning and formed one singular word as Bren leaned down to kiss the shy, brave mess of a lad beneath him—mine.

20

Bren's arm brushed against A.J.'s as he shifted on his spot next to him. Rather than pull away as his instinct urged him, A.J. let himself lean against Bren's side. They'd been half-watching My Big Fat Greek Wedding for the last half an hour. Bren had made a joke about Brokeback Mountain being a better pick, but dropped the idea after A.J. suggested he pop down to Xtra-vision and rent it for them.

A.J.'s hand twitched towards Bren's, but he diverted the energy into scratching his leg again. If he kept it up, Bren was going to think he had a rash or something.

Some part of him understood how stupid it was to be so scared to hold his hand, given what they'd been doing all morning. He kept picturing Bren pulling away—or worse—gritting his teeth but doing it anyway. "So, you gonna tell me what your name means now?"

"What?" A.J. had drifted so much Bren's voice almost made him jump.

"You even watchin'?"

He hadn't been, but he'd seen the movie enough to know where they were. They were still early on, Ian and Toula were still mid meet-cute. A.J.'s mind whirred trying to puzzle together what Bren was talking about. Then he saw it, the two of them walking home after his first day.

It's A.J., yeah? What's that short for?

Had he been thinking about that since September?

"It doesn't mean anything, it's just my name."

Bren groaned. "That's what you said before. No one's named after letters. It's a nickname and y'know it."

"Alright, *Bren,*" A.J. said, clapping him on the shoulder. It wasn't his hand, but it was something.

"St. Brendan of Clonfert, the navigator." Bren said and shrugged A.J.'s hand off. "Your turn."

"Didn't know I was in bed with a saint," A.J. replied before he could stop himself.

"Named after one. Think Mam had high hopes or somethin'. Now cop on."

"You're really not going to let this go."

"Nope."

A.J. let himself slide sideways to flop down by the foot of the bed. "Fine, but if you tell anyone, I'm changing schools."

He was trying his best to be annoyed about it, but he had to admit, it was cute how curious Bren was.

"Arlo Jonathan."

He braced for the laugh, the piss-take that was sure to come.

"Arlo . . ."

Bren said it so softly, like he was seeing how it felt against his lips. For the first time since he was five, hearing the name didn't make A.J. cringe.

He sat up and, without looking at Bren, took his hand. A.J. had enough time to regret his decision before Bren's fingers wove into his.

"Still gotta call you A.J., don't I?"

Cheeks burning, A.J. returned the pressure.

". . . maybe not all the time."

***

A.J. sighed as he stared at the sea of grey icons that was his contact list, never hating the time difference more. If he were back in Moose Jaw, he and Nat would already have been deep into dissecting what went down. Instead, he'd spent the last few hours trying not to tremble in front of the McCarthys. Not satisfied with simply throwing Bren at him lip-first, the universe had decided today was a good day for them to show an unusual amount of interest in him.

He'd done his best to enjoy the company, but he couldn't help feel like the time spent together had been more for their benefit. After some surface-level questions about how he was enjoying his time in Glenbridge, they'd launched into an endless stream of chatter about themselves. It had been impossible to follow most of it, but he'd understood enough to clock that they were planning a trip to the Canary Islands over Christmas. They didn't say, but he hoped he wasn't expected to go with them.

Even though he'd been waiting since dinner, his hand stayed hovering over the mouse when Nat's icon turned green. Where the hell was he supposed to start?

It became a moot point as Nat beat him to the punch.

LittleMoshpitKid46: "Ok so drama club hasn't been the same without you, but guess who got a kickass part for fall play?"

Part of A.J. groaned at the signal to stop thinking about himself, but another—more loyal part—shifted gears right along with it.

AJWalker90: "Please god tell me Morgan didn't get the lead again."

LittleMoshpitKid46: "Ugh, kind of, but that just means she dies in act two"

AJWalker90: "And I'm guessing you get to live?"

LittleMoshpitKid46: "Yup! I'm Ouiser! Can't keep an old bitch down"

AJWalker90: "Like Steel Magnolias? Congrats! I'm happy for you and just a little jealous. How come we do the cool plays the year I leave?"

LittleMoshpitKid46: "I know right? Oh! Yu's here too by the way. He's stage manager"

The piece of himself he'd left back in Canada drooped. They'd gone to hang out at Nat's house the day the cast list came out since grade nine. For the first time in weeks, he wished he was back in Moose Jaw, until he remembered why he'd been waiting for Nat in the first place.

AJWalker90: "Hi Yuuuu! Tell him sorry he has to manage you without me."

LittleMoshpitKid46: "He says he'll manage"

"Oh, and fuck you btw"

A.J. snorted.

AJWalker90: "Seriously though, congrats! Ouiser's perfect for you."

LittleMoshpitKid46: "Right? I just get to be me in 40 years but with great tits"

A.J. willed Nat to ask about his day, and whether it was coincidence or the universe deciding to cut him a break, she obliged.

LittleMoshpitKid46: "So how about you? What the heck are you going to do instead of drama club?"

A.J. checked over his shoulder, as if one of the McCarthys might be lurking, then forced himself to breathe.

AJWalker90: "Probably try and figure out what the hell's going on with me and Bren."

LittleMoshpitKid46: "You mean your Irish stand-in for me? What's up?"

AJWalker90: "I don't know if we can call him that anymore. You know . . . 'cuz I don't make out with you."

A.J.'s stomach did a backflip as he re-read what he'd typed. No going back now. It was a full minute before Nat responded.

LittleMoshpitKid46: "Wait . . . are you kidding?"

AJWalker90: "Not kidding . . . send help."

Nat Nudged the conversation so many times the screen froze. When it finally returned to normal, the chat exploded.

LittleMoshpitKid46: "HOLY SHIT!"

"I KNEW IT!"

"I KNEW YOU LIKED HIM!"

"I KNEW THAT FUCKER WAS INTO YOU!"

"GET FUCKED YU!"

"HE SAID I WAS IMAGINING THE VIBE!"

AJWalker90: "Yu's still there right? Like, you didn't kill him for second-guessing you?"

LittleMoshpitKid46: "He's fine"

"Laughing"

"But fuck!"

"Tell us!"

"NOWWWWW!!!!"

Nat Nudged the conversation again, but thankfully didn't spam him.

A.J.'s hand trembled as he typed out what had happened in as much detail as he could put into words. Even though it had all happened to him, bits of it had gone fuzzy around the edges since he'd had to head home.

AJWalker90: ". . .and then he said he didn't want me to go, but his mom was going to be home soon and . . ."

LittleMoshpitKid46: "And he didn't want her to see his new boyfriend going full koala mode on him?"

AJWalker90: "I wasn't! I almost passed out from holding his hand!"

LittleMoshpitKid46: "Even though you two sucked face all morning?"

"Yu says get over it and blow your boyfriend already"

A.J.'s cheeks grew hot, but because it was Nat, a smile found its way there, too.

AJWalker90: "Punch him for me please."

He waited long enough that he thought Nat had delivered on his ask then got back to it.

"And he's not my boyfriend. I'm still kind of worried he was just doing it 'cuz he felt bad for me."

"Is that crazy?"

LittleMoshpitKid46: "Ok, that is crazy but I still love you"

"Look, if you guys got wasted and fooled around that would be one thing. But he ditched school, let you put on his clothes, and spent the day watching movies with you"

"In"

"His"

"Bed"

"Yu wants to know where you're registered"

132

Despite his best efforts, an image of Bren and him in matching suits forced its way into his mind.

Don't be stupid.

AJWalker90: "Ok, but even if he DOES like me like that . . . I have to go home in June. I can't actually date him or anything . . . can I?"

LittleMoshpitKid46: "Look, it's gonna suck when you've gotta come back. But I know you, and it's going to live rent-free in your head forever if you try to ignore it"

"And hey, there's MSN and shit"

A floorboard shifted as the McCarthys' muffled voices chattered away—no doubt getting ready for bed.

AJWalker90: "I don't think we're going to wind up doing anything like that."

LittleMoshpitKid46: "Not if you don't want to"

"But you do want to, right?"

A.J. started typing out "I don't know," but was stopped by the image of him and Bren in those stupid suits.

AJWalker90: "I really do . . ."

21

"Still think Home Ec is a shite class there, Micko?"

Mickie said something in German that A.J. was sure wasn't anywhere in the curriculum.

"A.J. and me are gonna be makin' White Puddin' and boxty while you're trying to figure out what the fuck Shardenfundeng means."

"Yeah, yeah," Mickie said, grabbing his bottle of Coke with a look that told A.J. he was picturing breaking Bren's neck. "It'd be one thing if we were mixed, but a room full of guys learnin' how to cook and clean? Too faggy for me."

"You seen Twomey, right? He teaches the fuckin' class, and he could put you through a wall with one hand."

Bren rumpled Mickie's hair and Mickie shoved him away, which got a laugh from everyone else. A.J.'s smile took some effort to surface. Aside from the occasional double-takes at his bruise, the morning had gone the same as always. He'd met Bren at the fork, messed around in the yard before the bell, then muddled his way through his classes. Bren had been his usual self—making jokes, taking the piss, and in general, making A.J. wonder where all that energy came from.

None of this would have been a problem if Bren had—for even one second—acknowledged what had happened yesterday. Every time they found themselves away from listening ears, A.J. fought with the urge to check with Bren to make sure it'd happened.

"Either way, it's gonna be an easy pass for certs."

"Gonna be real funny when your dumb ass fails everythin' besides dress makin'," Mickie replied.

"At least he'll be able to make you something pretty for graduation," A.J. said, trying hard not to picture Bren putting his domestic talents to use with the phantom girl he'd been picturing in his head. A.J. didn't know who she was, but he hated her stupid, imaginary face.

Feeling nettled, he was about to add another dig when there was a clatter on the other side of the room. Judging by the clapping, someone had dropped their tray. A.J. craned his neck to get a look at who it was when a hand clasped his knee and gave it a squeeze.

A.J. froze. He could see Bren out of the corner of his eye, but didn't dare do anything but pretend like he was focused on the tray dropper. Bren squeezed his knee again, then gave him an almost imperceptible wink as he slid his hand up his thigh.

By the time the others turned back, A.J. had joined in on the clapping.

***

The bell to Niamh's jingled as the door clattered shut behind them. Even though he was still full of Boxty, A.J. wasted no time biting into his tart. What was effectively apple pie with no cinnamon was still strange to him, but each mouthful warmed him like a hug nonetheless.

"How come Canada gets his free then?" Mickie asked, looking like he had a mouth full of Warheads rather than sausage roll.

"Yeah," Brick said, popping in a mini cake as though it were meant to be bite-sized. "You've known us longer."

Bren shrugged. "Brothers in flour." And when the two of them blinked back at him . . . "A.k.a., A.J.'s got the stones to take Home Ec, like a real man."

From the way they launched into overlapping arguments, A.J. assumed they'd taken Bren at his word. Rory, on the other hand, looked at Bren like he was trying to work out a riddle. A.J. was right there with him. He didn't know if the tart meant anything, but after he'd spent the morning obsessing over what went on in Bren's head, he was trying to let things be what they were. Bren had bought him a tart. It tasted nice and made him happy. That was enough.

They cut into an alley before reaching the end of the street, and after squeezing through a pair of overgrown hedges, found themselves on a narrow wooded path. It wasn't a forest, or so Bren said. But the trees were tall enough that the city sounds all but vanished once they'd walked for about a minute.

A.J. watched the bits of dappled sunlight shifting as they went, the breeze making the overhanging branches dance in a dreamlike sway. He'd never say it out loud in front of the guys, but something about the place felt magical to him—although to be fair, he thought the same thing about the old creek near his house in Moose Jaw.

Not only did the woods cut a good five minutes from the walk to Bren's house, but there was even a clearing with a makeshift firepit along the way. Some days they ran into other groups killing time after school let out. From the sound of laughter up the path, today was one of those days.

A.J.'s bruise throbbed when they stepped into the clearing to find Cian sitting on the edge of an old wooden table that had somehow found its way into the "woods." Tadhg was with him, along with another guy and three girls A.J. had never seen before. He remembered Bren pointing out the maroon uniforms once to tell him about Crossgroves, Glenbridge's all-girls school.

A girl with shoulder-length box braids and a square jaw was rolling her eyes as she took a drag from the cigarette between her fingers. Cian said something that A.J. couldn't make out, and another girl with strawberry-blonde hair giggled.

A.J. didn't know if he was imagining it, but he thought he heard Bren grunt.

Mickie stepped forward, having noticed nothing.

"Alright there, Orlaith?"

The girl took a drag from her cigarette, exhaling as she spoke. "Better now you lot are here." She sounded bored, though A.J. thought there was a hint of softness to her voice.

"Yeah? Cian givin' you trouble?"

A.J. couldn't be sure, but it looked like Mickie was puffing his chest out.

"Just remindin' me why I swore off datin' till uni."

She shook her head and hopped off the edge of the table, then her eyes fixed on A.J.

"I don't know this one."

All too aware Cian was glaring at him, A.J. took a half step forward.

"Hi, I'm A.J. I'm here on exchange. From Canada"

Orlaith's friends perked up at that, their attention shifting off of Cian and his group.

"Orlaith," said the one with the cigarette, while her blonde friend chirped up, "I'm Aoife," and the third—a pale girl with a heart-shaped face and enough freckles to give Bren a run for his money—smiled and said, "Mary."

"You come all the way from Canada and choose this lot?"

She smiled as she said it, and after looking back at Cian, shrugged. "Could be worse, I guess."

Aoife leaned over and whispered something to Mary, and they slapped their hands over their mouths to stop their giggles.

"Somethin' wrong with O'Shea?" Orlaith asked, peering towards Bren as she flicked her cigarette to the ground. "Don't think I've ever seen your mouth shut before."

Bren opened his mouth to reply, but Tadhg cut across him.

"Probably still pissed his boyfriend got banged up."

A.J.'s entire body clenched as the words hit him. He looked at Bren, who looked for a split second like he'd been cold-cocked. His fist clenched at his side after he'd recovered, but he didn't say anything.

"Shut the fuck up, Tadhg," Mickie snapped, much to A.J.'s surprise.

"Not my fault you decided to adopt the Canadian queer."

"Nah, Mickie had it right, Tadhg, shut the fuck up," Orlaith snapped before turning back to A.J. "Sorry 'bout them. We're not all like that."

A.J. nodded. "It's ok . . . so, uh, you go to Crossgroves, right?"

"Lucky thing, too, or I'd have to deal with pricks like them every day," she replied. Mary chuckled at this, but Aoife looked like she'd found Mickie's imaginary Warheads.

"Seriously, Orlaith, careful talking to that one. Shite like that rubs off," Cian said, his voice booming out.

Orlaith raised her middle finger.

"And seriously, Cian, I'm not interested. So go pick up those marbles you call balls and fuck off."

The other guy A.J. didn't recognize snickered, and Cian shoved him.

It took some grumbling, but they milled out of the clearing. From the brief exchanges A.J. caught, it sounded like they'd talked themselves into believing they were about to leave anyway.

Once they'd disappeared into the overgrowth, some of the tension left A.J.'s shoulders.

"God, Orlaith, you're gonna get smacked one of these days," Aoife said, sounding caught between impressed and annoyed.

"Grand, it'll give me an excuse to rip his balls off. Been wanting to do that since class five."

Aoife huffed like she wanted to argue, but contented herself with folding her arms across her chest.

"Seriously, O'Shea, you broke or something?" Orlaith asked, taking another step forward with her head cocked. "Not like you to let pricks carry on about your mates like that."

She was right, of course. If Cian had said that about anyone else, A.J. was sure Bren would have stepped in. Something in A.J. curled up as he worked to maintain the neutral look on his face.

"Mickie had it covered," Bren said, jostling Mickie, who brushed him off.

Did he really not care?

Orlaith narrowed her eyes but cracked a smile. "Guess he did."

She sat back down on the edge of the table and looked over at A.J. "Canada, huh? How you liking Glenbridge?"

The next thirty minutes dragged on more slowly than they should have. Orlaith and her friends seemed genuinely interested in him and his life back home. It should have been one of his better moments since coming to Ireland. He'd forgotten how nice it was to get to share things about himself without an innuendo every five minutes. Despite this, he couldn't stop fixating on why Bren had kept quiet.

By the time Orlaith was telling a story about some teacher A.J. had never heard of, he'd come up with two possible explanations. Either Bren really didn't mind what Cian had said, or he did, but had realized what standing up to him in that moment might look like. A.J. couldn't blame him if it was the latter. Changing the way everyone thought about you, all for some weird foreign guy who'd be gone by next summer. Not many people would choose that for themselves.

"Right, you seem like a good time," Orlaith said, snapping A.J. out of his head. "Dunno if you already heard, but my parents are out of town for Halloween."

"Fuck yeah!" Mickie cried.

A.J. turned to Bren for explanation but forced himself to look at Rory instead.

"She throws a good party."

"Cheers," Orlaith said from behind a fresh cigarette. "Come by around eight."

"Wear a costume!" Mary added.

Mickie groaned.

"If you're too cool to wear one, you can fuck off," Orlaith replied.

"Or we could pick one out for you," Aoife said.

A.J. could tell from the honeyed tone that Mickie wouldn't like what they chose.

"Fuckin' fine,"

"I'll be there," Brick added.

There was a pause in which Bren stared, unfocused at the trees on the other side of the clearing.

"Look alive, O'Shea," Orlaith said, flicking ash in his direction.

"Oh, yeah, sounds like good craic," Bren said and checked his phone. "We gonna get in some CoD?"

He sounded eager to get out of there, but Mickie looked at him like he was crazy.

"More fun here, isn't it?"

Brick glanced over towards Mary and turned pink. "Yeah, gonna stay here."

Rory looked between A.J. and Bren like he was working something out before he nodded. "Yeah, I'm in."

A.J. thought Orlaith looked disappointed as the three of them made their way to the other side of the clearing but couldn't dwell on it.

By the time they'd clambered their way through to the other side of the woods, they hadn't spoken much. The second Bren reached out to push open the front gate, Rory clapped his hand to his head.

"Bollocks, I forgot Mum wanted me to help set up her new computer."

"Can't it wait? We just got here." Bren groaned, sounding more like himself.

"She's gonna be fuming already. Raincheck."

With that, he gave an airy wave and turned down the road at a jog. A.J. got the distinct impression that Rory's mom had no idea her son was supposed to be home early. This added another twist to the knot that had been building in his stomach. He knew Rory wasn't going to run his mouth about what he suspected, but if he'd picked up on it, it was only a matter of time before others did.

"Want me to raincheck, too?"

In answer, Bren took a step forward and let his forehead bump against A.J.'s

"Just, get inside . . . ok?"

22

By the time Bren realized what he was doing, the kettle was on and the mugs off the shelf. His hands were shaking as he pulled the milk out of the fridge. A.J. was standing off to the side of the table, bruise still plastered over his eye like a stubborn stain. He looked like he wanted to say something, but his lips were shut tight.

"You're pissed at me. Fuck!" He marched back to the kettle. "I didn't mean to—fuck!"

The back of his throat quivered, and he could feel tears threatening to well up behind his eyes.

The scene played again. The Canadian queer bit, the way Tadhg had laughed about what happened to A.J. Neither of those disgusted him more than his own silence.

Bren wouldn't have blamed A.J. if he turned around and left right now. What the fuck kind of guy lets a waste of space like Cian run their gob about their mate like that? He looked back at the kettle as if it might have started to boil in the thirty seconds since he'd plugged it in.

A hand squeezed his shoulder.

"Bren, it's not a big deal. Really."

A.J.'s attempt at a smile only made things worse.

"It—fuck it is, though! I let Mickie, fuckin' *Mickie*, defend you."

143

A.J. shook his head. "No one needed to defend me. We should have just ignored them."

"Pricks like Cian don't go away just 'cuz you ignore them. Fuck. I shoulda said somethin'."

A.J.'s voice fell, but he kept his strained smile on his face.

"Then why didn't you?"

"I—"

The gurgle of the kettle cut Bren off. He dropped in the tea bags, then filled the mugs.

"I wanted to, but I was so fuckin' pissed."

A.J.'s head tilted. "I've seen you mad, you're pretty loud."

Bren bit his lip. "No, I was like, *pissed* pissed. Like, I knew if I started in I wasn't gonna stop."

"Oh . . ." A.J. said, unreadable.

"And I know Cian," Bren said, resisting the urge to pace. "He would have thrown it back twice as twisted, and if it was about you, I woulda lost it."

He clenched his fist and swung it down at the table, but stopped at the last second, so it landed with a soft thud. "And then everyone woulda . . ."

A.J.'s eyes shimmered. "Would have known you liked me."

Bren sniffed. "Yeah. And I do! Like you. I just—" He left his tea on the counter and collapsed into a kitchen chair. "I'm a fuckin' coward."

The words hung in the air before A.J. moved. He plucked the tea bag out of the mug and dumped in a spoonful of sugar and a splash of milk.

"You're a lot of things, Bren . . ." he said, setting the tea down in front of him. "But I don't think coward is one of them."

144

He walked back to the counter, and Bren considered the mug in front of him. Extra big splash of milk, sugar not stirred in all the way. He'd never told A.J. that was how he liked his tea.

He was about to ask how he knew when A.J.'s lips pressed against the top of his head.

"Thank you."

"What the fuck for?" Bren didn't dare look at him given how hazy his vision was.

"You cared."

***

"So, what do you think?"

A.J. leaned back from the piano and popped a few pieces of chin chin into his mouth. At least he thought that's what Mrs. Davies had called the little pieces of fried dough. They were good, whatever they were.

"It's good, but . . ."

Rory took out his bow and played the first few measures of "I suck at composition In E". The longer Rory played the more obvious it was that he was trying not to laugh. By the time he was done, A.J. had shoved another handful of chin chin into his mouth.

"Hear it now?"

A.J. swallowed. "It's My Immortal, but happy."

"At least you changed the key."

"I really thought I'd be better at this," A.J. sighed.

He was tempted to vent his feelings on the piano but decided he should probably wash his hands first.

"Not like mine's any better."

Rory positioned his cello and played a single aching note. He kept saying he didn't know what he wanted to write, only that it needed to start with C.

"At least you didn't commit copyright infringement."

A.J. pulled himself away from the piano and stared around the room. Like every room in Rory's house there were books everywhere, and no shortage of comfortable places to read them. He wiped his fingers on his slacks and pulled out the copy of *The Importance of Being Earnest* that Rory had lent him last week.

Rory put away his cello and popped a few pieces of chin chin into his mouth.

"You'd think you'd be a little more inspired. All things considered."

A.J. froze mid page-turn.

"What do you mean?"

Rory crunched away with an eyebrow raised, and when A.J. didn't say anything, set the bowl down.

"How was CoD yesterday?"

A.J. felt a surge of panic for all of two seconds before he remembered who he was talking to. He'd be shocked if Rory hadn't clock him from day one.

"We didn't wind up playing. Just had tea and . . .talked."

"Thought you two might have needed that," Rory said.

"Yeah, thanks for that, by the way. I uh, mean, picking up on that." A.J. forced himself to take a breath, his nails digging into the couch. "So, uh . . . what exactly did you . . . pick up on?"

Rory flipped the clasps on his case shut then sat up. There was the faintest trace of a smile tugging at his lips, like his favourite song had come on the radio.

"I've known Bren since I was ten. Don't think I've ever had a better mate." His smile broke into something more familiar to A.J. as he spoke. "But he's the least subtle bloke on the planet. I can tell he likes you."

A nervous laugh left A.J. before he could stop it. "Bren likes everyone."

Rory looked like he was chewing over what he wanted to say. "Ok, so . . . do you like Bren?"

"Of course! He's," A.J.'s heart swelled as the words formed in his mind. "One of the best people I've ever met."

Rory leaned back in his chair. "Yeah, sounds like like to me," a Bren-like glint in his eye. "So, you're really not gonna say it then?"

A proud ember flickered in A.J. "It's like . . . I've known who I am since I was ten. I didn't tell anyone until I was in grade nine, and after that, I sort of just told anyone who asked. But now, it's not just my secret. And I don't know if Bren's . . . like that or not."

"Well, we do know that he's a bit of an idiot, so it's probably going to take him a while to figure that out." Rory shifted back and fixed his eyes on A.J.'s. "Just stick with him until he does, yeah?"

23

"Seriously, fuck math."

A.J. flung his textbook across the room, where it landed with a muffled thud in a pile of Bren's discarded T-shirts. They'd been trying to make sense of linear inequalities for the last half hour, and the only thing A.J. had to show for it was a brain that felt like it'd been put through a laundry mangle.

"Your fault for thinkin' my dumb arse could help you," Bren replied from where he lay sprawled on his bed.

A.J. brushed away a discarded trainer and let himself slide sideways onto the floor. His eyes met a small collection of dust bunnies and a plate with a half-eaten roll that was a lot greener than bread had any right to be.

"You're not dumb. You are messy, though."

Bren laughed and let his textbook drop to the floor, setting some of the dust bunnies scurrying in the breeze.

"Dumb and messy. That's why you like me so much? Charity case, like?"

A.J. pulled himself onto the bed to find Bren with his face buried in the mattress beside his pillow. A.J. slid beside him and lay his head down.

"Fine, you can be dumb, but not a charity case." He ran his hand along Bren's back. "We can be dumb together."

Bren propped himself up on one elbow and leaned in.

A familiar heat rose in A.J.'s chest as Bren's hand found the back of his neck. Math was a lot more enjoyable when you could kiss your study buddy.

Bren broke the kiss and ran his thumb along the spot where it rested on A.J.'s neck.

"One sec, yeah?"

He bounded off the bed before A.J. had a chance to reply. The dresser creaked as Bren pulled the top drawer open and dug around what A.J. knew was a hoard of mismatched socks and underwear.

He was about to ask Bren if he was going to model boxers for him when he leapt back on the bed in a creak of springs that sent the mattress shaking.

"Got you somethin'."

He was looking at the other side of the room as he thrust something silver under A.J.'s nose. Confused, A.J. pulled back so it wasn't eclipsing his vision.

"What did yo—"

His breath caught. It was a Discman. Not the same as the one he'd had, but remarkably close. Although it had to be several years old at this point, it looked new—shiny and silver and smelling like plastic that hadn't had time to air out.

"Where did you even . . ." A.J. took the gift from Bren as the lump in his throat grew. He couldn't remember the last time he'd seen anything that played CDs in a store. It even had batteries.

Bren rustled something in his pocket and chucked a pair of earbuds on top of the gift.

"Felt weird, seein' you without your wires."

A.J. swallowed hard, then sat up and pulled Bren into a kiss, trying to put some of what he felt into it. Maybe Bren understood, because he didn't push things deeper.

When A.J. opened his eyes next, Bren's room was glowing around the edges.

"Seriously, where did you even find this?"

Bren shrugged. "Over in Cork." Despite the shrug, he looked like he was trying not to be too proud of himself.

"What were you in Cork for?" A.J. asked, clicking in the earbuds.

"Gotta have my secrets, don't I?"

"You didn't just—"

Bren poked him in the chest before he could finish. "No, I didn't go just for you, like. Relax, Robolad."

It was an obvious lie, but A.J. found it hard to care.

"Seriously, though, thank you," A.J. said, doing his best to keep steady as he looked into Bren's eyes. "Not having anything to listen to has sucked. Big time."

"Well, now you can go back to drownin' me out with music all you want."

A.J. ignored him, rolling off the bed and pulling a CD from the stack next to Bren's boombox. He loaded it in and popped in an earphone before offering the other to Bren.

"Ah, come on." Bren groaned as the ladies of B*Witched started up.

"Hey, you're the one who gave me back my wires."

"Shoulda burned that shite years ago."

Bren's arm wrapped around A.J.'s chest as the first verse started. It was only then, as music poured from the bud snuggled in his ear, that he realized it—even without his Discman, there was always music when he was with Bren.

***

Bren's arm had been asleep for the last fifteen minutes, but there wasn't any part of him that wanted to move it. A.J. hadn't questioned when Bren pulled him close, only let out a sigh and started breathing deep—then the snoring had started.

Bren worked hard not to sigh. Quarter past six. Mam would be home soon. As much as she liked A.J., Bren didn't know what she'd do if she walked in to find the two of them like this.

The thought pulled at him. He'd started off telling himself that it was just a bit of fun. Something he hadn't expected. It was getting harder to believe that, though. The lad was burrowing down deeper with every kiss and fit of red-faced stammering. If things kept going like this, Bren didn't know if he'd ever be able to let him go—no matter what people might think.

A.J.'s snores petered out in one, and he stirred in Bren's arms.

"You know, for such a quiet lad, you snore like a fuckin' jumbo jet."

He expected stammering, but A.J. grabbed the hem of his shirt and wiped the pool he'd made off Bren's forearm.

"I drool, too, sorry about that."

Sor-ry. Two months on, and that accent was still cute as fuck.

"Little bit of spit never hurt anyone," Bren said, then licked the length of A.J.'s ear.

As expected, A.J. yelped and leapt out of bed.

"What the hellllll."

Bren flung himself up and ran his tongue across his lips.

"What, not like it's the first time you've gotten up close to my spit."

A.J. looked like he was trying his best to look cross, but was having a hard time of it. "Yeah! But not in my ear."

"Well, it's my kink, so get used to it."

A.J. groaned. "I'm going home. Like, Canada home."

"Alright," Bren said as he pulled himself off the bed. "Get your goodbye present before you go, then."

A.J.'s smile flickered into something more nervous.

"Don't go reachin' for the wires yet, Robolad. It's nothing special."

He walked over to his closet and pulled out half of the stuff he'd bought in Cork, then tossed it to A.J.

"What's this?" A.J. asked as he held up the bright red and white top.

"You've seen hurlin' plenty. That's your costume to Orlaith's party. You said you didn't have one."

It was true. A.J. had mentioned more than once that he had no idea what to wear to an "Irish Halloween party"—no matter how many times Bren told him that there weren't any special rules.

"Isn't that like—I don't know—culturally insensitive?" A.J. asked, sounding like he meant every word.

Bren managed not to laugh, but it took some effort.

"Christ, Arlo, we're not that sensitive."

Bren glowed at the look that appeared whenever he used A.J.'s full name. "You like hurlin' and wanna show it. You're fine. Irish boyfriend-approved and all."

He realized what he'd said a second after A.J. did. His heart was beating like he'd downed an entire case of Red Bull, but he was sure of what he'd said even if he hadn't meant to say it.

"I-I. A-are you? I mean, you're . . . ?" A.J. took a half step forward then hopped back as he talked, looking like he didn't know if he wanted to laugh or cry.

"Want me to leave you alone with your wires for a bit?"

A.J. shook his head and grabbed the side of his trousers before stepping forward. He threw his arms around Bren's neck and pulled him into a frantic kiss. Their teeth bumped a couple of times before it settled into something less frenzied.

Bren forgot Mam was due home any minute and kissed A.J. back like he might run out of air if he didn't. A.J. pushed them forward so the back of Bren's legs banged into the edge of the bed, and they almost toppled over.

A.J. broke the kiss, panting through shimmering eyes.

"Sorry!"

"Sor-ry," Bren replied, in a singsong rhythm.

A.J. brought his fist down on Bren's chest with a soft thud.

"You've got an accent, too, you know."

"Irish people got accents now, do they, bai?" Bren said, laying it on thick enough that he made himself cringe. "Someone tell the Taoiseach!"

A.J. laughed hard at that, and for some reason, it made Bren spin him around onto the bed. He was about to join him when a click drifted in from the front of the house.

"Bren! I stopped by the shops. Come help me unload!"

A.J. went from red to white so fast he looked like his Halloween costume for a split second. Panic spiked in Bren's chest too, but he was able to shrug it off. Mam had no reason to be suspicious.

"Come on, let's go help your new mam-in-law with the shoppin'."

He'd meant it as a joke, but something that looked almost wistful perked up behind A.J.'s eyes—and for once, Bren let the joke lie.

24

Boyfriend.

The word echoed in A.J.'s mind for the thousandth time as he pulled the hurling jersey closer to his chest. He knew Bren hadn't meant to say it, but he had said it. And more than that, he hadn't taken it back.

He had a boyfriend. For the first time in his life. A cute, funny . . . Irish boyfriend he was going to have to say goodbye to in June. A.J. thrust that last thought from his head so fast he felt like he cricked his neck.

He wasn't going to let something as stupid as reality ruin the afterglow of hearing Bren say that one beautiful word.

The flame in his chest flickered again as he opened the door. He could hear voices coming from the kitchen, sounding as if they were in a particularly good mood. A.J. had gotten to know the McCarthys well enough to know that meant they had something to brag about.

A.J. slipped off his shoes and crept towards the stairs like he was trying to avoid waking a sleeping tiger. His foot was coming down on the first step when an airy voice rose from the kitchen.

"Oh, A.J. could you come here for a second?"

Not seeing how he could say no, A.J. reversed course and wandered into the kitchen, hoping his delirious happiness didn't show on his face.

"Is everything ok?" A.J. asked as he came to find the McCarthys sitting around the kitchen island.

"Oh, everything's fine!" Meredith said, her vowels elongated in a way that A.J. didn't hear from the people in town. He'd been trying to figure out where in Ireland they were from for a while now. "Niall and I just wanted to run something by you. A little opportunity!"

"Oh? What's that?" A.J. asked, trying not to sound like he'd already decided to say no.

"There's an event that Mere and I have been invited to for Halloween," Niall said.

"Over in Dublin," Meredith added.

"Yes. And we were thinking it might be nice for you to come along and meet some people."

"Some people?"

"Some of our friends, of course, and their families. The event's to celebrate the upscale neighbourhood that one of our old clients is developing."

Something jostled in A.J.'s memory. An awkward dinner the first week here, where Meredith and Niall humble-bragged about how well their real estate ventures had been paying off the last few years.

"We thought you might want to play a couple of pieces for everyone!"

A.J. had to work to keep his brows from knitting together. He couldn't remember ever talking to them about being able to play.

"Your music teacher tells us you're quite good!" Meredith continued.

Oh.

156

"Uh, that's . . . I'm not—I mean, I just play for fun. My articulation sucks, and my left hand likes going off-rhythm."

"Oh, nonsense! I'm sure you play beautifully," Meredith said, flashing a smile that showed every one of her bleached teeth.

"You wouldn't have to spend the entire night with us adults either," Niall added, sounding as though he thought A.J. was about five years old. "Most years, the kids your age sort of drift off for their own little party at these sorts of things."

"That sounds nice and everything," A.J. said, trying to keep from inching towards the door. "But I don't really have anything impressive prepared, I mean—I don't really know *how* to play anything impressive."

"What about something slow and dreamy, like 'Moonlight Sonata'?" Meredith said, staring past A.J. like the room was filled with stars. "That's such a beautiful piece."

A.J. suppressed a groan. Why did everyone always go for "Moonlight Sonata"? It was like Propofol for piano.

"Well, I could probably manage if I practiced . . . but I was kind of hoping I could go to a party here in town with some friends."

Meredith pursed her lips as she fiddled with the clasp of her bag. "I'm sure it would be a better use of your time to come to the gala."

A.J. tried not to frown. Between the two options, being paraded out in front of a bunch of strangers, to play a piece that made him want to slap Beethoven, sounded like the bigger waste of time.

Niall took a sip from his mug before adding to Meredith's argument.

"I'm sure your friends are nice, but it would be a shame to come all the way to Ireland and not make connections with people who matter."

"I like the connections I've made."

A.J. was sure some of his disgust must have shown on his face for a second because Niall looked taken aback.

"I mean, people who can help you out in the future." He took another sip of his tea and shook his head like A.J. was missing something obvious.

"These are people from Ailesbury Road, not Meadow Park."

Though the fire that had ignited back at Bren's place had all but flickered out, heat rose in A.J.'s chest again. That was the street Bren lived on.

"Thank you for inviting me, but . . . I'm allowed to say no, right?"

"Of course you are!" Meredith said in a rush.

"Then I'm saying no."

The McCarthys shared a look that A.J. had to force himself to ignore—his hands could only sweat so much.

Meredith looked like she was on the verge of saying something, but in the end, she hitched her smile back on her face.

"Of course you want to spend time with your friends, that makes sense."

She reached into her purse and pulled out a BlackBerry, fingers flying across the screen. A.J. got the feeling she'd already told some people there'd be music courtesy of Canada.

"Well, just think about it some more, alright?" Niall asked, covering up his annoyance less skillfully than his wife.

"I will," A.J. said, not caring if his smile looked as awful as it felt.

He left the McCarthys in the kitchen, trying not to hate them too much. They couldn't have known how oily their offer sounded in the end—or at least he hoped not.

His hand twitched as he fished his phone out of his pocket, the happier fire rising in his chest again. There was no need to wait for Nat to come on to vent—he could just tell his boyfriend.

25

BOOM!

The sky bloomed with streaks of colour from the firework that someone had launched from up on the hill. He'd been sure Bren was putting him on when he told him that fireworks were big on Halloween in Ireland. Not only had he been telling the truth, but he'd undersold it. People had been shooting them off since the start of the week, and they'd been increasing in number the closer they got to Friday.

He tugged at his shorts as if he could will the hem down past his mid-thigh. If it were for anyone other than Bren, there was no way he would have been out in anything that didn't cover his knees. Bren had been adamant that A.J. had to go in full hurling gear, that his own costume wouldn't land as hard without it.

He let his borrowed hurley clatter against the crooked fence as he made his way through the gate. Lopsided jack-o'-lanterns flickered on either side of the door that now bore an outline of a witch flying over a full moon. Judging by the car in the driveway, Bren's mom was home. The thought made him smile, even though he was sure she'd have something to say about his costume.

Long since done stressing over it, A.J. knocked and pushed the door open in one as a blast of turf-warmed air hit his face.

"Trick-or-holyshit!"

A.J. stumbled back from the figure standing inches from the threshold. A burlap sack with eyes that were all sunken pupils stared back at him, its jagged, needle-hewn grin dripping with red.

Heart still somewhere in the stratosphere, A.J. took in the rest of what he hoped was a costume.

A patchwork of burlap and denim lined with jagged stitches and gaping tears, from which tufts of bloodstained hay were sticking out. It was holding a sickle in one hand, and there was a kitchen knife buried to the hilt in its left shoulder.

"B-Bren?"

The figure brought a slender finger with a blackened nail to its stitched mouth and shook its head.

A.J. was considering the possibility that he'd wandered into the start of a horror movie when a laugh rang out from behind the mask.

"Sorry, love! Saw you comin' and couldn't help meself."

A.J. was sure he recognized the voice, but waited for Mrs. O'Shea to pull off her mask before he stepped inside all the same.

"Have you been doing that to the kids, too?"

"Course I have!" She plucked a snack-sized Mars bar from a plastic cauldron full of dry-ice fog. "You shoulda seen what Bren's grandad got up to when I was coming up. Someone called the Garda one year."

She popped the sweet into her mouth, looking A.J. up and down.

She smirked through her mouthful of chocolate. "You don't have to go doin' every mad thing he comes up with. Must be freezin' your arse off."

She wasn't wrong. Fall in Ireland was tropical compared to back home, but the damp made what chill there was stick to A.J. in a way that the dry winds of Saskatchewan didn't.

"I don't mi—"

A booming whoop cut A.J. off as Bren came barrelling into the room. He was wearing a Team Canada jersey—white with a silhouette inside a black and red maple leaf—black shorts, and actual hockey socks. A cardboard hockey stick that he'd clearly made himself was swung over his shoulder, next to a mullet that he hadn't had that morning.

A.J. had been wondering why Bren was letting his hair get so long. The part of him that wasn't horrified had to admire his commitment to the bit.

Bren looked more pleased with himself than he had any right to as he strutted, singing at the top of his lungs.

"O Canada, our home and native land . . . ofwhereroboladisfrom."

A.J. couldn't help but laugh, but something else came with it. Bren had done this for him. He looked to Mrs. O'Shea. Her expression was caught somewhere between exhausted and amused. He didn't think he saw anything that looked like disapproval, though.

"Whaddya think, eh? I pull it off?" He was speaking with what A.J. was sure he thought was a Canadian accent, but just made him sound like he was already ten drinks deep.

"Is that why you grew out your hair?" was all A.J. could manage.

"Oh yeah, for sure, eh?" Bren said, the accent now sounding Minnesotan. "Looks good, eh?"

A.J. snorted, though his Canadian DNA was wondering what Bren might look like with a chipped tooth or two.

"Where did you even get a jersey?"

"Bribed Brick to take me to Cork, eh?"

"Wait, is that when you got—" A.J. began, but remembered Mrs. O'Shea was there. "I mean, I can't believe you messed up your hair like that."

A.J. looked at Mrs. O'Shea in silent apology.

"I know this wasn't your idea." She sighed and waved them towards the door. "Come on, let's get a picture and get you out of me house. I can't look at that hair much longer."

A.J. let himself be jostled towards the door, Bren's arm thrown over his shoulder. Whatever Bren had used to pad out his shoulders pressed into A.J.'s cheek as the camera clicked.

"You done fawnin'?" Bren asked.

Mrs. O'Shea rolled her eyes. "Oh yeah, seein' me son lookin' like he walked off Jeremy Kyle, proudest day of me life." She turned to A.J. "Don't let him embarrass himself too bad, yeah?"

"I'll do my best," A.J. replied, though he wasn't sure there was much he could do about it.

"Alright, let's go, O'Sullivan!"

A.J. didn't have enough time to wonder who the hell that was before Bren pulled him out the door.

"Somethin' the matter, eh?"

A.J. flinched. He'd been focused on two witches and a skeleton jogging towards the next house, candy pails swinging.

"Have you literally ever heard me say 'eh'?"

Bren smiled and bumped his shoulder against A.J.'s.

"Just said it right now, didn't you . . . eh?"

"Ha-ha."

They walked in silence as a firework burst from somewhere off in town. When the light faded, Bren's voice came out sounding worried.

"I do somethin' wrong? You're quiet, and not your usual kind."

162

"I just . . ."

"Don't like my costume? Fuck, thought you'd think it was gas, like."

A.J. tugged at his jersey as they cut through a side street. "I do! It's—ok, you look dumb as hell, but fuck, it's cute."

"Think I should keep my hair like this then?" Bren asked, running his fingers through his mullet like he was shooting a shampoo commercial.

"Like I said, it's cute."

"But?"

"I don't know, just . . . You're all Canadian, I'm all Irish."

"And?"

A.J. tugged at his shorts again.

"And people are going to notice we're, like, both sports guys and stuff."

Bren snorted. "That brain really never shuts off, does it? It's just a laugh. Mickie and Brick went as a couple of old birds last year. Purses and all."

A.J. bit the inside of his cheek. "They can do that because they're straight! I'm pretty sure most people have figured out I'm decidedly not."

"Lad . . ."

"I wasn't even sure I was going to be able to wear this." He gestured at his too-short shorts. "And now you look like you're trying out for Team Canada which is fine, but also kind of hot, and people will see me looking at you thinking, 'Oh, my boyfriend looks weirdly hot with a mullet,' and they'll figure it out."

"A.J."

A.J. couldn't hear Bren. He was too busy sifting through the shitstorm he knew was coming.

"And these shorts are so fucking small. I know it's how hurling kits are, but I don't play hurling. It's going to look like I'm trying to be a sexy hurler. Or like I asked you to dress up like a hockey player 'cuz it turns me on. I don't know. It would work if I were better at passing, Bren, but I really think I should go home and chan—"

"Arlo!"

The ringing that had been building in his head snuffed out like a blown amp. He was back on the side of the road, palms throbbing from how hard he'd been clenching them.

"It's a laugh. No one's gonna think that deep on it except you." He grabbed A.J.'s hand and pressed it to his lips as they slipped into a dark patch between two streetlamps. "And if they do, fuck 'em. Eh?"

26

The party was already in full swing by the time they made it to Orlaith's house. They passed a guy in a jumpsuit and a Jason mask holding a baguette like a machete, trying to impress a girl in a black skirt and cat ears.

Bren had to resist the urge to give A.J. a pat on the back as they neared the door. He'd calmed down over the rest of the walk, but Bren still thought the lad could do with a drink or five.

Sound hit them like a wall once they pushed their way inside. It was lucky that Orlaith's place was bigger than his, or people would have been standing on top of each other.

"O'Shea! What the FUCK did you do to your h-hair!"

He knew who it was from the first syllable and wasn't at all surprised to find Orlaith wiping a tear from her eye when he found her in the crowd.

"We're gonna talk about my hair, eh?"

Orlaith's braids were sticking out at odd angles across her head. She must have wrapped them around some kind of wire to help hold them up. She'd swapped the blue beads she normally wore for emerald green ones, and for some reason that was beyond Bren, several of the braids had googly eyes and little slips of red ribbon at the end.

He'd been ready for Orlaith to go for a hug. Instead, she stared at him like she was trying to make his head explode. He stared back, trying to figure out what the fuck she was doing. Next to him, A.J. let out a squeak and froze with his hands stretched out over his face.

This made Orlaith beam.

"See, he gets it!"

"You wanna explain what's goin' on?" Bren asked, nudging A.J. in the side.

"Can't—stoned," A.J. said out of the corner of his mouth.

"Alright, can one of you tell me what the fuck you're on about?" he asked, waving his cardboard hockey stick like it might make it make sense.

"Christ, O'Shea," Orlaith groaned. "Medusa? I was in that class with you!"

"Ohhhh," Bren said, rubbing the back of his neck. "Guess the mullet's makin' me dumber!"

"Gowl."

She looked at A.J. who was still frozen at Bren's side. She looked perplexed for a second, then snapped her fingers.

"Alright, unfreeze. I only stone people I don't like."

A.J.'s arms fell to his side, a smile spreading over his face. "It looks really good! I knew who you were right away."

"It'd better! There's four coat hangers and like fifty safety pins in there."

She returned A.J.'s smile and took a sip from her cup.

"How come I like your mate better than you, O'Shea?"

"'Cuz you've got good taste."

He clapped A.J. on the shoulder and snuck in a squeeze that he was pretty sure no one noticed.

"You gonna like me better if I get you another drink?"

"Fair chance of it."

A.J. was bobbing his head along to the music as he looked around the room. It didn't seem like he was ready to bolt, but Bren still thought he looked twitchy.

"How 'bout you?"

It took a second for A.J. to realize he'd been asked a question.

"As long as it's not Smirnoff and Tanora, sure."

"Get him a Fat Frog," Orlaith said, leaving no doubt that Bren was expected to bring her one, too.

Bren had to work hard not to look like too much of a dopey idiot at the confused look on A.J.'s face. He was sure A.J. thought she was talking about actual frogs.

"Good enough start. Better have something stronger, though."

"Shut your gob and get me my drink!"

***

A.J. thought he heard the slap of Orlaith's hand against Bren's ass above the thud of club music. Bren didn't look the least bit abashed, and after rubbing the spot, started pushing his way across the room.

"Arse like that almost makes me sorry we didn't work out."

A lump rose in A.J.'s throat.

"You two dated?" he asked as someone in a cheap rubber mask walked past.

Orlaith made a sound in her throat.

"Nah. Tried, but he kept annoying me. Never got past shifting." She considered him from across the room as she ran a finger along the laurel crown she was wearing. "Might need to give it another go. Feel like maybe he's learned to sit still or something."

167

"I don't think Bren ever sits still," A.J. said, as he watched him bounce around the drink table. It looked like he'd gotten roped into a conversation with a zombie that might have been Jord.

Orlaith sighed, "He's got no right pulling off that chop job on his head."

She changed the angle of a couple of her snakes to the beat of the music while A.J. did his best not to implode next to her.

"How about you? Got your eye on anyone?"

A.J. was saved from collapsing into a black hole as a marrow-rattling "YESSS" exploded behind him.

A ruddy-faced Brick threw an arm over A.J. so hard he had to throw his whole weight back to keep from falling over. Brick was dressed in leather sandals, a pair of black shorts, and was shirtless but for a red cape tied around his neck.

"Fuckin' . . . hurlin' hero Canada!"

The fumes on his breath made A.J.'s eyes water as he was jostled around.

"We . . . gotta get you to a league match!"

"Gonna be hard to go if you break my neck," A.J. said as he wiggled free.

Brick wobbled as he looked over A.J., his smile lopsided.

"That's my old hurley." He pulled the strip of wood from A.J.'s hands before A.J. knew what was happening. "Outgrew it two . . . fuckin' seasons ago."

He looked misty-eyed as he ran a hand over the hurley. A.J. thought he saw something dangerous flicker across his expression. Orlaith must have seen it, too, because she tugged the hurley out of his hands and thrust it back at A.J.

"Swing that in here, and I'm throwing you out the door myself, yeah?"

Brick squinted at her like he hadn't noticed her before then.

"Snake ladyyyyy!"

He laughed at this in a way only someone several pints in could.

"Thanks for the free booooozeeee."

Orlaith ducked his hug and pushed him back so he didn't topple forward.

"Heyyy, isn't that Mary over there?" she asked, nodding to the opposite end of the room. "Looks like she might need someone to get her a water."

Brick's arms dropped to his side as a different red crept over his cheeks. His mouth hung as he made a less-than-subtle attempt to smell under his arms. It was with a dopey smile and smaller steps than A.J. had ever seen him take that he made his way across the room.

"Are they . . . ?" A.J. asked, unable to hear what Brick said when he started talking to Mary—a first.

"They've been tiptoeing around it since class six."

"Aww, that's really sweet," A.J. replied, feeling a new fondness for Brick.

Orlaith groaned, but the corner of her mouth twitched.

"Exhausting is what it is."

"Whaffs exhfastin'?"

Bren had chosen that moment to reappear, holding a cup in each hand, a third clenched by the rim in his mouth. If Orlaith found this strange, she didn't show it and took the cup in his right hand.

"Brick and Mary."

Bren pushed the other cup into A.J.'s hand, their fingers brushing in the handoff. A.J. took an overly large gulp of the drink. It tasted like a melted popsicle with bite.

"Ahh, yeah," Bren said, downing half his drink in one so that when he spoke next, blue dribbled down the corner of his mouth. "They're either gonna end up married or combustin' from holdin' it in, like."

With Bren standing beside him, looking like he could play for the Warriors, A.J. thought he knew the feeling.

"Thanks for inviting me, by the way," A.J. said, only realizing how weird the timing was after he'd said it.

"Oh. No worries." Orlaith said, looking somewhere between confused and mildly embarrassed.

"Sorry."

"So-rry."

Bren's "apology" rang out in perfect time with A.J.'s, and the next second he burst out laughing. A.J. joined in, but Bren's laughter cut short in a jarring note. A.J. didn't have long to wonder what had caused it as Orlaith's face contorted.

"Oh, hell fucking no!"

A.J. followed Orlaith's death-glare to the door where Cian had just walked in, Tadhg and the nameless boy from the clearing trailing in his wake. None of them were wearing costumes.

"Right then," Orlaith said, throwing back the rest of her drink.

Before she could take a step towards the new arrival, a gleeful giggle broke out above the music. Aoife, dressed in a gauzy pink babydoll dress with glitter on her cheeks, flitted across the room.

A.J. looked between Orlaith and Aoife, who, wings flapping at her back, was trying to wrestle a pair of kitty ears onto Cian. Though he was feeding off Aoife's attack, his eyes were fixed on Orlaith, mouth curled into a triumphant grin.

She glared back, but some of the fight seemed to leave her.

"She's got the worst fucking taste I've ever seen."

She said that part so only the three of them could hear it, but when she spoke next, her voice carried.

"He's not even fit!"

Bren stood rigid beside A.J., his look darker than Orlaith's, who seemed not to notice.

"If they start shagging, I'm gonna light myself on fire."

With that, she marched off towards the drink table, Bren still looking like he'd gotten the full Medusa treatment.

"Maybe I should go . . ." A.J. said, resisting the urge to reach for Bren's hand.

"You're stayin'," Bren said, his voice even before it shifted into something more dangerous. "He comes near you, and I'm puttin' him through a fuckin' wall."

A.J.'s hand found Bren's shoulder before he could stop himself. He tried to pass it off like he was brushing something from it.

"Alright, I'll stay just . . . don't cause any property damage. Even if he's an asshole."

He appreciated the loyalty, but a scene was the last thing he needed.

"Fine, but we're gettin' you a shot. I want you havin' fun, not spinnin' out over Cian. Deal?"

"Deal."

***

Bren's shoulders twitched as the chill night air made his mullet tickle the back of his neck. It had been happening all night, and he still wasn't used to it. He was worried about leaving A.J. in the house, but last he'd seen, Cian was sucking face with Aoife off in a corner.

That was when Orlaith had hissed she needed a smoke and dragged Bren stumbling behind her.

Drunk as he was, he had enough brainpower to be proud of his shy Canadian lad. He'd had three shots and a couple of beers and had only gotten into one stammering loop all night. Bren would have spent the entire night by his side, but A.J. had slipped off a couple times. Something about not wanting to look like they were at the party "together" together—not even alcohol turned that brain all the way off.

Orlaith shifted, and their shoulders brushed. They were sitting on the steps at the back of her house, getting some air. Well, Bren was getting some air. Orlaith sat beside him, grumbling as puffs of smoke billowed around her like some kind of cross teapot.

"Gotta fuckin' . . . quit those things, Orls." His voice sounded normal to him, but A.J. had told him he was getting pretty slurry about three shots ago.

"Fuckouttahere with that." She swayed on the spot, squinting her eyes in the dark.

She flicked her ash as a smile crept across her face.

"Hey . . . this remind you of that time at your place?"

"Uhhh, what time?" Bren asked, his mind had drifted back to how cute A.J. looked in his shorts.

"Fuckoff, what time!" She shoved him with one hand, and he overbalanced to one side before pulling himself straight. "The time we were shiftin', and you wouldn't let me smoke in your room." She flicked the stub of her fag to the ground, where it rolled over in the breeze. "Your room already smelled like turf and socks."

Bren laughed. He remembered, though it was pretty hazy at the moment.

"Turf an' fag smoke aren't the same."

Orlaith slumped to her side and pressed her head against him. He could feel her breath on his shoulder.

"Doin' ok?"

Orlaith grunted.

"Just resting."

Bren let his eyes close as the world spun. A.J. really did look good in that hurling kit.

"Smells nice."

Bren's drink-addled brain stirred at that, but he couldn't put his finger on why.

"My shoulder?"

He turned to fix her with his wobbly gaze and found her pressing in on him. He tried to lean out of her way, thinking she might be about to hurl. His brain lagged behind his body by about five seconds as she followed his movement, pressing down on top of him.

Their lips met and Orlaith sighed.

Bren's eyes fluttered for a split second, then went wide . . .

She was kissing him.

"Whoa!"

He lurched up, doing his best to get free without sending Orlaith flying. She followed his motion again and sat up, staring at him with half-lidded eyes.

"What'ssa matter?"

Bren shook his head. Bad. This was bad.

"Orlaith, I—" Bren stammered, the adrenaline cutting through the fog. "I can't."

Orlaith blinked, her mouth half open.

"Wha? Whynot?"

"I'm . . ." He thought of A.J., his cute, stammering, brave-in-the-weirdest-ways lad. He couldn't lie. "I'm seein' someone."

Orlaith's expression morphed from confusion, to hurt, to amusement in about the space of three seconds. She lit up another fag.

"Fuck, we're thick." She took a drag and, after holding the smoke in for longer than usual, sighed. "The fuck didn't you tell me?"

She was still slurry, but there was more steadiness to her words now.

"We're not really . . ." Bren paused as the world spun again. "Tellin' people."

Orlaith sat up straighter, her head cocked to the side. It was hard to tell with his heart beating so hard it was making his eyes vibrate, but Bren thought she was grinning.

"Cop on! You're dating someone secret?" She suppressed a shudder like she'd taken a shot. "Do I know them? Fuckkkkk. If you're shaggin' a teacher, O'Shea, I sweartogod."

Bren wasn't sure if he regretted his last Jägerbomb or wished he had another as he answered.

"Yeah, you know them. And it's not a teacher, you sicko," Bren said, trying to sound indignant instead of terrified.

"Well then, who the fuck is . . ."

Orlaith looked like she'd been hit over the head with Brick's hurley as she let the sentence trail off. She looked at Bren, then over her shoulder towards the party. He wasn't drunk enough to think she could see through walls, but all the same, he knew she was looking at A.J.

27

"Forty-five . . . fifty."

A.J. counted along with the handful of people gathered in the kitchen. Conor had, for whatever reason, gotten into it with Brick over whether or not he could do a hundred push-ups given how hammered he was. After peering at Mary, who was engrossed in a conversation with a girl with fake spiders in her hair, Brick had gotten to work.

The back door clattered open, and Orlaith stormed through the room, not acknowledging the two-hundred-pound giant doing push-ups on the hardwood. A.J. was wondering if Orlaith hadn't looked upset when Bren appeared at his side.

"You're ready to go?" he asked, slurring more since the last time they'd spoken.

"Oh, uh, sure," A.J. said, still half watching Brick, who had passed seventy and was looking green. "Is everything ok?"

"Yeah, just wanna head 'ome."

They left the kitchen as Brick stumbled to his feet and made a mad dash to the door with a hand over his mouth.

He was considering whether or not he should go check on the guy when Bren gagged behind him. A.J. turned to find him mid-shudder from the shot he'd downed. Despite what he'd said, he didn't look ok.

Hoping Brick would be alright on his own, A.J. looked around for Orlaith. She was sitting on the bottom step of the staircase that led upstairs. She wasn't crying, but her face was blotchy, and her mascara had migrated to the area around her eyes.

"I'm gonna go say goodbye to Orlaith first, ok?"

Bren shook his head. "Come on. Lessgo."

"I'll be fast, promise."

A.J. wended his way into the crowd before Bren had a chance to reply. He found himself in front of Orlaith in time to watch her wipe her face on the crook of her arm with a loud sniff.

"Is everything ok?"

Orlaith jumped at his words.

"Oh, yeah," she began, adjusting a snake that was now missing its ribbon-tongue. "Everything's grand. What's up?"

A.J. had spent too much time smiling like that not to know a mask when he saw it. He knew better than to try and peer behind it.

"I just wanted to say thanks again for the party." He looked around the room and frowned. "They must be a lot of work."

The corner of Orlaith's mouth quivered, and she wiped her eyes with the back of her hand.

"Fuck, you really are nice, aren't you. Not fake at all."

Her eyes darted around the room, and when it looked like she decided no one was listening, she was so quiet A.J. had to lean in to hear her.

"I can see why he likes you."

A.J.'s stomach plummeted like he'd jumped out of an airplane. He had to have heard that wrong.

"W-what?"

Orlaith scanned the room again.

"Don't worry, I'm not gonna tell anyone. I—" She sniffed, and her breath caught in her throat as a half-sob forced its way out. "Fuck—Sorry—I think you need to talk to Bren. Just . . . don't blame him. I was the slime that did it."

A.J.'s heart hammered as he left Orlaith on her step. Bren was waiting by the door, swaying with his hands in his pockets, his eyes bloodshot.

A.J. braced for whatever he was walking towards and, with Bren stumbling beside him, left the party behind.

The night air hung heavy with silence as they made their way down the darkened path that wended its way towards town. Bren kept listing to one side as they went, so A.J. had to tug at his jersey to keep him from wandering into the ditch.

A.J.'s head was spinning like he'd matched Bren drink-for-drink even though he'd switched to water almost two hours ago. Orlaith knew, full on knew, that he and Bren were together. Worse, she thought that he and Bren needed to talk. "You two need to talk" was probably the one sentence in the English language worse than "We need to talk."

A shiver traveled up his arms as they moved through the darkened streets. If Bren wasn't so drunk that he might wander into traffic on his own, A.J. thought there'd be a fair chance he'd break into a run. But Bren was hammered. They weren't going anywhere faster than he could stumble, and A.J. needed to know what was going on.

"Bren, is everything ok?"

He had to stop asking people that.

Bren took a couple of uneven steps before coming to a stop. He stared down at the road like it had said something nasty about his mom.

"I-I . . ." he swayed again, the crease on his forehead growing. "I really like you, Arlo."

A.J. clenched. There was a but coming any second now.

Bren sniffed and wiped his nose on the back of his hand. "Really like you . . ." he repeated. "I-I fucked it up though."

"What do you mean?" A.J.'s lip quivered as he forced himself to speak. "Orlaith? She knows about us, right? How?"

"Fuckin' told her." A huff that was caught somewhere between a laugh and a sob escaped Bren. "After we kissed."

For the second time that night, A.J. felt like the ground had dropped out from beneath him. He should have run after all.

"You kissed Orlaith?" He'd tried to sound steady, but there was a definite break in his voice.

Bren launched into the story as if he'd been waiting for the question—which A.J. supposed he had. Between Bren's accent, his slurring, and the two times he had to stop to retch, it took longer than it should have for A.J. to understand. When Bren finished talking, he looked up with eyes shining.

"I'm so fuckin' sorry, Arlo. I didn't know she was gonna do it, like. an' I pushed her right off. But I still let her—"

Bren grabbed at his knees and made a motion like a cat trying to hork up a hairball. He was able to keep it down and looked relieved before misery settled back on his face.

A.J. looked back at the mess of a guy standing in front of him and laughed. Really laughed. He hadn't meant to do it, let alone as loud as he did, but he couldn't help it. He only stopped once he caught sight of Bren's tortured expression.

Not willing to let Bren look that way for a second longer, A. J. stepped forward and, grateful for the cover of night, kissed his boyfriend right on his half-opened mouth.

Bren kissed back for all of two seconds before pulling away.

"I tell you I cheated an' you go kissin' me?" he asked, squinting as he tried to bring A.J. into focus.

A.J. stopped himself from laughing again and let his forehead come to rest against Bren's. It was covered with sweat, but he couldn't have cared less. He wasn't sure he'd ever loved Bren more.

"Bren I lo—" A.J. caught himself just in time. "Like you a lot, too, but you're really silly sometimes." He kissed the spot where his forehead had been resting.

Bren hiccoughed, bringing up a cloud of spirits rather than words.

"Look, I don't love that it happened. But Orlaith kissed you, and you stopped her. And you told her you were . . . with me."

Bren blinked back at A.J. like he still didn't get it.

"You aren't pissed?"

"I'm not pissed, but you are." A.J. laughed, the night feeling ten degrees warmer. "That means drunk over here, too, right?"

Something close to a smile spread over Bren's face.

"Really?"

"Yes, really, you eejit," A.J. said in an earnest but awful attempt at the Glenbridge lilt.

Bren stared at A.J. with his mouth hanging open, raised his hand like he was about to say something important, and hurled into the ditch.

The mood for the rest of the walk couldn't have been more different. After Bren vomited up his last couple of drinks, he reverted to his usual drunk self—which was to say Bren with more energy and less filter. He'd wasted no time in blurting out that he was sure that he'd never been more nervous in his life. That he was sure A.J.

was going to ditch him. A.J. didn't know how much of it was the alcohol, but he appreciated the sentiment.

"Wish we lived in Cork!" he declared to the night, wobbling to the left so A.J. had to lean against him.

"Why's that?" A.J. asked, feeling like he was entertaining an overexcited toddler.

"'Cuz then the Centra wouldn't be the only shite open! I want curry chips!"

Drunk-Bren had even less volume control than the sober model, and A.J. was therefore thankful he was thinking about his stomach and not their relationship.

They walked past shuttered shops and a handful of other stumbly people as they made their way home. At one point, Bren locked eyes with a guy in a full-on Master Chief suit, and the two of them exploded in rapid-fire dude speak. Between the slurring and their accents, A.J. had to wonder if what they were speaking could be considered English anymore.

It had taken some work, but A.J. had gotten Bren's mind off of curry chips by pointing out that Centra had other food. He had, horrifyingly, opted for an egg-mayo sandwich that he'd munched on while mumbling that it could do with curry sauce.

"Now I'm kind of glad you puked," A.J. said as they approached the fork. "I don't know how I'd feel about a goodnight kiss after midnight egg-mayo."

Bren, who had finished his questionable purchase, balled up the wrapping and shoved it into his pocket. He stopped mid-step and groaned, his arms swinging like a gorilla's. "Fuckkkk, didn't mean to get so pisssssssed. Mam's gonna be . . . pissed." He laughed at what A.J. was sure he thought was a joke, but looked worried.

"Oh, right, she's not big on you drinking, is she?"

Bren sighed, throwing his head back before letting it fall forward, stumbling as he did. "Thinks I'm gonna turn into me da 'cuz I have a few drinks, like." He ran a thumb under his nose, his cheeks flush with more than vodka. "I'm not gonna be like that."

A.J. wavered on the edge of what he wanted to say. There was no doubt Bren was way too drunk to fool his mom—if it was even possible to fool her about anything. It felt cruel to send him home to that.

"Hey, uh. The McCarthys are in Dublin until Sunday, so you could sleep it off at my place."

Bren perked back up at that, a twinkle breaking through the haze clouding his eyes.

"You askin' me to sleep with you? Takin' advantage of yer drunk b-boyfriend?"

A.J. imploded. If Bren was thinking it too, then that must be what he was doing.

"N-no. I mean, you don't have to! I just—" He fiddled with the hurley he was white knuckling. "I don't want you to get in trouble with your mom."

Bren reached into his pocket and shoved both his phone and the crumpled-up wrapper into A.J.'s hands.

"Too pissed to spell. Be me 'n tell her what I'm doin, yeah?"

A.J.'s brain went into overdrive as he found the contact labeled "Mam." Nice and simple, no reason to overthink it.

Hey, Mam, is it ok if I spend the night over at A.J.'s?

He pressed send before he could workshop it and forced himself not to worry. A shiver ran across his shoulders. Despite his pride as a winter-forged Canadian, his costume showed way too much skin for a night this chilly. He huddled closer to Bren, who was radiating heat like the turf stove back at his place.

Bren wrapped an arm around his waist and pulled him closer, letting out a soft grunt. A warning formed on A.J.'s lips, but he pushed it away. It was dark and he was cold. The chances of anyone passing by this late at night seemed minimal.

"Sorry you saw me hurl." Bren said out of nowhere.

"It's fine," A.J. said. He meant it. Of all the things that had given him pause since coming to Ireland, Bren's puking hardly registered.

They didn't have time to move on from the reminder of that particular level of bonding when Bren's phone buzzed. He flipped it open, read the reply, and tried not to laugh.

"Crap. I'm sorry."

"Wahfor?" Bren asked, trying to read the screen, though from the face he was making, the letters weren't standing still.

A.J. cleared his throat.

Hi, A.J. Tell my son we'll talk about his decision-making once he's sobered up. Chuck him out if he gives you any trouble. Fresh air might do him some good.

"Fuckkkkkkkkk." Bren groaned, letting his head fall against A.J.'s shoulder.

"Still wanna come over?" A.J. asked, thinking maybe it might be some kind of a test from Mrs. O'Shea.

Bren shook his head. "Already gonna get chewed out. Let her cool off before she starts."

He stepped towards the hills, tugging A.J. along with him. "An' since I'm already in shit—I wanna see yer bedroom."

28

Bren's eyes shone with childlike wonder as A.J. set down the sky-high plate of Canadian comfort food. It was lucky he'd been craving poutine last week, or Bren's obsession with chips smothered in sauce would have had to wait until tomorrow. At the last second, A.J. had split the packet gravy in half and stirred in a generous amount of curry powder. Now half the plate was curry-flavoured gravy, and the other half was good old brown gravy, chips, and chunks of mozzarella cheese. No matter how hard he'd looked, A.J. hadn't been able to find cheese curds since touching down in Ireland.

"What's this called again? Putin'?" Bren asked, clenching his fork in his fist.

"Poutine," A.J. corrected, popping a chip in his mouth before Bren could defile the mound. "Sort of. I couldn't find cheese curds, because Ireland hates my culture, I guess."

"What's a cheese curd?" Bren asked through a mouthful from the curry half of the plate.

"Little chunks of white cheese that squeak when you rub them together. They get really melty when you heat them up."

183

Bren stared at the half that was something close to poutine and shoveled a forkful into his mouth. Judging by how fast he went back for seconds, it was a hit.

"Scratch the itch?" A.J. asked as he filled up a glass with water.

Bren closed his eyes and nodded.

"Poutine's fuckin' class."

"You haven't had poutine, but I'm glad you like it." A.J. said as he set the water down. "Now, do me a favour and have some water, please."

Bren dropped his fork with a clatter and chugged the glass before tucking back in. He peered around the room as he chewed, a stray droplet of gravy clinging to the gingery scruff above his chin.

"This place is feckin' huge, Arlo. Always knew you were posh, like."

A.J. rolled his eyes but smiled all the same.

"Meredith and Niall are posh. This place is three times as big as my actual house."

A.J. sat down next to Bren and sipped from his own glass as he picked at the point where the curry chips met the cheesy fries.

"Yeah, an' it's like . . . five times bigger than mine, so your place is still posher 'n mine."

A.J. shrugged. "I guess. But I still like your place better than here."

Bren frowned, swaying as he peered around the room again.

"Kinda feckin' creepy. Bit cold."

"You're not wrong."

That's what he'd thought his first night, and it wasn't just about the draft the place seemed to get after the sun went down. He didn't know how he said the next part, but somehow, he did.

"Guess you'll just have to keep me warm tonight."

He regretted it before he'd finished talking. A feeling that was only reinforced by the booze-addled grin that spread across Bren's face.

"Yeah? Wanna do somethin' that"—he inhaled a final forkful of cheesy fries— "gets you hot?"

He didn't wait for A.J. to reply before he threw his arms around him, rocking forward in his chair to do so. Bren's hand slid down to rest just below the small of his back and groped hard. A.J. had no doubt that if he wasn't sitting, Bren's hands would have traveled even lower.

Bren looked up at A.J. with unfocused eyes and leaned in for a kiss. A.J. almost met his lips before he remembered and ducked his head.

"Puke mouth!"

Bren pulled away.

"Well, fuck you, too."

"No! I—" A.J. shook his head as he spluttered, "You puked on the walk, remember? I kind of want you to brush your teeth before I kiss you."

"Ohhhh, right," Bren replied, like he was only now remembering. "Where's the jacks in this yoke?"

"There's one in my bedroom."

A.J.'s cheeks burned as Bren leapt off the stool and stumbled out of the kitchen.

"You have no idea where you're going, do you?" A.J. asked as he hurried after.

"Yeas, I do!" Bren slurred, "I'm goin' to my boyfriend's bedroom."

Bren didn't see in his quest to find his way through the house, but his boyfriend combusted into a pile of ash.

"You sure someone lives here?" Bren asked after he'd looked around the room with his wobbly gaze.

A.J. couldn't deny he had a point. Between the stark white walls and curated pillow collection on the bed, his room looked more like something out of a catalogue than a teenager's bedroom. The only difference between now and when he'd first moved in was a clunky boombox and his CD binder.

"I'm honestly not sure," A.J. replied, too frazzled from the fact that he had a very drunk Bren in his room to worry about how honest he should be. "I had more of my stuff out the first week, but Meredith kept coming in to organize things for me. So now I keep everything in my closet and try not to take up space."

Bren stumbled over to the king-sized bed and fell to his knees. From the sound they made against the hardwood, A.J. was sure they'd be hurting once he'd sobered up.

"Christ on a fuckin' bike, it's even clean under here. Is that polish?"

"Probably," A.J. groaned. With how Meredith cleaned, it wouldn't surprise him in the slightest. "But even if Meredith didn't clean under there, I don't think you'd find anything green."

Bren chuckled as he wobbled to his knees. "I keep forgetting about that feckin' plate."

"So, do you hate it as much as I do?" A.J. asked, more than happy to have an ally against the place.

Bren shrugged. "Dunno, got some perks, I guess," he said and made his way towards the overstuffed papasan on the other side of the room.

"Hey, uh, how about we get you into something less easy to knock over?" He'd almost sent the thing toppling his first week here, and he hadn't been drunk off his ass.

Bren changed course and wrapped his arms around A.J.'s waist, hands finding his ass and squeezing. "You just want me in your bed, don'tcha?"

A.J. turned red and stepped away from Bren's grabby hands. "I just think you'd do less damage if you were lying down. Let me get you some pyjamas first, though."

"Fairnuff."

Without another word, Bren pulled off his jersey, or at least he tried. He seemed to be having trouble navigating his head out of the neck hole, and after flashing his ginger treasure trail at A.J. flopped down on the bed in a huff.

"Just wait a second and I'll help you."

A.J. bustled towards the dresser and rummaged around until he found a pair of pyjama bottoms and a baggy shirt. He heard Bren get off the bed behind him, and so wasn't surprised when he turned and found him standing. What did surprise him was that Bren was now standing bare-chested, gleaming under the light.

A.J.'s eyes roved over Bren's form. His pale chest with its tuft of gingery hair at the center. A stomach with just the barest suggestion of abs.

Without warning, Bren dropped his shorts, taking his underwear with them. A.J.'s eyes snapped upward, realizing only now that his life's mission was to figure out how many panels made up the crown moulding that surrounded the room. If nothing else came from this night, he'd never doubt whether Bren was attracted to him anymore.

"Bren!" A.J. yelled, eyes still counting crown moulding.

Bren giggled, low and drunk. "Whoops, sorry, Robolad, wasn't thinkin'."

A.J. would have been mad at him if he wasn't sure it was the truth. Bren had heard the words change into pyjamas and sprang into action without another thought.

"Here, just put these on. Please."

***

The world went dark as the checkered pyjamas fluttered down over his head. He heard Arlo cross the room and open a door behind him.

Despite the heroic amount of alcohol he'd thrown back, Bren still felt scarlet as he pulled the bottoms off his head. He'd heard A.J. say he wanted him to change, and his body had acted without another thought.

He couldn't blame him for spiraling. The poor lad had got a peek at the backside, too. No one should have to see anything that pasty.

Bren had pulled on the borrowed clothes by the time A.J. came back, clutching a toothbrush like a lifeline.

"I found a new one in the cupboard," he said, looking relieved that Bren had put his arse away. "There's mouthwash next to the sink."

Bren pawed at the toothbrush, the hem of his shirt lifting enough that a breeze lapped at his belly button. Arlo's clothes were a little too small.

"Can't I just go to bed? Wanna spooooooon."

Bren knew he was probably making Arlo regret inviting him over, but he couldn't help it. He was so fucking cute, blushing in his little hurling jersey. Like he might have been a lad from down the lane. Someone he might be able to keep.

The world spun, and the floor slid until it was too steep for Bren's feet to grip. Arlo's arms wrapped around him, and he grunted with the effort of keeping them upright.

"Stronger than you look," Bren said, letting himself be held as his head nuzzled against Arlo's shoulder. It smelled like chips and laundry soap.

"Ok, we need to get you horizontal, just help me out. Please?"

Bren let himself be led into the jacks and sat on the edge of the counter. He was vaguely aware of the taste of mint as his hand fumbled to brush his teeth. Arlo reminded him, more than once, not to swallow the mouthwash that came next, which of course made Bren want to try it—just to see.

He fell into bed with a sigh. It was the first time he'd ever been in a king, and boy, did it live up to its name. Not a single lump or sag, and no questionable smells either. Just cool sheets and cushy memory foam. Bren rolled over to pull Arlo close and found only air. He peered out from the bed and saw Arlo looking like he wasn't sure how to get in.

"Doin' ok?"

Arlo shifted in place. Bren hadn't realized until now, but at some point, he'd changed into his own pyjamas.

"Maybe, I should sleep in the guest room . . ."

"Wha?"

Bren tried to push himself up, but his hands slipped on the sheets, and he fell back. He laughed at himself, then focused back on Arlo.

"You invite me over 'n, then wanna go sleep in a different room? Don'tcha wanna . . ." His cheeks puffed as he stifled a burp. "Score?"

He'd meant it as a joke, but when Arlo answered, his voice was as serious as Bren had ever heard it.

"I do. Want to . . ." He looked away, but his eyes snapped back before they roved too far. "Do that stuff with you." He took a deep breath. "But I want you to be here for it. With me."

Bren thought he might be having a heart attack for a split second. Whatever it was, it sobered him up enough that some of the fog lifted. He didn't slip this time when he sat up and looked A.J. straight in the eyes.

"Ok. Not tonight."

A.J. still looked nervous.

"Promise?"

"Promise."

The world wobbled again and Bren slid back down, his head cradled by the downy pillow. "Now get y'arse in bed and cuddle your boyfriend."

A.J. rummaged around in the nightstand and got into bed. He'd put *Wicked* on low.

Battle won.

Bren sighed and wrapped an arm around A.J., nuzzling his forehead against the back of his neck.

It felt so good lying there with him. Feeling their chests rise and fall together and hearing the way his breath sounded against the satin pillowcase. When Galinda—not Glimma, he remembered that much at least—made her entrance, a question bubbled through the bliss.

"Wazzit with you an' this show anyway?"

A.J. shifted in Bren's arms and sighed. "Weird girl doesn't know how to people and is scared of the secret she's keeping from everyone? Gee, no idea why I like it so much."

Bren kissed the back of A.J.'s neck as gently as he could.

A.J. sighed and, in a softer voice than before, went on.

"It was the first musical I ever heard that wasn't Disney. It wasn't all cartoon and happily ever after. It was weird and funny and messy and so heartbreaking, and it just . . . it made me want to be there so bad." A.J.'s hand found Bren's and squeezed it. "It would be a lot easier if I could just sing a song when I get feelings instead of freaking out. Like when I met you."

Bren was drifting fast now, but he wanted to stay in the moment. With A.J.

"Yeah? What song'd you sing when you met me?"

A.J. snorted and, in a voice that Bren had never heard him use before, he sang, "Loathing, unadulterated loathing."

Bren's heart gave a funny flutter.

"You . . . loathed me?"

A.J. sighed again. "Kind of? I thought you were laughing at me."

Bren frowned and pressed his lips to the back of A.J.'s neck again.

"I wasn't laughin'. I—" he hadn't thought about it until now. Or, maybe he had, but he hadn't let himself be honest about it. "I thought you were cute but . . . sad." He kissed the spot again. "Wanted to make you smile."

A.J. didn't say anything, but his hand trembled as it squeezed Bren's.

"What song'd you sing now?" Bren asked, returning the pressure.

A.J. didn't reply for the longest time, and when he did, it was little more than a mumble. Bren tried to ask him what he'd said but found his body wouldn't listen. His thoughts had blurred at the edges. He shifted still closer to A.J.'s warmth, and swearing that he'd ask again in the morning, let his mind drift away.

***

191

A.J. lay awake long after Bren's breathing slowed into a dreamy rhythm. Though the room was pitch black, A.J. could still see it, the looming shape on the horizon. The end of the school year. His return to Canada. It had been popping up ever since he realized how happy he was whenever Bren was around.

It usually took him hours to push his mind off that particular train of thought. Tonight was different. He closed his eyes and, louder than before, sang out the answer to Bren's question.

"Just for this moment. As long as you're mine."

29

The ice pick lodged behind Bren's left eye scraped bone as he rolled onto his side. A groan escaped his lips as—after two failed attempts—he forced his eyes open. He could tell that it was sometime in the afternoon, but a set of heavy curtains drawn over the windows was keeping the worst of the light out.

Bits of last night danced half out of reach as he stretched. The party, the kiss with Orlaith, something about chips and pyjamas. It was all a foggy mess. Well, everything except one fact. He was in love with A.J. Flat out in love with the lad. He had no idea what that meant for him, but there was no getting around it anymore.

His eyes found A.J. curled up next to the bed in a chair that was shaped like the bottom half of an egg. He was humming along to whatever was playing from his headphones as he stared down at a bright blue binder. Bren lay still in the bed, unable to take his eyes off A.J. as he did whatever it was he was doing.

His left hand fiddled with a pencil, his brow creased like he was trying to work out a tricky maths problem. Bren's heart swelled as a light shone behind A.J.'s eyes. The pencil found its way to the page and scribbled out something Bren couldn't see.

"Whatcha workin' on there, Robolad?"

The words left Bren without his conscious thought, and A.J. kept scribbling away.

Right. The headphones.

Bren grabbed the pillow he wasn't using and was surprised to see the sleeve of a T-shirt he didn't remember putting on. A fuzzy memory shifted in the back of his mind. Shit—had he stripped in front of the lad?

Hoping he hadn't scarred A.J. too bad, Bren tossed the pillow into the chair where it landed with a muffled fwoosh. A.J. startled, but not as badly as Bren thought he would.

"Good morning, Starshine," he said as he pulled the earphones out, "how're you feeling?"

Bren rubbed his temple as a groan forced its way out.

"Like I drank a whole feckin' brewery."

"Well, you were already pretty messed up before your last two shots," A.J. replied, setting down his binder, then sliding out of the chair. "One sec."

A.J. scampered out of the room before Bren could reply, oversized shirt flapping. Bren slid his way to the edge of the bed and, after stretching out as far as he could, grabbed the corner of the folder. He knew enough about music to know that's what he was looking at, but beyond that, he didn't have a clue.

"What the feck's a legato?" he asked the empty room as A.J.'s footsteps traveled back up the stairs. "Hey, what the feck's a legato?" he asked again as A.J. walked in holding a breakfast tray.

A.J. blushed at the sight of Bren holding the binder but recovered. "It's a music thing."

"Yeah, but what's it mean? I knew you played. Didn't know you wrote."

A.J. set the tray down on the bedside table and tugged the folder away.

"It means tied together, so you play the notes smoothly. And I don't write, I mean, not really. It's just a project for music class."

He tucked the binder away, then looked at the tray. "Think you could eat something? You should probably have a drink, too."

Bren recognized the redirection and let it lie. He put a hand on his stomach. A bit rocky, but food sounded kind of good.

"Long as it isn't vodka."

"Oh yeah, that's what I got from the shops for my hungover boyfriend. Booze."

He rolled his eyes as he placed the tray on Bren's lap. It held a tall glass of something bright orange, a bottle of Panadol, and a curved bowl full of—

"The feck is this?"

A.J. turned pink as he sat on the edge of the bed, careful not to jostle the tray.

"The glass is Lucozade. That's right, right? I asked the guy at the till, and he said that's what people here drink when they're sick."

"Better than penicillin, swear down." He took a swig with a fistful of pills.

Bren wrinkled his nose as he peered down at the bowl A.J. had brought with him. It looked like porridge that someone had turned into soup and thrown a fried egg on top.

"You can eat around the egg if you want," A.J. said like he'd just handed Bren something totally normal.

"This some kind of Canadian thing?" Bren asked, shaking the bowl to see if it jiggled. It did.

"Korean-Canadian, I guess. It's juk, my friend Yu taught me how to make it. It's really good when you're sick."

"The hell kind of a name's Yu?" Bren asked as he brought the spoon to his mouth.

"A Korean one."

Bren chewed the porridge. There were strips of chicken in it and something more than heat that warmed the back of his throat.

"Well, fuck, guess I like Korean food."

He devoted himself to the juk as A.J. looked on. He got the feeling A.J. was pleased that he liked it. When he was about halfway through the bowl, A.J. shifted on his part of the bed. He had a look that told Bren something was weighing on him.

"Whaffs up?" he asked through a mouthful of juk.

"I was just wondering, how much of last night you remember?"

Bren washed down the bite with a swig of Lucozade and leaned back into the pillows.

"Enough that I think you're probably pissed at me."

"What? Why would I be mad?"

Bren cocked an eyebrow. It didn't sound like sarcasm, but maybe he was more hungover than he thought. He scooped up the dregs at the bottom of his bowl and let them fall back in a trickle.

"I mean. I kissed Orlaith, then I'm pretty sure I was a pain in the arse all night, and"—he frowned in an effort to bring the memory back into focus—"did I go showin' you me bits?"

"Uh, well . . . kind of," A.J. said, his cheeks turning pink, "but not like, in a weird way. You were just changing."

"And you're still here after seein' all that? Christ, you must really like me." He let his spoon clatter into his bowl and pushed the tray aside, wanting to sit up for the next bit. "Arlo, I'm real sorry about the kiss. Honest. I didn't know it was comin'."

"It's ok, Brendan."

A.J. was looking at him so lovingly as he said it, but Bren couldn't help it—he laughed.

"What?" A.J. asked, frowning.

"I'm sorry, but who the fuck is Brendan?"

"Uh, you?"

Bren shook his head. "Nah, Brendan's some gowl who sips martinis and complains about the stock market."

"Alright, and who the hell do you think Arlo is? You realize you're the only one who calls me that, right?"

Bren slid forward and reached an arm around A.J.'s lower back, pulling him close. "He's this real fit lad from Canada. Cute, nervous, has real shite taste in boyfriends."

A.J.'s eyes shone as he opened his mouth like he was about to say something. Instead, he leaned forward, head tilted. Bren made to mirror him but forced himself to stop before their lips met.

"Look. The Orlaith thing, it's—" he slid back so he could look A.J. in the eyes. "You don't know the whole story. We used to kinda go 'round together."

"If go 'round together means almost date, I know." And before Bren could ask, added, "Orlaith mentioned it last night."

A.J. reached out and took Bren's hand, running his thumb along the knuckles.

"I don't love that it happened. But you didn't know she was going to do it, and she didn't know she shouldn't have done it." He brought Bren's hand to his lips and kissed it. "In a weird way, it makes me like you more."

Bren let his hand be kissed but frowned all the same.

"Ok, I'm pretty hungover, like. you wanna run that one by me again?"

A.J. let their hands fall back to the bed but didn't let go.

197

"You could have tried to hide it, or lied about it, or something. But you didn't. And you looked so torn up before you told me. That's enough for me."

Bren leaned forward without meaning to and pulled A.J. into the softest kiss they'd ever shared. When they pulled away, A.J.'s eyes were shimmering like they might spill over. Bren's vision was getting cloudy too.

"Still feel like I should make it up to you," he said, sniffing as he dragged his arm across his face. "Wanna see me arse again?"

A.J. laughed but looked down at the bedding like he was embarrassed.

"Well, I'm supposed to hang out with Nat today. It would be really cool if you could meet her."

"With me arse covered, yeah?"

A.J. laughed again but still looked anxious.

"As long as you don't mind her seein' the mullet, sounds like good craic." Bren reached out to take A.J.'s hand this time and let himself fall back against the pillows. "Wanna see the kind of people who put up with you back home."

He said it with as much bravado as he could muster, hoping A.J. couldn't tell that he was the nervous one now.

***

"Oh my god! Why does he have a mullet?!"

Bren stared at the screen with his mouth half open. There'd been no lead-up to this. The call had connected, and a girl with a chunk of acid green hair appeared on screen and slagged him like they'd known each other since birth.

"Don't be a dick! It was for a Halloween party."

"What was he supposed to be? That weird guy who pulls beer for grade schoolers?"

"Fuck off, you're just jealous I landed someone who looks like he could play for the Canucks."

"Oh yeah, rabid for that hockey hair over here. Ireland's made you dumb, dude."

If it weren't for the ache behind his left eye, Bren would've thought he was dreaming. He'd never, not for one second, heard A.J. talk to anyone like that before.

"Is he gonna say anything? I thought he was supposed to be the loud one."

Bren jerked away from his thoughts and fixed what he hoped was a casual grin on his face.

"Hey. I'm Bren."

"Yeah, no duh." Nat laughed. "Is he still drunk or something?"

Bren laughed along with A.J. but was trying to figure out how the hell this was his best friend.

"With how much he drank last night, maybe. So be nice."

"Right, sorry, sorry," she said so-rry the same way A.J. did. "Didn't mean to sound like a bitch. I'm Nat, nice to meet you."

Bren nodded, his mullet tickling the back of his neck. A.J.'s hand found Bren's knee and squeezed it.

"Aww, the hand on the knee and everything." Nat brought a hand to her mouth like she was trying to hold back her joy. "I miss your face so much."

"I miss you, too. Ireland would be a lot more fun if you were here."

"It looks plenty fun to me. Seriously, look at you two!"

A smile crept across A.J.'s face, and he let his head rest against Bren's shoulder, which made Nat swoon even more.

"Everything ok?" A.J. asked, reminding Bren of himself.

"Grand. Just tryin' to figure out how the feck the two of you are friends."

"Oh my god, the accent! I'm kind of jealous Agee."

"Oh yeah. Glenbridge accent's real sexy," Bren replied, still refusing to believe that anyone thought it was charming. "But seriously, the fuck did you two happen?"

Nat and A.J. shared a look, then burst out laughing.

"I didn't really have a choice. A bunch of us were playing Power Rangers back in kindergarten, and both of us wanted to be Kimberly, so it pretty much had to happen."

"You were so fucking gay even back then, dude."

"Yeah, yeah, took me another six years to figure it out, though."

"How about you, Bren?" Nat asked, sounding more controlled than she had for the entire conversation. "When'd you know?"

"Nat!"

She grinned and shifted toward the camera. "What? Is it some big secret he likes you?"

Bren's palms broke out in a sweat as he fumbled to find his voice. "Uh . . . since I met this one, I guess."

He thought the truth was more complicated than that, but it seemed like the easier answer. Nat squealed again as A.J. grinned next to him. Bren, for his part, was having a hard time ignoring the sound of his heart hammering in his ears. Was this what life was like for A.J.? If so, he needed to give the lad more credit.

A thought occurred to him as Nat launched into a story about the play she was in. He thought he'd gotten to know A.J. pretty well in the last three months. He'd seen him spiral and smile and open up in so many ways, but this side was something different. He wondered what else he might see if he was lucky enough to keep him.

30

"Bren! Mickie's at the door!"

Bren watched the ribbons of Harpic disappear down the toilet and wrinkled his nose. The strange blue goo may have disappeared, but the reek of bleach and artificial orange threatened to stick around for a while.

"Comin'!" he shouted back, peeling off his gloves. "I'm allowed to talk to him, am I?"

Mam had been less annoyed than he'd thought she'd be. That or she was getting soft in her old age. Cleaning the jacks and taking care of the washing for the rest of the week was a lot less than he'd thought he was going to get.

The thought was reinforced when he passed her in the kitchen, and she waved him on.

"Alright there, Micko?" Bren said when he got to the front door.

Mickie was standing outside with his hands thrust into the pockets of his windbreaker, looking like he was nursing one hell of a hangover.

"Hey, got a minute?" he asked, looking at Bren but not quite meeting his eye.

"Probably just a minute, yeah? Mam's pissed about me drinkin' last night."

For some reason, this made Mickie dig his hands deeper into his pockets. He looked like he was hovering at the edge of saying something but kept glancing over Bren's shoulder towards the kitchen.

"You alright?"

"Grand," Mickie said in a voice that didn't sound like his. "Just wanna talk."

In the course of their twelve-year friendship, Bren could count the times Mickie had come over just to talk on one hand, and all of those had been before Secondary. Knowing Mickie well enough to assume that this was something Mam wouldn't want to hear, Bren tried his luck.

"Hey, Mam, can I go out for a bit? Mickie's feelin' all soft like, and needs a mate."

Bren could see the gears turning behind Mam's eyes as she rose from her chair to get a better look at the two of them. She grabbed a piece of paper off the fridge and jabbed it into his chest.

"You can talk while you go to the shops. Don't linger."

"Yes, ma'am," Bren said, taking the kindness for what it was.

"So, what the fuck's so important? You look like shite."

Sodden leaves squelched under their feet as they trod towards the fork in the road. It made Bren smile to picture A.J. coming down from the hill to meet him there.

"Party went late," Mickie said, sounding almost Rory-like.

"Right, how was it? A.J. and I bailed a bit early, like."

Mickie made a convulsive movement beside him before he answered.

"Orlaith was real upset after you left."

"Fuck, really?"

Bren knew full well why she'd been upset, but fuck if he was about to talk about that with Mickie.

"Yeah, real weird for the rest of the night." They moved out of the way so Mrs. Farrelly could shuffle by, shopping trolley creaking as she went. "I asked her what was up, and she got real cagey."

"Don't try an' understand girls, Micko, you'll lose your effin' mind."

Mickie looked over at Bren but didn't laugh.

"Why'd you leave with Canada anyway?"

The hair on the back of Bren's neck stood up.

"No reason, I guess," Bren said, wishing he hadn't agreed to this walk. "Why's it matter, anyway?"

They were getting close to the shops now, and Bren was thinking maybe that would save him from this conversation when Mickie nodded to the alley that led off to the woods.

"Ah, I don't got time. You heard Mam, shoppin' and back."

Mickie looked around them, and Bren got the feeling he was doing an inventory of who was within earshot.

"Fine," Bren grunted, pushing past Mickie towards the path. "Hurry it up then."

The clearing was deserted when they got there. Everyone who might be there was probably still hungover after Orlaith's party.

"Right, what is it?"

Mickie looked like a goldfish as he opened and closed his mouth for a while. He snapped his mouth shut and, looking off into the trees rather than at Bren, launched into it.

"Look, I'm not dumb. I've seen the way A.J. looks at you sometimes."

"Like a Canadian?" Bren asked, still hoping he could make this not happen.

"Like a fuckin' puppy droolin' over his favourite bone."

"Jesus, Mickie!"

Mickie took a step towards the splintered bench and ran his finger along the uneven grain.

"So I thought, fine. He's queer. Whatever. He's sound enough, isn't hurtin' anyone, who cares."

"Alright, glad we had this chat then."

Mickie shook his head, still looking at the table.

"Then I started noticin' that you kinda get that look 'round him, too. Then you showed up in those fuckin' costumes and go home with him before the party was even windin' down."

Bren's mouth felt like it had never known a drop of water as Mickie continued not looking at him, so it was a surprise when he heard himself reply.

"Look, Mickie . . ." He felt both a thousand and five years old as he forced the words out. "It was a laug—"

Bren saw A.J. smiling as he lifted his pencil to scribble something in his folder and found he couldn't finish that sentence.

"I'm sorry you don't like the way I look at him."

Mickie sat down in the spot Orlaith had been in a few weeks ago. He stared into the fire pit like he might take a swing at it.

"So, what, are you just, inta lads now?"

Bren checked the time on his phone, Mam was gonna be pissed if this took much longer.

"Look, I'm still hungover as hell, do we gotta do this right now?"

"You know, I was kinda happy when you stopped goin' after Orlaith. Always thought she was hot." He was running his hand along the wood grain again, still looking everywhere but at Bren. "Kinda wish you'da shagged her and stayed normal."

"You wanna say that again?" Bren said, anger coming to his defense now.

Mickie pulled himself off the bench and looked like he was going to take Bren up on that. Instead, his shoulders drooped, and he shook his head.

"Right, well, guess that's my answer then."

Bren considered taking a swing as Mickie shouldered past him, but the impulse left him almost immediately. His fury, much like a twelve-year friendship, crumbled to dust.

31

"Come on, Brenny, if you're not gonna jump, the least you can do is give us a smile."

Brick's voice boomed above the whistling wind as Bren shivered at the edge of the bridge. Twenty feet down, icy black water churned in the November breeze. Bren didn't look at the camera and instead dropped the back of his heart-spotted boxers.

"Aw, come on!" Brick groaned.

Bren smiled when A.J. joined in. He sounded disgusted enough that Rory and Brick would buy it, but Bren heard the trace of a squeak that told him A.J. had liked what he'd seen. Two months into dating, and Bren still had trouble believing A.J. liked his pasty cheeks.

The breeze picked up as, next to him, Rory let out a resigned groan.

"Let's just get it over with."

"What was that? Speak up for the camera!" Brick yelled back, clearly enjoying himself.

"He said fuck off, you ruddy bellend," Bren said in his best-worst imitation of Rory's accent.

"Yeah? Tell him it's not my fault his dumb arse bet against Bally-wood!"

"Their defense has been shite all season, and you know it!" Bren cried, hating their yearly wager for the first time.

For two years, they'd all bet on who'd make it into the county finals, with the losers having to jump in the river. Bren had stayed dry both years and had the immense satisfaction of watching Brick, Mickie, and Rory each take their turns shivering.

He started to wonder if Mickie would have been shivering beside him but shoved the thought away. That was done.

Almost three weeks since the clearing, and Mickie hadn't said more than two words to him. It hadn't taken more than one Mickie-free lunch for the other lads to start asking questions, but Bren had shut it down. Mickie was a prick. That's all they needed to know.

"Are you sure it's deep enough?" A.J. said, sounding worried.

"Water's up past the second rivet on the middle post. They're fine," Brick said.

Taking his mind off of both Mickie and the cold, Bren gave his cheeks a flex and was pleased to hear A.J. try and pass off a squeak with a round of coughing.

"Alright, Canada's gettin' chilly. In the water now," Brick cooed.

Bren took another step towards the edge.

"Canada's a fuckin' traitor, sidin' with you."

He'd meant it as a joke, but a part of him was upset A.J. hadn't trusted his advice on which team to be on, even if it'd been wrong.

"Don't blame the lad for figuring out you've got shite for brains."

From the sound that followed, Brick had slapped A.J.'s ass.

"Just in time or he'd be in his jocks, too."

Bren grunted and took another step, toes now curled along the edge.

"On three?"

He took a breath.

"One . . . Two . . . Thr—"

Bren didn't get to finish before an A.J.-sized blur pushed past him and jumped into the river with a panicked laugh. Sense left Bren as he whirled around, expecting to see A.J. still standing behind him. Instead, he saw a crumpled hoodie in a heap next to a whooping Brick.

Bren turned back to the water as the splash broke through Brick's manic laughter. The next thing he knew, he was falling.

A thousand icy knives pierced Bren's body as he broke through the surface of the water. The world was a dark, writhing mess of bubbles and thrashing. He kicked his legs hard and forced his head into the icy air above.

"Shit! Holy shit, that's cold! Shit! Shit!"

The part of Bren's brain not concerned with getting the fuck out of the water as fast as possible had locked on to A.J. bobbing a few feet away, as an echoing splash announced Rory had joined them somewhere to Bren's right.

"W-what the f-fuck, Arlo!" Bren shouted, half-stammering, half-laughing.

A.J. gritted his teeth and made a sound like his soul was trying hard to leave his body.

"B-bit colder than you thought?"

A.J. groaned again, but nodded, face red.

Bren got a lungful of water as a laugh forced its way out.

"A-alright, let's get the f-f-uck out of this f-fuckin' river," Bren said and started paddling towards the shore with his rapidly numbing arms.

Rory was already shivering under the bridge when Bren got there and offered him a hand. He thought for a second about pulling him back into the water, but wound up pulling himself out.

Between their shaking arms and A.J.'s soaked clothes, it took all three of them to pull the lad up. A.J. was smiling through the whole thing, but when he got out of the water, his arms wrapped around himself.

Bren looked at the soaked, trembling mess in front of him and realized that he'd be shaking even if he wasn't stripped down to his jocks in the middle of November. His arms moved towards A.J. on reflex, but he caught himself in time.

"L-let's get up to the c-ca—"

"Oh, go on then."

Rory was looking at him like he was the thickest person on the planet and rolled his eyes with what looked like a massive effort.

Bren's heart froze.

He looked at A.J., who, through chattering teeth, was smiling back at him.

Bren tried to say something. There was still a chance Rory didn't know. They could laugh it off and go back to normal. Rory didn't need to leave.

Sense caught up with Bren as A.J. took a step forward. Bren met him in the middle and wrapped his arms around his waist. Water squelched out of A.J.'s sodden jumper as they kissed, but Bren was so numb with cold and adrenaline that he didn't care.

"About time," Rory said through chattering teeth.

Bren would have flipped him off if he wasn't worried his finger might snap off like an icicle.

"Hey, you ladies die down there? Car's all warmed up!"

A.J. started to pull away, but Bren pulled closer. Who cared if Brick saw.

32

By the time Bren realized A.J. had come over, he'd already flipped on the stereo and flopped beside him with a groan of springs.

"Mmmphing hhfh thfh mchtchses"

Bren paused FIFA, then rubbed A.J.'s back.

"You wanna run that by me again, like?"

A.J. huffed and lifted his head off the pillow.

"I said, I fucking hate the McCarthys."

"What'd they do this time?" Bren asked, remembering when Meredith had gone into A.J.'s closet and sorted his outfits by colour.

A.J. groaned and fell back onto the pillow.

"Stop shiftin' the pillow, lad."

A.J. turned his head to the side and let out a sigh.

"They want me to go to the Canary Islands with them."

"Bastards," Bren said, trying not to laugh. "Bring me back a tweety-bird."

"For Christmas. The entire holiday."

"Bastards. . ."

Bren tried not to let the ache show, but wasn't sure he managed it. This was their first Christmas. Maybe their only one.

"Do you think Rory will hide me in his basement if I bribe him with books?"

Bren's heart soared like a canary out of a coalmine.

"Or you could just, you know, stay here."

A.J. peered up from his pillow like Bren had said something insane.

"What?"

"Mam likes you. She doesn't know what we get up to when the door's closed. Why not?"

A.J. rolled onto his side as his face took on an expression Bren knew too well by now.

"Come on Robolad, don't go overthinkin' this one."

"Bren. . ."

"Aw, fuck."

Bren flopped down next to him, resigned.

"What's up?"

"Wouldn't that be weird? I mean, she thinks I'm just your friend, right?"

"Yeah? What's the problem?"

"It feels like lying to her I guess?" A.J. took Bren's hand and rubbed his thumb along his knuckles. "Like, 'hey Mam, can my friend A.J. stay over for two weeks? Oh by the way we're going to be groping and shite every time your back's turned.'"

Bren didn't react to A.J.'s imitation because of how worried he looked, but made a mental note to take the piss out of him later.

"It's not like we're gonna go rattlin' the headboard every time Mam's out of the house," he pulled A.J. closer and gave him the best smoulder he could manage. "Unless that's what you want for Christmas."

A.J. laughed and pulled Bren into a kiss. When it broke, he pressed their foreheads together.

"I want to spend Christmas with you."

"Gonna let me ask Mam if you can stay then?"

A.J. stayed quiet for an entire chorus but nodded in the end.

Bren sat up and filled his lungs.

"Hey Mam!"

They would have landed on the floor if Bren hadn't been ready. He used the momentum and twisted so A.J. wound up under him. A.J. looked surprised by the turnabout, but still reached a hand up to cover Bren's mouth. He licked across the length of A.J.'s palm and laughed when he pulled it away.

"She's not even home, lad."

It looked like A.J. had forgotten, judging by the blush creeping in on his cheeks.

"Right. Just, promise me you won't yell it at her when you actually ask, ok?"

Bren shook his head.

"Nah, gotta butter her up first for something like this. I got a plan."

***

"Whoops, casualty of war."

Mam laughed as Bren held up a gingerbread man, its leg left behind on the counter for all its brothers to see.

"Poor little gingerbren man."

Bren rolled his eyes, but couldn't keep from smiling. He could still remember the year the tradition started. Whether he'd misheard her or his six-year-old self had been self absorbed, he'd really thought Nan had told him they were going to be making gingerbren men for Christmas.

"Oh well, needed to taste this batch anyway," Bren said, dipping the wounded cookie into the bowl of royal icing.

"Still think the maple was a good call?"

Bren chewed his bite carefully before he swallowed. The combination wasn't the worst, but there was a certain candle-like quality that was hard to get around.

"Good enough," he said and popped the rest of the cookie into his mouth.

"I'll let you hand out those ones then. Let your mates risk it."

She went back to her own biscuit, leaving Bren to stare down at the gingerbren men who hadn't lost limbs in the Great Baking War of 2006.

It's no big deal. Just pretend it's Mickie.

"Hey, Mam," Bren asked, scraping the last of the red icing towards the bottom of the bag.

"Hmm?"

Bren's eyes found the maple flavoured biscuit without red hair. The one he'd given an icing Discman down by his hip. He could feel his heart thumping in his throat.

"We're not doin' anything for the hols, right?"

"Not unless you've got anything planned," Mam replied, focused on sticking a gumdrop button in place.

"Sound."

He squeezed a trail of icing dots down the front of his biscuit.

"Since we're not doin' anything, woulditbeokifA.J.stayedover?"

There was a split second where he thought maybe Mam hadn't noticed his verbal stroke, but her laughter put that hope to bed.

"You wanna try that again?" she asked, still only half paying attention.

214

"A.J.," Bren said, being careful not to look at the biscuit version of him, "You know how I told you his host family is going away for Christmas?"

Mam stopped her frosting to look at him. She was smiling at least. That was a good sign.

"I do."

"Well he doesn't want to go. He's only got," Bren's stomach clenched as it always did when he thought about how A.J. wasn't going to be here forever, "One Christmas over here. He wants to spend it in Ireland. Is it ok if he stays here?"

"For how long?"

Bren took a breath. It was a big ask no matter who it was.

"The whole thing?"

Mam stared at him for a few seconds, still smiling like she was looking at a picture from back when he was a kid.

"As long as the McCarthys and his parents are ok with it, sure."

"Wait, really?"

Mam nodded.

"Yes really. What did you want me to say? No?"

A smile broke across Bren's face.

"No. I mean—thanks Mam. Feck, guess I better let him know."

Mam made a movement like she was going to go back to frosting, but stopped.

"Bren?"

The misty look was gone now.

"Yeah?"

"Whoever's taking the camp bed is staying on the camp bed, you hear me?"

Bren almost dropped the piping bag. He couldn't have heard that right.

"W-what?"

Mam gave him a look.

"Bren."

Bren stared back at her, heart thudding out of his chest.

"Mam?"

He tried to sound like he had no idea what she was talking about, and when she didn't break eye contact, went back to his biscuits.

The back of his neck prickled as he tried to pretend he gave a fuck about gumdrops. He could still feel her eyes boring into him.

"Bren, it's ok."

He made one last attempt to give a gingerbren man a button with his shaking hands before admitting defeat.

"Mam, I. I mean I'm not—I mean, I still like—how did you know?"

Mam stifled a snort and clapped a hand over her mouth. Her eyes went wide as she fanned herself with her free hand.

"What the fuck?" he asked, not sure if he was angry or terrified.

Mam waved her hand one more time and swallowed her laughter.

"Sorry, sorry. But Bren," She fixed him with the kind of smile that always made him feel about five. "I've heard you talk more about that boy in three months than Mickie, and you've known him since you were five."

"I don't tal—"

Mam rose on her tiptoes and pushed her chin out in what he thought might have been a horrible impression of him.

"Nah, Mam, A.J. doesn't take sugar in his tea. A.J. was saying that his little sister gets picked on cuz she's so shy. Guess it's genetic. Hey, Mam, did you know A.J. learned how to ice skate when he was four? Parents just pushed him out on the ice, like."

216

Bren would have liked to crawl in the oven with the next batch of cookies as Mam forced herself not to laugh again. He'd really thought he'd done a good job of covering it up.

"So you're not. . ."

"I do have a question though."

180c for 12 minutes, or until brown around the edges.

"Y-yeah?"

"Had you two already kissed that night he brought the tart over?"

Bren made a sound caught somewhere between a groan and a cough.

"I'm gonna go tell A.J. he should go with the McCarthys," Bren said, shoving another biscuit in his mouth as he went.

"Give him love from his mam-in-law!"

Bren slammed his door shut, heart still racing. "Home For The Holidays" started up from the kitchen, the volume loud enough that it carried through the door. Now That's What I Call Christmas, Nan played that at least a dozen times each December, and always on gingerbren day.

Bren leaned against the door, as Mam's voice rose up with Perry Como's.

"Thanks Mam."

33

An impatient huff pushed past Bren's lips as he bounced his foot to the rhythm that always cropped up when his mind had nothing to settle on. Term had ended twenty minutes ago, and he was sitting around in the music prefab like he was hoping for Christmas homework.

He flipped his phone open and frowned. A.J. had asked to meet here twenty minutes ago and then gone silent.

Rory had texted right after saying that some of the lads were meeting up at Niamh's. She could usually be counted on to slap on a holiday discount on the last day of term. If they waited around much longer, the place would be cleaned out by the time they got there.

"Sorry!" The door behind Bren clattered open, letting in a burst of chilly air and a very windswept A.J. "I had to fill out some exchange stuff with Mr. Kelleher, and it took way longer than I thought."

Whatever frustration Bren had been feeling evaporated. A.J.'s cheeks were flushed, and there was a catch in his voice that told Bren he'd run here.

"S'alrigh, just gonna miss out on free pastries down at Niamh's," Bren said, rising to poke A.J. in the shoulder. "Ready to go?"

A.J. shook his head and pulled a bright blue folder out of his bookbag.

"I still have to give you your Christmas present," he said, sounding like he was trying not to pant.

"Bit early, isn't it?" Bren asked, looking at the folder and trying to remember why it looked familiar. "Christmas is a week away."

A.J. breezed past him and stopped in front of the piano.

"I know, but uh, I kind of need a piano to give it to you."

Bren perked up at that. Éclairs could wait.

"You finally gonna play for me?"

"Yeah. Remember that term project I've been working on?"

The folder clicked into place.

"Oh! The one from back in fuckin' October?"

"That's the one. Well, I got it back, and I wanted to play it for you."

"Must be a hell of a feckin' song if it took you all term, like," Bren said as he sat back down. "Whatcha get on it?"

It was hard to tell since he was still pink from running, but Bren thought A.J. was blushing now.

"Ninety-eight. Mrs. Doherty said the two percent was just because there's always room for improvement."

"Well, go on then, let's see if she was gradin' you easy 'cuz you're Canadian."

A.J. ignored the jab and lifted the cover off the keys. He paused and took a deep breath, like he was bracing himself for something. Before Bren could ask what was up, A.J. squared his shoulders and turned to face him.

"'The Navigator, composed by Arlo Jonathan Walker for Brendan Finley O'Shea.'"

219

Bren's heart beat faster as A.J. took his seat. He straightened his back, lifted his arms, and with a grace Bren had never seen on him, played.

The notes came in slow, dreamy waves. It reminded Bren of something that might have come out of a music box. He was wondering if Mrs. Doherty had been taking it easy on him after all when the song changed. It looped back to the beginning, but A.J.'s hands were busier this time. More notes were layered in, and the sounds blurred as A.J. rocked back and forth to the rhythm of the song.

In the four months since Bren met A.J., he'd made his way through the entire dictionary trying to describe him. Cute, shy, sometimes gloomy, often twitchy, fit in a strange way Bren could never explain to himself. This was the first time the word beautiful came to mind.

He was beautiful.

The music swelled into echoing strains that filled Bren with their sound. "The Navigator"— Bren had told him that's who he was named for, right before he'd called him Arlo for the first time. Arlo Jonathan. A name for the feeling in his chest whenever he was around. His lad. Arlo.

The last note faded into silence before A.J. let his hands come to rest in his pockets. His chest rose and fell to the rhythm of the piece he'd finished playing, his body still synced to the moment.

"I got you a real present, too, obviously. But, I really wanted you to hear that, I guess." He picked at a piece of lint in his pocket as a new thought occurred to him. "Maybe it was a present for me, huh?"

The sound of steel against linoleum made A.J. look away from the piano he'd delivered his speech to. Bren was striding towards him. His eyes were red above a jaw clenched so tight it looked more like a grimace than anything. A.J. rose to his feet, sure that he'd done something wrong. He didn't have time to give the thought words before Bren's arms pulled them together.

"B-bren?"

Bren sniffed and buried his head in the crook of A.J.'s neck, his arms pulling them still closer. The knot in A.J.'s chest relaxed as his own jaw struggled to hold in the feelings that threatened to overtake him. For once, he didn't try to make words come. Instead, A.J. closed his eyes and let himself be held by the boy who'd given him the notes to the sort of song he never thought was meant for him.

The wind outside whistled against the music prefab, its bitter chill unseen and unheard by the couple inside. Bren let out a watery chuckle as A.J. mumbled something into the top of his head, just as the figure peering through the cracked door pulled it shut again.

34

"Whatthefuckshitsorry!"

A.J. rolled onto his back as the looming figure above him braced against the chest-high dresser. He yanked his earphones out as Bren, dressed in nothing but a pair of checkered pyjama bottoms, forced himself upright.

"Good morning to you, too," A.J. said, smiling despite his throbbing ribs.

"Sorry! Forgot you were there, like. You ok?"

"Only 'cuz you're skinny as hell. If I was dating Brick, I'd be dead."

Bren groaned in a way that told A.J. it was too early for quips.

"Wouldn't have happened if you just took the bed."

Bren had offered to sleep on the camp bed so he could have the proper one, but A.J. had been adamant about sticking it out on the floor. The O'Sheas were already putting themselves out by having him for the holidays—he wasn't about to go kicking people out of their beds.

Then there was the ginger elephant in the room.

"Alright, say I did. What are the odds I'd wake up getting spooned by some weird Irish dude?"

"Pretty high," Bren said as he scratched at the scruff on his chest. "You sayin' you don't wanna cuddle yer man?"

A.J. made himself push past the "your man" comment to avoid a short circuit.

"I do, it'd just feel weird . . . your mom invites me in, and then I defile her firstborn?"

Bren hunched down in the space between the bed and A.J.'s cot.

"Look, I amn't askin' you to shag whenever we got the house to ourselves. But I don't wanna spend the holiday worryin' that you're worrin' about, like, breathin' too loud while you're here."

"I do snore pretty loud . . ."

"So, lemme ask you again." He hopped off the floor and let himself fall back into his bed. "You wanna come up here and cuddle with yer man?"

The soft refusal was halfway out of A.J.'s mouth before Bren had finished, but something pulled him short. He rose off his cot and flipped on Bren's boombox. The Fall Out Boy CD he'd been listening to last night started up as he slipped in beside Bren, whose arms pulled him close.

Bren's lips brushed his neck with the barest trace of warmth, driving away some of his more stubborn hesitation. A.J. flipped around to kiss Bren but paused halfway there. He somehow looked even paler than usual, his eyes had faint shadows of lingering sleep, and he was rocking a pretty serious case of bedhead. Still, A.J.'s heart stirred.

"You're thinkin' again, aren't you?" Bren asked, brushing his lips against A.J.'s.

"Just that I kind of wish I lived over here. It's a lot nicer."

A look of surprise flashed across Bren's face. A.J. was sure he was comparing his house's square footage with the McCarthys', but somewhere along the way, it seemed to click.

223

"Well, you do live here for the next two weeks," Bren said, pulling A.J. so close he could feel Bren's heart beating next to his. "So just relax, ok?"

A.J. let out the breath he'd been holding since he'd dropped his duffel bag on Bren's floor last night.

"Ok."

***

"Oh, come on, Mam! This is child abuse! It's freezin'!"

A.J. moved out of the way as a Brussels sprout whizzed past and bounced off the side of Bren's head with a satisfying thunk.

"Now you've gotta wash that off *and* go to the shops," Mrs. O'Shea said as she returned to the mountain of sprouts she was double-checking.

Bren sighed as he bent to pick the sprout off the floor. It came flying back past A.J. and landed in the sink.

"Dunno why we gotta get punished just 'cuz Mrs. Farrelly don't have anyone to spend the hols with."

A quiet part of A.J. had to agree with Bren. The first few days of the holidays had been laid back, but ever since Mrs. O'Shea had announced she'd invited one of her patients for Christmas dinner, there'd been an edge in the air.

"Oh yeah, my poor neglected child. He has to get off his arse on Christmas Eve so a lovely old lady has something decent to eat. Call the Guards."

A.J. wasn't sure there was any danger of a lack of decent food, even if Bren stayed home. The mountain of vegetables and buttered and stuffed turkey waiting in the fridge was enough to feed a small army by themselves. If you counted the Christmas pudding and mince tarts Niamh had sent over last night, they could probably feed the entire block without breaking a sweat.

Bren let out another sigh, and his mom's hand twitched towards the assortment of wooden spoons next to her. Sensing danger, A.J. pushed away from the pile of potatoes he'd been peeling.

"Here, you finish these and I'll go to the shops."

"Ah, you don't gotta, I was just—"

"It's fine," A.J. replied, already grabbing the list from the fridge. "Wouldn't want that big bad two degrees to make you chilly."

He would have given Bren a kiss for how adorably indignant he looked if his mom wasn't right there.

"No, you're a guest, too. You don't gotta go runnin' errands," Mrs. O'Shea said, though she was already fishing around in her purse.

A.J. took the bills with no intention of spending any of them. The McCarthys had left him with enough food money for a family of four for the holidays, and this seemed like the only way to spend some of it on the O'Sheas. He'd have to ask Bren to sneak the cash back into her purse later.

"I don't mind. It's almost January, and I haven't risked frostbite once. Gotta fix that."

Bren looked like he was going to object again, but settled on a chuckle before taking his spot at the mountain of potatoes.

A chest-high Santa covered in fake snow stared at A.J. with beady eyes as he pulled on his bunnyhug. He was one of at least a dozen jolly Santa Clauses that dotted the bungalow, though this one was by far the largest.

"Alright, try not to freeze your arse off!"

225

A.J. waved a dismissive hand at the comment. If he couldn't manage a walk to the shops in what passed for cold over here, he might as well turn in his passport.

"Have fun with the potatoes," A.J. called back, and before he could stop himself, added, "Not too much fun though. We still have to eat them later."

Bren looked shocked, but burst out laughing as A.J. headed out the door. Bren really was rubbing off on him.

35

The wind nipped at A.J.'s hands as he made his way back towards the O'Sheas'.

It hadn't taken him long to find the handful of things on the list. He'd also spotted a tin of biscuits that Mrs. O'Shea swore were for guests, but kept disappearing faster than he'd been eating them. Without thinking, he turned halfway up the street to take the short-cut through the woods.

He hummed along with the women of B*Witched, having taken the CD off of Bren's hands a couple weeks ago. The music was low enough that the sounds of the day weren't lost on him, and so when he heard rustling branches behind him, A.J. looked back. There was a figure strolling along the path A.J. had just walked. He couldn't be sure, but he thought it was vaguely Tadhg-shaped.

He popped his earphones out and picked up his pace.

Now that the music was gone, A.J. could hear voices bubbling up from off towards the clearing.

Maybe it wasn't them.

When he broke from the trees, Cian was sitting around the empty fire pit with the other guy whose name A.J. had never learned. Heart racing, he gave one pointless glance over his shoulder.

"Hey there, faggot, been meaning to have a word with you."

A.J.'s stomach turned; there was something animal buried under the slur.

"Sorry, uh, kind of busy, Cian. Merry Christmas, though."

A.J. kept his gaze fixed on where he was going and for a moment, he thought that might be the end of it. The delusion shattered when a powerful hand clamped down on his shoulder.

"Don't fucking talk to me like we're mates. Wouldn't be mates with a fucking faggot like you if you paid me."

A tinny ringing started up in A.J.'s ears as the world came into cruel clarity.

"Sorry, I was just . . . trying to be civil. I'm just going to go, though, ok?"

Tadhg appeared at the edge of the trees and looked on at the scene in surprise. It didn't last long. After a nod from Cian, he took his place beside them as if this had been a long-standing plan.

"Where? Back to your boyfriend's?" Cian asked, spitting by A.J.'s feet.

The ringing was an alarm bell now. He needed to get out of here.

"I-I don't have a boyfriend . . ."

Tadhg and the other one laughed at this but Cian looked more serious than ever.

"You know, I've known Bren since I was eight. First communion and everything."

"I actually didn't know that. But what's Bren got to—"

"I don't know what the fuck made him even talk to you. But he shoulda dropped you the second he found out what you were."

He needed to run. But Tadhg and the other one had inched their way between him and the path back to town, and Cian was blocking the way to Bren's.

"Look, Cian, just—" A.J. was disgusted by the note of pleading in his voice, but he had to at least try to reason his way out of this. "I'm not doing anything to you, or to Bren, so can I—"

"Ah, but you are, and you know it," he said, taking a step forward. "Every time I think about the two of you by that fucking piano, I wanna puke."

A.J.'s terrified brain struggled to make sense of what Cian had said. By the piano? What was he—

"You shoulda never come to Glenbridge, Arlo."

And then Arlo broke.

36

Bren chucked the last potato into the pot where it landed with a splash. They were finally done. Nothing more to do for the effing things than to bung them on the back steps.

The VCR read three-twenty as he fell onto the couch, feet propped up on the coffee table. Arlo would be back any second now. Maybe they'd get a minute to do something that didn't involve veg.

"Hey, Mam, need anythin' else?"

"Bathroom floor needs moppin'," she replied, distracted by whatever recipe she was looking at now.

"Did it this mornin'. So can I pop in a movie or somethin'?"

"What? Yeah, just, don't make a mess."

Bren thought about asking her how he'd make a mess watching a movie, but stopped himself—she might decide the roof needed new shingles or something. He rolled off the couch and crawled to the cabinet under the TV. It didn't feel like Christmas until they'd watched Home Alone. He wondered if Arlo felt that way, too.

***

Bren's foot twitched as he flipped his phone open again.

You get lost or something?

His text hung there, unanswered. It had been twenty minutes since he'd sent it—forty since Arlo had gone to the shops. He'd thought about texting Rory or maybe Orlaith, but what would he say? He was getting antsy because his boyfriend was taking his time at the shops?

"Hurry up, lad . . ."

***

"I'm sure he's fine, Bren."

Mam was using the same voice she used whenever he was sick, but her expression told him she thought this was worse than a cold.

"It's been an hour and he isn't textin' back. A.J. always texts back."

He pulled a woolly hat over his ears and made for the door. Mam flipped on the kettle and pulled a trio of mugs from the cupboards.

"I'll call you when he comes back."

When he comes back.

God, he hoped she was right.

***

The sun was threatening to dip past the horizon by the time Bren recruited the others. He'd checked the shops, Niamh's, both chippers, and the schoolyard—nothing. He'd hesitated at the point of texting Mickie, but swallowed his pride in the end. Who knew if the bastard would actually help? At least Bren could say he tried.

***

"A.J.!"

Bren's voice rang out through the dark as he swept his torch along the path. His fingers had been numb since the sun went down two hours ago, but that only made him clench the plastic cylinder tighter. He had to keep looking, keep calling his name. If he stopped for even a second, the black hole in his chest was bound to swallow him up.

Where the fuck are you, Arlo?

Bren pushed through the thicket that bordered the hidden path, taking a shower of icy droplets to his face in his hurry—of all the nights for it to rain.

He couldn't believe it had taken him so long to think of the place. A.J. had mentioned once that it reminded him of a creek near his house back in Canada. Bren was sure he'd find him sitting in the clearing, distracted by memories, or maybe inspired to write a new piece. That had to be it.

"A.J.!"

Flickering light roved across the battered picnic table, the pile of wet ash surrounded by fist-sized rocks. It didn't look like anyone had been here . . . but that didn't mean anything. Maybe he'd just missed the lad.

Bren hopped the fire pit and jogged to the other side of the clearing. He turned sideways to slip into the tangle that bordered the narrow path, careful not to snag his jumper on the brambles.

His heart plummeted.

The path was a mess. Missing leaves and snapped branches pointing every which way. Like someone—or a whole group of some-ones—had barreled through here.

Bren's feet carried him forwards, breath tearing fissures in his throat. He swept the torchlight in wide arcs as he barreled on, sure that Arlo had to have come through here. He was barely three steps in when his foot kicked something soft. Hand trembling, he shone the light down to find red and yellow—a crushed loaf of Pat's.

He tried to call his name again, but no sound made its way out. A branch swiped his cheek as he followed the trail of spilled shopping. A stray onion, a packet of crisps, more snapped branches.

The trail veered to the left, and so did Bren, torchlight scrambling. It found a lid gleaming next to a pile of soggy biscuits and—

"Arlo!"

He moved the beam up from the trainer to find the rest of him. He was lying face down, cheek swollen and caked with mud. Bren lunged forward, foot catching on the underbrush. His knees slammed into the wet earth. He tried to get to his feet and stumbled, hands breaking his fall with a jolt of pain next to Arlo. His arm was outstretched, like he was trying to reach out for something after he'd fallen.

Bren heaved Arlo onto his lap. His head lolled like a ragdoll's. His hand flinched as it brushed Arlo's cheeks. Then Bren pulled him closer, willing some of his heat into the skin that felt like ice as he rocked.

"I got you. I got you. I got you."

"—got you. I got you."

Bren's useless puppet fingers fumbled with the seam of his phone three times before he could pry it open. He dialed home without conscious thought.

"Hello?"

"Mam! I found him! He isn't movin'!"

His voice caught despite his best efforts. He squinted down at A.J.'s too-pale face and leaned forward to try to keep the worst of the rain off it.

There was a single, agonizing second where Bren thought Mam might not know what to do. But when she spoke next, her voice had taken on the tone he'd heard her use with some of her more stubborn patients.

"Bren, listen to me. I'm ringing an ambulance right now. Where are you?"

He heard his voice trying to describe the path off the clearing as he stared down at the limp figure in his arms. If Mam found his words confusing, she didn't show it. There was rustling in his ear and the muffled sound of her parroting his words to the 999 operator.

"Mam! He's not movin'!"

Didn't she understand? There wasn't time for an ambulance to get here.

"Mo chroí, I need you to listen to me right now. Where are you? And does he have a pulse? What about breathing?"

"Mam! I don't know, I don't think—"

"Brendan!" The snap in her voice cut through his words like a scalpel. "I need you to put two fingers under his jaw on the left side. Then lean down and watch his chest. Try and feel if there's breath on your ear."

Bren flinched again as he pressed his fingers against Arlo's icy neck. He leaned down as far as he could with him in his lap and waited.

Please. Fucking PLEASE.

There! A pulse, and, it was hard to tell if he was imagining it or not, but he thought he felt a puff of air on his cheek.

"H-he's got a pulse and I think he's breathin'. But Mam, he's so cold. Should I try and make him warm?"

"Bren, just stay where you are, and try not to move him too much." There was more rustling on her end now and the jingle of what might have been keys. "I have to hang up now."

"Mam, no!"

"Bren! I have to stay on my mobile with the operator. I'll be there right away. I know exactly where you are. You're doing great. Keep talking but don't go moving him."

"Mam, I alread—"

The line cut out before he could finish. He let his phone fall from his hand, his fingers moving to stroke the rain-slicked hair from Arlo's forehead. It was just hair. This couldn't count as moving.

"Ok, Mam said keep talkin' so I'm gonna keep talkin'." His legs were starting to cramp, but there was no amount of discomfort that would make him shift. "Fuck, Arlo, you're all banged up, I mean . . . you're gonna be ok. Just stay with me, yeah?"

He couldn't keep himself from staring down at the shallow rise and fall of Arlo's chest. His right eye was swollen shut, and there was a vertical slash cutting through his eyebrow.

Bren's heart lurched as a low moan left Arlo. His arm twitched, then rose off the ground by an inch, like he was trying to reach for something.

"Arlo? Can you hear me? It's me, Bren. Mam's on the way, just hold—"

Something new erupted in Bren as Arlo's arm fell back to the ground with a muffled splat. His left hand was a mess, swollen and stiff, the fingers curled and splayed at unnatural angles. That was bad enough, but it wasn't the detail that made Bren's blood ignite. Across the back of his hand was the unmistakable shadow of a shoe print.

Bren was saved from having to sit with what that implied when Mam called his name from somewhere in the brush. She materialized out of the foliage, wrapped in a raincoat with a beanie pulled down past her eyebrows. She was holding an umbrella in one hand and her mobile in the other.

"Mam! He tried to say something! Moved a bit!"

"Good, Bren, that's good." She brought her phone to her ear. "Yes, I just got here. My son said he's semiconscious. He's got bruising and lacerations to his face. It . . ." Her eyes flitted towards Bren before continuing. "It looks like it might have been an assault."

Fury stirred in Bren again. "It was, there's a—"

"Here, take this and hold it over him."

Mam shoved her umbrella into Bren's free hand, and she dropped to her knees, mirroring the instructions she'd given him over the phone.

"He's got a pulse, it's slow but steady. Breathing, but it's shallow. He's cold. Hypothermia, for sure."

Arlo groaned again. It looked like he was trying to open his eyes but couldn't manage it.

"He's responding to sound. A.J., can you hear me? Try and stay still. It's Maura O'Shea. Bren's got you. Everything's going to be fine, love. Help's on the way."

Bren could hear sirens growing louder in the distance now. For the first time in his life, he was glad Glenbridge was small.

Light blinded Bren as a pair of voices emerged from the darkness.

"Yeah, we're on scene. Unconscious adolescent male, fifteen—"

"He's sixteen!" Bren's voice cut across them.

They ignored him.

"Maybe sixteen. Yeah, it looks like it could be an assault. Right. Ok. Garda will meet the caller and her son at A&E. Right."

The paramedic said all this between crackles from their radio that Bren couldn't make sense of. His partner set down a stretcher next to them, her reflective vest gleaming in the torchlight.

She tried to ease Arlo off his lap, but Bren's hands dug into his sodden hoodie and he shook his head.

"Son, we need to get him into the van so we can help him."

Bren started to shake his head again, but forced himself to look at Mam.

"You've done great, mo chroí, but you need to let them do their jobs. They'll take care of him."

Mam's words reached Bren in a way the paramedic's hadn't, and he felt his fingers loosen their grip.

"Was he like this when you found him?" asked the man with the radio.

"What?!"

Bren's pulse hammered in his ears. He could feel the fury pushing its way past his lips when Mam cut in.

"They mean, was he on his back?"

Bren's chest relaxed.

"Oh," now that she'd said it, it was obvious that's what he'd meant. He wiped his eyes with the back of his mud-slicked hand. "N-no. He was lying f-face down. I-In the mud."

"Might have aspirated some," said the woman as she and her partner lifted Arlo off Bren's lap and onto the stretcher. Arlo groaned again, low and slurred.

"Right, you'll follow in the car, Maura?"

"Yeah, I'm parked on Willow."

They'd maneuvered the stretcher through the overgrowth, back towards the place they'd materialized from.

"Wait!"

Bren tried to jump to his feet, but his legs had gone numb, and he had to grab onto a branch to keep from faceplanting back into the mud. "I'm comin'!"

The duo slowed their pace but didn't stop.

"Bren, we can meet them there. They know what they're doing."

"No!" Bren shoved her hand away and took a step towards Arlo. "He was alone in the rain all fuckin' night! I amn't leavin' him again."

The paramedics shared a look.

"Alright. Come with us then."

238

38

The tang of antiseptic filled Bren's lungs as his legs carried him across the room for the dozenth time that minute. His hand clenched into a fist without meaning to as he stared at the clock again. He would have thought it was broken if he couldn't see the second hand ticking along like everything was fine. Had it really only been twenty minutes since they'd chucked him out of the A&E?

He tugged down his sleeve, wishing that he could have kept his own clothes, soaked as they were. The whim vanished as he remembered his shirt being stuffed into a plastic bag—caked with mud and tinted red from where he'd wiped blood off of Arlo's—

"The fuck is taking so long?!" Bren barked, not caring that he'd made Mr. and Mrs. Sprained Wrist jump on the other side of the room.

"Bren, you need to calm down."

Mam rose from her chair, but he shrugged her off and kept pacing.

"Why can't they at least tell us somethin'? What if he's—"

Mam's hand twitched like she was going to reach out again.

"If . . . that happened, they'd have told us. The fact that they haven't been out yet is a good thing."

Bren stopped his pacing to look Mam in the eyes. Every part of him wanted to believe her, but the writhing ball of fire in his stomach wasn't having it.

He'd made his way across the room another seven times when he became aware of the sound of shuffling feet.

He'd just finished his about-face when Brick, Rory, and Orlaith shuffled their way into the waiting room. The shadows under Rory's eyes were deeper than ever, and it looked like Brick was working hard to keep his jaw set. The shoulders of Orlaith's jacket were soaked through, and a stray droplet of water clung to her cheek.

Bren didn't know how to say what their showing up meant to him, but a strange part of him wished they had gone home.

"Hey, thanks fo—"

Bren didn't have time to finish before Orlaith's arms were around him. She hugged him so hard that he felt something crack. When she pulled away, her eyes were more dangerous than he'd ever seen them.

"It was fucking Cian, wasn't it? I swear to God if you tell me it was, I'll—"

Bren grunted. On the list of things he wouldn't let himself think about right now, that was right at the top. Orlaith seemed to understand and took a step back, though she still looked like she was ready to tear someone's throat out.

Bren wiped his eyes with the sleeve of his borrowed scrubs and scanned the group.

"Mickie not come with you lot?"

He'd tried to sound like he didn't really care, but wasn't sure he managed it.

Orlaith's head whipped around and she let out a loud tut.

Without another word, she marched back the way she'd come, leaving Bren to look to Rory for an explanation.

"He was right behind us."

Brick looked uncomfortable, but nodded along. Bren couldn't be sure, but from the way Brick was avoiding his eyes, he guessed the big guy had figured it all out.

A new terror bubbled in Bren's chest. He'd known Brick almost as long as Mickie, and look how that had gone. There was no avoiding it now, though.

"Thanks for comin'," Bren said, trying but failing to look Brick in the eyes. "And for lookin' for h-him."

Bren didn't have time to cringe at the catch in his voice before Brick laid a meaty paw on his shoulder. They locked eyes long enough for Brick to nod. It was all they needed, which was good because Orlaith walked back into the room, followed by a sheepish-looking Mickie. Like Orlaith, his hair was still damp from being out in the rain. Mickie's jaw was set in a way that made Bren sure he was trying not to say something awful, so it was surprising when he opened it and instead asked.

"He's ok, right?"

Bren's lip trembled. He tried to say that he didn't know, but didn't trust himself to get through it. Instead, he shrugged, which pushed him a step towards sobbing, anyway.

Brick and Rory were both looking everywhere that wasn't the two of them, while Orlaith stood with her arms crossed. She made an angry clucking sound, and Mickie jerked forward.

"Look, I was a shitehead, yeah?" He let out a sigh that traveled all the way through his body. "I just, didn't—I mean, I'm sorry, ok?"

Something inside Bren threatened to crack a smile. He'd known Mickie since he was five and couldn't ever remember him sounding this sincere, even once.

"Fuckin' right you are," Bren said, something close to a laugh forcing its way out as he ran his sleeve along his nose.

Orlaith rolled her eyes but uncrossed her arms as Mickie flipped Bren off.

"Maura?"

Bren whipped around so fast he almost toppled over. A woman with a blonde bun and a stern expression stood between the now open doors that led to Resus. Mam stood up without a word and made to follow the doctor past the doors.

"Wait! What is it? Is he ok?!"

Mam looked for a second like she'd forgotten he was there.

"Is it ok if Bren comes, too? A.J. is—" She looked at the group assembled around him, "very important to him."

The doctor looked at Bren like she wasn't sure it was a good idea. He tried to relax his expression as much as possible, which seemed to work.

"Hi, Bren, I'm Dr. Williams. I'm Arlo's doctor—"

"A.J."

"Excuse me?"

"His name's A.J. He doesn't like bein' called A-arlo."

Dr. Williams shared a look with Mam before she went on.

"Right, I'm A.J.'s doctor. If the two of you will just follow me, I can give you an update."

Bren was already through the doors before he realized he didn't know where he was going. Dr. Williams followed after him and waited for Mam to cross the threshold before waving them to an alcove off the main hallway. Dr. Williams couldn't have paused for more than a second after they'd gathered, but that was still too long for Bren.

"Is he ok?"

The question came with more bite than he'd meant, but after frowning, Dr. Williams' expression shifted back to its professional mask.

"He's stable enough that we've moved him from Resus to the high dependency unit. We—"

"High dependency? Is tha—?"

"Bren," Mam said, her tone firm, "you need to let her finish."

Bren swallowed a huff, but shut his mouth.

"High dependency means we still need to keep a close eye on him, but not so much that he needs to be in intensive care." She turned her attention to Mam for the next part. "He's got a grade two concussion, but he's showing signs of increased awareness. We've got him under a Bair Hugger for moderate hypothermia and started a drip for pain. His ribs are bruised pretty badly—no breaks, though."

Bren opened his mouth to ask another question, but caught himself in time.

"He has multiple metacarpal fractures on his left hand. We've put him in a splint for now. But we should be able to get a cast on him in a day or so, as long as the swelling goes down."

Bren waited to make sure she was done before asking the question that had been screaming in his chest since the Resus team took him away.

"So, is he going to be ok?"

Dr. Williams gave half a nod, looking like she wasn't sure if she should commit to smiling or not.

"He's responding well to treatment. We'll have to watch for afterdrop." She'd started talking to Mam again but caught herself. "Afterdrop can sometimes happen when someone with hypothermia is warmed back up. It's rare, and we can treat it, but we need to be watchful for the next few hours."

Bren thought he'd feel more relieved after they'd told him Arlo was alive, but the dread in his stomach didn't let up. It sounded to Bren like Arlo might go at any minute if fate was anything less than kind about it. Some of his fear must have shown on his face because Mam put a hand on his arm. Bren didn't pull away this time.

"He's alright, mo chroi." She kept her hand on him as she addressed Dr. Williams. "Thank you, Caroline."

"Of course," Dr. Williams said, smiling properly for the first time.

Bren shifted under Mam's hand in the silence that followed. The screaming in his chest was quieter now that he knew Arlo was alive, but there was only one thing that would make it shut up all the way. But Bren wasn't sure if he was allowed to ask. As always, Mam came to the rescue.

"Is it ok if Bren sees him now?"

"As long as he stays calm and lets A.J.'s nurses do their job," Dr. Williams said, looking sternly at Bren.

Bren clenched his fists to stop his hands from shaking and met her eyes.

"Good. He's right over here."

39

Bren stared at the sleek double doors like they might reach out and bite him. Dr. Williams had told them Arlo was on the other side, second bed in, before hurrying back to Resus. This is what he'd wanted from the second they'd taken Arlo out of the ambulance, so why were his feet welded to the floor? And where the fuck did all his spit go?

He swallowed hard and took a step forward, but Mam put her hand on his arm again. "Bren, I know I can't stop you—"

Bren's throat hitched as he met her eyes. He must have looked as hurt as he felt, because Mam rushed on.

"I don't want to stop you. I'm proud of you, but after tonight—Bren, people are going to talk. You're not going to be able to keep how the two of you feel quiet anymore."

Bren squared his shoulders as a flame flickered to life in his chest. "I don't fuckin' care."

A grin flashed across Mam's face as she pulled him in for a hug. Bren let himself, for the first time that night, relax, his body returning the pressure with interest.

"It's gonna fuckin' suck."

It wasn't a question; he knew what he was in for.

Mam held him tighter, and when she spoke next, her voice sounded rocky.

"It is. But I'm not going anywhere, you hear me?"

Bren sniffed and nodded as Mam hugged him tighter.

Her eyes were watering when she broke away.

"I'll be right outside if you need me."

She pressed her palm against his cheek, then left him in front of the door.

With the flame still burning, Bren took a shaky breath and stepped forward.

Bren squinted as he walked into the gloom on the other side of the door. The overhead lights were emitting a dim orange-ish glow, so it felt like walking into dusk and dawn at the same time. The room was smaller than he had expected. A narrow aisle ran between a set of four beds, two on each side, with curtains serving as the walls that divided them.

A middle-aged man with circles under his eyes that would have put Rory's to shame was sitting at the nearest workstation, scribbling away.

"You're here for A.J. Walker?"

Bren tried to speak, but a shaky cough was all he could manage.

"He's in the second bed on the left. Pari just stepped in there. She can get you sorted."

The lump in the back of Bren's throat bobbed as he made his way across the room. It was quieter here than the rest of the hospital, so Bren could hear each whir and beep of the machines that were holding the patients together.

He froze outside the curtain that marked Arlo's room with his hand clenching the stiff fabric. What the fuck was wrong with him?

He let his eyes close as he forced himself past the curtain. In that brief window, he'd told himself he was prepared for what was on the other side—he'd been wrong.

A horrible, choked sound left him despite his best efforts. Arlo was lying on his back, sterile hospital blanket pulled up so high that it didn't look like he had a neck. A clear piece of tubing was strung around his ears and came to rest under his nose, hissing faintly among the whirs and beeps of the room.

His dark hair had been brushed out of his eyes, so there was no hiding the angry purple bruise that dominated the right side of his face. Bren swallowed in an attempt to get the tightness out of his throat. It didn't help, but did make the nurse who was scribbling on a clipboard turn around.

She had long, black hair braided down the center of her back and eyes just as tired as her coworkers'. A smile spread across her face as her gaze landed on Bren. Strange as it was, it made him feel better.

"Hi, Bren, right? Dr. Williams said you'd be coming by."

Her voice had the familiar lilt of Glenbridge to it, but there was something else there. The way she formed her vowels, the rhythm of her words. He didn't know what it was, but it was strangely soothing.

"Y-yeah, I'm me. I mean, that's me. Bren."

The knife in his heart twisted. He was reminding himself of Arlo back on that first day.

"I'm Pari. I'll be looking after A.J. for the rest of the night."

She kept an eye on Bren, but leaned towards the monitor to finish whatever it was she'd been doing before he'd interrupted her.

"Is he . . ." Bren hesitated as his eyes ran over the room. Wires, tubes, a heart monitor, an IV drip with a clear vial of something attached to it, they were all running into Arlo. He couldn't imagine how anyone could be okay with all that, but finished the question anyway. "Ok?"

Pari looked down at the clipboard, and her smile faded into something less reassuring.

"He's stable and showing increased signs of consciousness. Those are both really good things." She made her way around Bren to reveal a chair to the left of Arlo's bed. "We're still warming him up, so he's going to be shaking for a while. It might look scary, but I promise, it's perfectly normal."

Bren swallowed again, the tightness in his throat spreading to his eyes.

"I've got to go check on my other patient," Pari said, parting the curtain. "You can sit in the chair over there, but be sure not to touch anything, ok?"

"Is it ok if I . . ." Bren found he couldn't hold Pari's gaze anymore and instead looked at the foot of Arlo's bed. "Hold his hand?"

"That's just fine," Pari said after a short pause.

Bren watched her feet walk past the curtain line, leaving him alone with Arlo. His legs turned him to face the bed, and his breath hitched again.

"H-hey th-there, A-a-arlo."

He sat down just as his legs felt like they'd turned to Jell-O, and he found himself at eye level with Arlo's pillow-raised head. Whatever force he'd tapped into since he found him in the clearing evaporated.

With nothing to hold them back anymore, the tears fell hot and fast. His sobs came in shuddering gasps as his eyes roved over the swollen mess of Arlo's face.

He was ghost-white, lips tinted blue among the sea of bruises. A row of four stitches smeared with something brownish held a swollen gash together above his right eyebrow.

Heat streamed down Bren's cheeks as he worked his hand beneath the blankets, searching for the one part of Arlo he was allowed to hold.

He'd been expecting skin and was confused when his fingers found plastic instead. His heart turned to ice when he pulled back the blanket. Arlo's hand was an angry purple to match the bruises on his face. Two of his fingers were twice their normal size and bundled together with gauze. Something worse than rage threatened to erupt in Bren's chest, but it had too much grief to compete with and fizzled out before it got the chance.

Bren slid the covers back over Arlo's hand and peered around the room. He was sure Pari wouldn't care which side of the room the chair was on. If he got yelled at, he could deal. At least he'd be able to hold on to Arlo until then.

Taking enormous care not to bump into any of the machines, Bren carried the chair to the other side of the bed. He locked his fingers around Arlo's good hand, refusing to pull away despite the chill it sent up his spine.

He'd expected to feel better once he was able to touch some part of Arlo, but all it did was make the hollow sensation in his chest worse. It was like trying to be close to someone on the moon.

"A-arlo, can you hear me?" he managed after a solid minute of trying to steady himself. "It's B-bren."

Arlo's chin twitched a millimeter in his direction, and relief flooded through him.

"H-hey, lad. Fuck, you're all—"

The joy curdled in Bren's chest as Arlo's swollen face contorted into a look of anguish.

His lips parted a fraction of an inch and formed a word Bren couldn't make out.

"W-what was that? Arlo?"

Bren leaned in as close as he could. A.J. made the sound again, and this time Bren could make it out over the sounds of the room.

"Cold."

He hadn't had enough time to absorb the meaning before Arlo started shaking. It built in a crest until the entire bed was vibrating from the force of his shivers, his teeth chattering so loud Bren's mouth throbbed in sympathy.

His eyes searched for the call button—it was on the other side of the bed, right where his chair had been. He leapt up before he remembered where he was.

"H-help." The word came out hoarse and way too quiet to do any good. "H-hey! Someone, help! H-he needs help!"

Bren watched, helpless, as Arlo, brow knitted in what could only be pain, shivered still harder before going still. Fury erupted in Bren and after a series of soft footsteps, Pari appeared through the gap in the curtain, looking annoyed instead of concerned. She strode over to Arlo and frowned at one of his monitors.

"We can't have you yelling like that. Everything's fine."

Bren wiped the tears from his eyes.

"He was shakin'! Like, the whole bed was movin' he was shiverin' so hard!"

Pari looked like she was going to snap back, but her expression softened again.

"I know it must look scary, but that's perfectly normal." She peeled back Arlo's blankets, revealing something that looked like a form-fitted air mattress. "This is called a Bair Hugger. His core temperature was very low when he was brought in. So low that his body wasn't able to react normally to the cold."

She tucked the blanket back around Arlo's neck, smoothing it out before she went on. "The hugger is helping to warm him up bit by bit. As it does, his body starts to wake up to the cold and do what it can to warm itself up. He'll shake a lot, but his colour will improve and so will his awareness."

She waited like she was expecting Bren to say something, but when all he did was blink back, she added, "It means he's waking up for us."

Pari hovered at the edge of the room like she was still waiting for Bren to say something. He was grateful for her explanation, but he didn't want to risk talking. He didn't need more people seeing him bawl today.

Bren waited until he heard her back at her workstation before he took his seat. The bed had stopped shaking, but Arlo's chin was trembling. Bren fussed with the blankets around Arlo's neck, even though they were pulled as high as they could go.

Arlo's teeth chattered as the shaking started again. This time, Bren took his hand and held tight. If he was cold, he could have some of his warmth.

"I amn't goin' anywhere, lad, just . . . hurry back, yeah?"

40

In the waiting room. I think I got everything.

Bren gave Arlo's hand a squeeze. The clock on his phone told him it had been about ninety minutes since he'd entered the HDU, even if it felt like he'd been there for years. Arlo was still shivering on and off, but the time between bouts had been getting longer, and the bed had stopped shaking about four rounds ago.

"I'll be right back, yeah? Right outside the room."

He couldn't help but feel kind of stupid talking to Arlo like that. All he'd done since Bren sat down was shiver and occasionally half-form disconnected words Bren couldn't make out. But, if there was even a chance some of what he was saying was able to reach Arlo, Bren would make a fool of himself until he woke up.

Pari was busy scribbling something down on a sheet of paper as he made his way to her station. She tilted her head in his direction as he approached, but didn't stop working.

"My mate brought me some stuff from home. Is it ok if I go change? I'll be right back. Five minutes, like."

Pari pushed away from the desk and got to her feet.

"I was just about to check on him anyway." She grabbed a clipboard from her station and brought it to hang by her hip. "It'll take me about fifteen minutes to finish documenting everything, so don't rush. Maybe grab a tea from the waiting room. You're looking pretty pale yourself."

"Yeah, cuppa sounds good," he said as Pari rubbed her thumb and index finger across her half-closed eyes. "Want me to grab you one, too?"

"That's sweet, but I've still got half a thermos to work through."

Bren made a sound that was as close to a laugh as he could manage and watched as she walked into Arlo's room. He made note of the time as he stepped through the double doors at the end of the hall. Fifteen minutes to get back. He wouldn't be using more than ten.

"Hey, how's he doing?"

Bren breathed a sigh of relief at the sight of Brick in the otherwise empty waiting room. Mam had said she'd convinced the others to head home for the night, but part of him had expected to find Orlaith still smoldering in her chair when he came out.

"He's not shakin' as much. Lookin' a little less pale I think."

"That's great! I mean, that means he's warming up, right?"

"Yeah. His nurse says he's doin' grand. Just . . ." Bren felt a lump rise in his throat and became intensely interested in the space to the right of Brick's ear. "Wish he would wake up."

"Still gotta get him to national match," Brick said, a familiar hint of fervor in his words. "He's not gonna sleep through that."

Bren half-managed a laugh and nodded at the bag slung over Brick's shoulder.

"Oh yeah, here!"

Bren accepted the bag and pulled the zipper open. A change of clothes, a container of mince pies, and Bren let out a sigh, Arlo's Discman and binder.

"Thanks, big guy," Bren said, cramming a pie into his mouth and almost moaning from how good it tasted.

"Need me to stay?"

"Nah, go home and get some sleep. I can call Mam if I need anything else."

Brick looked around the empty room and frowned. "She still trying to get a hold of his folks?"

"Yeah," Bren said, now pulling off his scrubs. He probably should have waited until he found the jacks, but he wanted the fucking things off him. "Took the McCarthys a while to answer, but she let them know what happened, then started phonin' Canada."

"Fuck. Whatddya think's gonna happen?" Brick asked, not paying Bren's half-nakedness the least bit of attention.

Bren shrugged, then pulled the hoodie Arlo had been stealing all week over his head. He'd been working hard not to think about what Arlo's parents might do once they found out what happened.

Silence stretched between them as he slipped into his trousers, finally free of the paper-thin scrubs. He balled them up and chucked them into the bin with great satisfaction, then looked over his shoulder at the HDU. To Brick's everlasting credit, he didn't need more than that.

"Tell him I say hi when he wakes up."

"I'll save a pie for him. Tell him it comes with all your love."

Brick snorted and, after making a motion that made Bren think he was going to go for a hug, headed for the door.

"Right, tea then back to Arlo."

He plunked the paper cup into the machine and held down the button for tea. What poured out looked more like dodgy hot chocolate, but it was at least hot.

He pulled Arlo's binder from the bag and flipped through as he took tiny scalding sips. He couldn't help but smile when he found what he was looking for, "A.J.'s BIG ASS EXCHANGE MIX" written in what he now knew was Nat's handwriting. He found an empty spot next to where someone had written, "Bring me back a pot of gold," trying hard not to roll his eyes. It had taken him at least twenty minutes of hard thinking back in the HDU to decide what he was going to write.

In the end, there was only one thing he wanted to say.

"Hey, is it ok if I eat in here?"

Pari, who was setting down the chart at the foot of Arlo's bed when he walked back in, nodded.

"Just don't spill anything."

"Thanks. Hey, want a mince pie?"

Pari looked thrown by the offer. "If there's any left when I come by again, sure."

"Sound."

He waited until Pari disappeared on the other side of the curtain and took his seat.

"Hey, Arlo. I got you somethin'. We gotta keep it low, but I figure you'll like it better than listenin' to all this fuckin' beepin'."

Bren started the Discman up and skipped straight to track three, remembering that tracks one and two got scratched back on their first walk to school. He pushed an earphone in as "Lady Marmalade" started up.

"Christ, lad, you gotta wake up soon so I can slag you for this shite."

His thumb brushed against Arlo's ear as he nestled the other earphone in place.

"Now, that's a wire I like seein' on you," Bren said, struggling against the reappearance of the lump in his throat.

Arlo didn't say anything back, but Bren was sure, impossible as it might be, that the lad's hand felt warmer as his fingers closed around it again.

41

"Bren . . . ?"

Bren jerked awake from his stupor with a slurring grunt. He'd only meant to close his eyes for a couple seconds, but the crick in his neck told him it had been a lot longer. He looked over his shoulder, expecting to see Pari behind him but found only air.

"B-bren?"

It was louder this time, he hadn't imagined it. Hoarse and whisper-quiet, but definitely—

All stiffness in his neck forgotten, Bren whipped his head around and almost fell out of his chair. Arlo was staring at him through half-open eyes, lips parted like he was having trouble forming his next words.

A sound Bren had never made in his life left him. It was some strange combination of sobbing, laughing, and cheering all at once, and he had no power to stop it. His hand scrambled under the blanket until it found Arlo's and held tight. A second choked sound forced its way out as, for the first time since yesterday morning, Arlo's hand squeezed back.

"A-arlo! Y-y-your're awake! Fuck." An insane laugh followed his words before he could cut it off. "Gotta get Pari."

He knew he wasn't supposed to yell, but the call button was still on the other side of the bed, and there was no way he was going to let go of Arlo ever again. Arlo let out a low groan as he shifted. It was hard to see through his tears, but Bren thought he might have been squinting out of confusion instead of exhaustion now.

"You . . . found me?"

Bren wiped the tears away with his free hand and tried to look as happy as he felt.

"Of course I found you. Always gonna find you, yeah?"

Every cell in his body was screaming for him to crawl into bed and kiss each unbruised inch of Arlo's face, but he settled on squeezing his hand again.

"How do you feel? Are you—fuck it! Pari! He's awake!"

There was just enough time for Arlo to throw a confused look Bren's way before Pari appeared from the other side of the curtain. She looked as tired as ever, but there was a glow about her that Bren hadn't seen before.

"Arlo? Can you hear me? My name's Pari. Do you know where you are?"

She said all this as she bustled over to his bed, pushing buttons here and there before putting her hand on his shoulder and squeezing.

Arlo's head tilted in Pari's direction but stayed focused on Bren.

"I-I tried to get up—in the woods. But I couldn't . . ."

A crease appeared between his eyes as he frowned in concentration.

"Arlo, can you hear me? Do you know where you are?" Pari repeated.

He looked confused again as he turned his head towards her voice.

"The hospitugh—"

A cough forced its way out of him and his face went crimson. His eyes squeezed shut as tears streamed down his cheeks. He tugged his hand away from Bren's and brought it to his chest, which only made him wince harder.

"Arlo, can you rank your pain on a scale of one to ten for me? One being fine, and ten being the worst pain you've ever felt in your life?"

Bren watched as Arlo shook his head, the tears sliding down his jaw now.

"I'm ok. Just hurt when I coughed."

"Arlo, you look fuckin'—" Bren caught himself as Arlo's eyes widened. The fuck was he scaring him for? "You're allowed to be in pain, yeah?"

He considered Bren, then closed his eyes in a wince.

"Like, a five?"

Bren started to protest, but a look from Pari told him she didn't buy it.

"Do you want something for pain? Dr. Williams has you on paracetamol, but has also approved a low dose of morphine."

He looked at Bren like he needed to ask for permission.

"Take the meds, lad, I'll still be here."

"Ok," Arlo began, his voice soft despite the rasp. "But can I talk to Bren first?"

"Of course. I have to go tell Dr. Williams you're awake anyway. How does ten minutes sound?"

Arlo looked like he tried to smile, but it came out closer to a grimace. Pari moved the call button over to his right hand.

"Hit the call button if you need it sooner."

She was barely out the door before Arlo gave Bren's hand a squeeze. Bren returned the pressure, still fighting to keep the occasional joy-sob from bubbling out.

"Hey, Bren?" Arlo asked, sounding much younger than he was.

"Yeah? You need somethin'?"

Arlo grimaced as he took a shuddering breath.

"Can I have a kiss?"

Bren was on his feet the second his brain had processed the words. He was doing his best to keep the pressure light, but wasn't sure he was managing it. His hand drifted towards Arlo's cheek but came to rest on the pillow beside him instead.

"Fuck. I'm so glad you're ok," he whispered, still close enough he could feel the heat from Arlo's lips. "I thought you wer—"

Bren's chest clenched as, without warning, Arlo began to shake. His thumb was already halfway to the call button when he realized these weren't the same shakes from before. Tears were streaming down Arlo's face as he trembled with suppressed sobs.

"Shit, does it hurt? Do you want me to get Pari?"

Arlo shook his head and tears spilled over his cheeks as he continued to shake, now looking like he was fighting with pain.

"What's wrong, then?"

Arlo sniffed and slowed his breathing enough to talk.

"I'm really sorry."

The words hit Bren like a punch to the gut.

"What the feck for?"

Arlo shuddered again, but sounded stronger when he spoke next.

"I should have just ran." He leaned his head back, face twisting in anguish again. "I ruined everyone's Christmas."

The fury that rose in Bren was so visceral that he wouldn't have been surprised if it tore a hole in his ribcage. In the relief of having Arlo out of his horrible twilight state, Bren had all but forgotten who had put him there.

Cian.

260

That bastard wasn't fit to lick mud off Arlo's shoes, but there he was, rooted in his head like a tumor.

He grabbed Arlo's hand as hard as he dared and looked him dead in the eyes.

"You didn't ruin anything. That was all that fucker Cian."

Arlo winced at the mention of Cian, which only fed the demon raging in Bren's chest.

"But, your mom's patient. And all that food . . ."

Bren let out something between a laugh and a scoff.

"Mrs. Farrelly'll get by just fine."

"But—"

"She'll be just fine. And if you think Mam isn't gonna cook all that food and fix you a plate anyway." His voice was sounding unreliable as the corners of his vision blurred, but he didn't care. "Then we need to get you back in that MRI yoke."

Arlo looked about five years old as he stared back with watery eyes. Bren leaned in and pressed his lips on the top of Arlo's head.

"You done apologizin'? Gonna take it easy with the fun drugs now?"

"Ok, but—"

Bren sighed. He really was in love with the world's most stubborn person when it came to being polite.

"I'll drug you meself if I have to, lad."

Arlo stared at Bren like he was trying to check if he was secretly pissed at him. Bren stared right back with the softest look he could manage. Arlo looked confused, then teary again. He closed his eyes and, through a wince of pain, pulled Bren in for another kiss.

Bren had done his fair share of kissing in his life, and a lot of it had been with Arlo. He'd thought he had the act pretty close to figured out. Lips, tongue, a bit of teeth if he was feeling frisky. It came as a surprise then when this kiss didn't say "I want you" or "this feels nice." Bren leaned in and sighed, as, for the first time in his life, a kiss said "thank you."

***

"Yeah, alright. Thanks, Mam. Yeah, love you, too."

Bren couldn't help but grin as he slid his phone back into his pocket. He was having trouble processing how different the world felt compared to an hour ago. It was like someone had thrown open a window and let all the doom out of the world. He knew there was plenty of shite on the horizon, but as long as Arlo was ok, who cared?

Mam had gotten ahold of Arlo's folks sometime last night and was probably on the horn with them to pass along the good news. Better still, Pari had said they planned to move Arlo out of high dependency as early as tonight, as long as he kept improving. He stuffed the rest of his muffin into his mouth as he reached the sliding doors, its twin cradled in his other hand.

"Excuse me, lad, are you Brendan O'Shea?"

Bren turned to find a pair of Guards behind him. Their highlighter-yellow tops looked especially awful under the harsh fluorescent lighting. Bren swallowed too fast.

"Yeah, that's me," he said, his voice straining as he tried to make the bubble in his chest go away.

"You ok there?" said the taller of the two.

"Yeah. Fine. You're here about A.J., yeah?"

"Is that Arlo Walker?" the second Guard asked, his pudgy fingers flipping through his notepad.

"A.J. Walker," Bren corrected.

262

"Right. We were wondering if we could ask you a few questions."

Bren had to work hard to keep himself from crushing the muffin into dust.

"You find him yet?" Bren asked, partly hoping the answer was no so that he had time to get to Cian first.

"Get who?" asked the taller one, whose badge identified him as S. Ryan.

The muffin was in definite danger of getting crushed now.

"Cian McConnell, the piece of shite that did this."

The Guards shared a tense look, but Bren barreled on.

"He already fucked with A.J. before. Gave him a black eye for just walkin' down the street."

"Son."

"Ask Mickie Walsh or Brian Sullivan, they both saw it!"

Lynch, the shorter of the two, raised a hand. "We appreciate the tip, but that's not what we're here for."

"Why the fuck not, then?" Bren snapped, trying but failing to keep his voice down.

"Can you start by telling us how you know A.J.?" Lynch continued like Bren hadn't said anything. "When we've asked people who he's close with, they've all pointed us to you."

Bren's jaw twitched. This was it then, just like Mam had predicted.

"He's my lad."

Lynch stopped taking notes to look at Bren.

"And when you say lad, you mean . . ."

Bren took a breath.

"I mean, he's my boyfriend."

Ryan became interested in the cuffs of his uniform, but Lynch plowed on.

"Right, well, that would explain why the two of you are so close."

"Yeah, and it explains why you lot better do your jobs before I put the shitehead in the fuckin' ground."

Ryan snapped away from his sleeve and opened his mouth like he was going to say something, but Lynch cut across him.

"I know you're going through it right now, so I'm going to pretend like I didn't hear that."

Bren swallowed down the bile rising in his throat.

"Sorry. What do you need from me?"

Both Guards looked relieved as Lynch got back to scribbling.

"We can start with where you were around five yesterday evening."

42

A.J.'s lips brushed the whorl of ginger hair at the top of Bren's head as they lay together in the bright afternoon sunlight. It was hard to tell if it was the morphine or the fact Bren was allowed in his bed in the general ward, but it was almost possible for him to forget about how much he ached. As long as he didn't breathe too deep. . . or move too much.

"A Dream Worth Keeping" poured from the earbuds they were sharing as his thumb rested against Bren's cheek. He stroked it in soft, clumsy circles—still not used to using his right hand for things like this. His eyes watered as a ray of sunlight caught Bren's hair. Jerk, ally, friend, boyfriend, the words he used to describe Bren to himself had shifted so many times in four months. Now, he had to add hero to the list, although that word didn't quite do it justice.

"Mmmmwhatisit?" Bren asked, his eyes fluttering partway open as A.J. brushed across his eyebrow.

"Sorry, I didn't mean to wake you up."

Bren nuzzled into A.J.'s shoulder and yawned.

"Wasn't asleep. Just relaxin'."

"Is that why my shoulder's wet? Relaxing juice?"

Bren grinned and wiped the corner of his mouth on his sweater.

"Not my fault you're comfy."

"Well, my head does feel like it's full of stuffing."

Bren's face fell.

"No, I mean, I'm not—sorry, that was stupid."

"Want me to ring the nurse?"

"No, it—"

"Or fuck," Bren scrambled up and swung a leg out of bed. "Should I let you stretch out? Fuck, shouldn't have got on the bed."

A.J. clapped his hand over Bren's mouth. His hand warmed from the heat of his lips, and the memory of the last time he'd done this.

"Bren, it was just a stupid joke. I'm fine."

Bren didn't pull away, but raised an eyebrow.

"Ok, not fine, but, I'm ok," A.J. said, letting his hand fall away. He nuzzled the top of Bren's head in its place. "And I feel a lot better with you up here."

Bren scrunched up his face like he wasn't convinced.

"Sure you don't need anythin'? How about a snack? I can run down to the can—"

A.J. stopped him with a kiss this time, and after a pause, Bren returned the pressure. It would have been nice to stay like that for the rest of the afternoon, but A.J.'s chest was already burning from sitting up like this. He fixed the most neutral look he could manage on his face and leaned back into his mountain of pillows.

Bren stared down at him as if he were looking for something else to worry about. He must not have been able to find anything because he slid down beside A.J. with his head resting on his shoulder.

"You can't just kiss me every time I try and help you, like. Gonna give me a complex or somethin'."

"I'll keep that in mind," A.J. said as a new song started up.

A.J. closed his eyes, letting the familiar lyrics wash over him. "A Case of You." This was a song from his childhood—played over the speakers in his living room, or else from the ancient radio his family took with them down to the beach at Diefenbaker.

"Hey, Bren?"

"Yeah?" Bren asked, sounding sleepy.

How did he switch emotions so fast?

"So, you know how I had that call with my parents before they moved me out of HDU?"

"Yeah."

A.J. winced as he sat up straighter. He'd avoided talking about the call until now, and Bren, bless him, hadn't asked either.

"They were, well . . ."

He knew his parents hadn't meant to make him feel worse, but his mom had spent the entire call crying. He'd felt so guilty he almost hadn't done what he'd promised himself he'd do.

"I'm trying to convince them not to fly over here to take me home. I think my dad's open to it, but my mom is still really upset."

Joni Mitchell sang on as silence hung between them. A verse later, Bren replied, although he didn't look at A.J. when he did.

"Do you wanna go home?"

A.J.'s shoulders shook despite his best efforts. There wasn't any part of him that wanted to say goodbye to Bren six months early. He couldn't lie to himself though. The thought of going back to school with everyone knowing what had happened made it hard to breathe.

Then there was Cian. An ocean between them still wasn't enough as far as A.J. was concerned.

"No," A.J. said, hoping he didn't sound as unsure as things were in his head. "But, I don't think my mom's going to listen to me."

Bren sniffed, and his shoulders shook against the pillows as he did. A.J. made himself look at Bren since Bren wouldn't look at him.

267

He was staring straight ahead, his jaw set, though his lower lip was trembling.

"Sorry, I didn't mean to—" A.J. said, wiping his eyes with the back of his good hand. "I meant, I think maybe if they got to meet you, they might not want me to come home so much."

"You sayin' all I gotta do is talk to yer folks, and you might get to stay?"

A.J. wiped his eyes again, ignoring Audrey III stirring in his chest when he did so.

"Yeah, I think it would really calm them down. To know I had someone like you."

A tinge of red appeared on Bren's cheeks. He leaned in, lips parted. A.J. closed his eyes and leaned forward, expecting to find a kiss waiting for him. When it didn't come, his eyes fluttered open. Bren was sitting straight up and wearing the faintest trace of a frown.

A.J. held Bren's gaze as best he could. It was like staring into a crackling fire, and A.J. had to fight to not look away.

"You sure you wanna stay?"

A.J.'s hand reached for the volume knob, but he caught himself. For all Bren had done for him, the least he could do was be honest.

"I'm sure I don't want to leave you, Bren."

"But?"

"But I'm scared."

A.J.'s chest heaved as a weight he didn't know he was carrying lightened. He'd been scared since he'd woken up in the HDU—before then, really. Scared from the moment he'd seen Cian in that clearing. Waking up to find Bren at his bedside had been more wonderful than he could put into words, but it didn't change the fact there had been a bedside to begin with.

"I'm so scared. I-I thought I was going to die out there."

268

A.J.'s breath was coming in shudders now; the warmth that had been protecting him from the pain in his chest had flickered out like a snuffed candle.

"It was cold, and dark, and I kept trying to get up, but everything kept spinning, and my legs wouldn't listen."

Bren tensed beside him, his freckled fingers clenching into the scratchy hospital blanket.

"That fucker isn't ever gonna touch you again."

"You can't know that."

Warmth spread across the top of A.J.'s hand as Bren's came to rest there.

"I can, Arlo, honest." He brought their hands up to his mouth and kissed the space where they joined. "He's gonna have to go through me, and Mickie, and Brick, and Rory, and Orlaith to get anywhere near you."

"You guys can't just drop your lives to keep me safe, Bren."

Bren's face fell, then softened into something almost mournful.

"Stop that, ok?"

"Stop what?"

Bren's voice sounded stuffy when he spoke next.

"Thinkin' that carin' about you's some big inconvenience, like." He sniffed again and squeezed A.J.'s hand harder. "You got a family here, whether you believe it or not."

A.J. was about to point out Bren was overestimating things. That they were only his friends by proxy of him, but against his better judgement, memories poured in. Working on "The Navigator" at Rory's house, hours of talking hurling with Brick, and to his surprise, more than one instance of Mickie telling Cian off. Even Orlaith's words at Halloween, "I can see why he likes you," made their way through the sea of doubt.

"And," Bren said, kissing the back of A.J.'s hand now. "You got a boyfriend who isn't gonna leave you the fuck alone. Unless you ask," he shrugged. "Maybe not even then."

Warmth ran down A.J.'s cheeks again. He tried to make himself say something, but things were just too loud. Instead, he pressed his head into Bren's shoulder and let himself exist in the gift he'd been given.

Bren's free hand traced a circle on his cheek, the same way A.J. had when he'd thought Bren had been napping.

"You don't gotta decide anythin' now. And if you go back to Canada early, it doesn't change anythin'. I'm still gonna be your boyfriend. Gonna get my sleep all kinds of fucked up talkin' to you and everythin'." He wiped a tear from A.J.'s eye, then kissed the top of his head. "Just, don't let that piece of shit make your decisions for you, yeah?"

A.J.'s throat worked to form a reply, but he still didn't have the words. He didn't think he ever would.

— · —

43

A.J. let out a stomach-rattling groan as he eased his back into the mountain of pillows at the head of Bren's bed. Both the slight movement and exaggerated sound caused his ribs to grumble, but he couldn't be bothered to listen just now.

"Ok, I know it's probably not funny, but I think your mom killed me."

He watched Bren's expression and was pleased to see that he smirked.

Thank you.

"Yuuuurrrrp," Bren said, leaning back and pushing a belch out of his stomach with his fist. "Mam always goes big for Christmas dinner."

A.J. thought that "big" was something of an understatement for the meal they'd had: Turkey, ham, mashed potatoes, roast potatoes, carrots, brussels sprouts, gravy, and—A.J. had almost cried when Mrs. O'Shea brought them out—a plate of pan-fried cheese perogies, piled high with sauerkraut and medallions of browned kielbasa.

"Alright, you ready for movies?" Bren asked, cradling his stomach like he was expecting twins. "Isn't Christmas 'til Marv and Harry kiss them paint cans."

Off in the kitchen, dishes clattered as Mrs. O'Shea cleaned up the remains of their feast. A.J. had offered to help as they were finishing dessert but had been shot down before the words had even left his mouth.

Bren sighed as he eased himself onto the bed and slipped a hand on A.J.'s knee.

"Right, need anythin' before we get started?"

"Are you actually offering me more food?" A.J. groaned, sure that he wouldn't need to eat again before New Year's.

"I could go for somethin' to nibble on."

A.J. saw Bren in his forties, pot-bellied and rosy-cheeked—a fate that was sure to befall him if he kept eating the way he did. It was one of the ways A.J. knew how far gone he was. Chubby or thin, balding or covered in back hair, there wasn't an image of future-Bren he could picture that didn't make his heart feel whole.

Every moment, as long as you're mine.

"Hey, Bren?" A.J. asked, working to keep the tears he felt lurking as theoretical as the phantom Brens.

"Yeah?"

"Thank you."

"For askin' if you want a snack?" Bren asked, raising an eyebrow.

"Come on," A.J. said, trying to match Bren's expression. "I'm new here, but I'm pretty sure Christmas on the thirtieth isn't normal in Ireland."

He'd been trying to figure out how to bring this up all day. No part of him had expected to open the door to the O'Sheas' and find it looking as it had on Christmas Eve. Kitchen full of food, lights blinking merrily, "Silver and Gold" playing from the old sound system under Maurice the ceiling horse. The only difference had been that there were somehow more presents under the tree than before.

Bren shrugged.

"Couldn't do it on the proper day, could we?"

Then he looked panicked, like he was sure A.J. was going to take offence.

"I just meant. You don't think we were gonna have Christmas without you?"

A.J. was in real danger of crying now. The way Bren said it, he might have been explaining that two plus two equaled four.

"What happened to all the food from first Christmas?"

Bren shrugged again.

"Think Mam took most of it down to the church."

Bren muted the movie so they didn't have to hear the menu music again.

"You up in your head over this?"

A.J.'s lip quivered. With his belly full of food, and the small mountain of presents—two books from Rory, a set of headphones from Orlaith, and a stack of CDs from Bren to name a few—it was impossible to ignore how much trouble everyone had gone through.

Bren had looked overjoyed when he'd unwrapped the box of Canadian snacks and the recipe for his grandma's Nanaimo bars, but it seemed like poor repayment, all things considered.

"I guess a little bit," A.J. admitted.

Bren leaned over and kissed him before he could say anything else. His hand trailed up to A.J.'s hip and their mouths parted. It didn't build the way their kisses often did. It was warm and steady, with the faintest trace of Christmas pudding lingering on Bren's lips.

"What was that for?" A.J. asked when Bren pulled away.

The corner of Bren's mouth twitched into a half-smile.

"I figure if I kiss you good enough, you might stop thinkin' you're a burden all the time."

Bren leaned back in and pressed his forehead against A.J.'s , warmth spreading from the spot where they met.

"We like you 'round here, Ar—"

"I love you, Bren."

The words hung in the air for one breathless second, then relief washed over A.J. They'd been rattling around in his head for weeks now. If nothing else, he was glad he let them out.

He couldn't read the look on Bren's face as they stared at each other. If he didn't know any better, he'd think it was almost smug.

"You don't have to say it back. I just didn't wanna keep sitting on it," A.J. said, his cheeks burning despite the peace he'd made with the decision.

Bren kept the strange look fixed on his face as he got off the bed. He rummaged around in the bag full of stuff from the hospital and when he turned around, he was wearing a shining disc around the tip of his index finger. He sat back down and gestured for A.J. to take it.

Without the faintest idea what Bren was on about, A.J. leaned forward and slid the disc off his finger.

A.J.'s BIG ASS EXCHANGE MIX stared back at him, decorated as always with signatures of home.

"GOOD LUCK, DUDE!"

"WE'LL MISS YOU, A.J.!!!!"

"BRING ME BACK A LEPRECHAUN!"

And—

Something in A.J. broke as new life bloomed in its place.

Off towards the bottom of the CD, written in electric blue Sharpie:

"I love you, Arlo Walker."

-Bren

He thought he'd learned everything there was to know about kissing Bren, but now, as warmth spread from both his lips and the talisman balanced in his hand, he realized how foolish that had been. He could kiss this boy for a thousand lifetimes, and there would always be something new to learn.

He thought it was unlikely he'd get it, a thousand of anything was a lot, a greedy ask, really. In light of that, A.J. made a silent bargain with the universe—he'd settle for one lifetime, as long as he could spend it with Bren.

44

"Oh, Arlo!"

Bren tried to shoot Arlo a covert look as the woman on screen hid a sob behind her hand. Five seconds and they were already in tears.

"Mom? What's wrong?" Arlo asked, sounding like he was worried he'd upset her.

"—y-your face!"

"Oh." Arlo touched the bruise under his eye. "I'm fine. It hardly even hurts anymore."

Through the tension, Bren couldn't help but notice Arlo's hair was the exact shade of brown as his da's. There was also something around his mouth that made Bren feel uncomfortable seeing on another person. He'd gotten his cheeks from his mam, along with the exact shape of his brown eyes—he thought there was something familiar in the way she held herself, too.

Arlo's mam blinked at the camera through watering eyes, but found her voice again.

"I didn't think it would look this bad. Are you sure you're ok?"

"I'm ok, Mom, really."

Bren wasn't sure if he was imagining it, but he thought there was an edge of doubt there now.

"Katherine," Arlo's da said, putting a hand on her arm. "They wouldn't have let him out of the hospital if they weren't sure he was ok."

"I know, but—"

"And he's staying with a nurse. Isn't that right, A.J.? She'd know if there was anything wrong."

Bren missed Arlo's reply. He was too gobsmacked by how much Arlo sounded like his da. He spoke with more confidence than Bren heard in A.J. most days, but he had no trouble picturing Arlo at forty-something sounding like that.

"We're not supposed to be talking about that right now, though, are we?"

Bren pulled himself back into the conversation just in time.

"I've gotta say, son, he looks exactly like I imagined."

"Dad!"

"Jonathan!"

Bren blinked as Arlo's da laughed at his . . . joke? Bren couldn't think why that would be so funny, unless he hadn't expected Arlo's boyfriend to be so funny-looking.

"Uh, yeah, hi there, Mr. and Mrs. Walker."

He thought about signaling Arlo for help, but wasn't sure how to do it without his parents noticing.

"Am I missin' somethin'?"

"What? Oh, shit!"

Bren's confusion only got worse as Arlo joined in the laughter.

"Seriously, you wanna fill me in, like?"

"Sorry," Arlo said, his accent coming out stronger than usual, "My uh—well. I guess I forgot to mention. My dad was born with optic nerve hypoplasia. He was blind from birth."

There was something about the way Arlo said that—like he was reading it from a card.

"You didn't tell him that before?" Arlo's mom asked, sounding reproachful.

Bren had to agree. It felt like something worth mentioning to your boyfriend.

"Well, I'm glad I didn't let you down. Six foot four and model fit over here. Perfect teeth, too," Bren said, seeing this as more of an opportunity than anything.

Arlo's da blinked at the camera—or now that Bren knew what he knew, it was obvious he was just looking in the general direction of the thing—and laughed again.

"You picked a good one, son."

Arlo turned beet red, but linked their hands outside the camera's frame.

"I know."

"He really is quite handsome, Jonathan," Arlo's mom said, "Gorgeous red hair and a very sweet smile."

Bren had to wonder if Arlo's da had any idea what red even looked like as he felt the tips of his ears move to match his hair. A silence stretched out after everyone's smiles faded. It was creeping past what Bren felt was normal when Arlo spoke up again.

"So, yeah, that's Bren. He's not usually so quiet."

The fact hadn't escaped Bren either. Arlo's parents hadn't been anything other than nice so far, but he didn't know what the heck he was supposed to say here. He didn't think anyone would be convinced by him yelling they needed to let Arlo stay in Ireland, and that was all he wanted to do.

"It's an awkward situation. I can't imagine how I'd feel if I had to meet your grandparents like this." He paused and smiled to himself. "Might have been better that way. Poor Keno."

Bren was about to ask what he was talking about when Arlo's mom picked up the thread. "He tripped over the dog when I brought him over for dinner for the first time."

"Like something straight out of The Three Stooges," Arlo's da added.

Bren snorted before he could stop himself.

"Was the dog ok?"

He was horrified to hear the note of humor in his words.

"Oh, they were both fine," Arlo's mom said with a dismissive wave.

Arlo's da straightened in his seat and shook his head mournfully.

"Everyone always worries about the dog. Never the poor blind guy on the floor."

They all laughed at that, and Bren almost forgot what the call was supposed to be about. When the laughter faded, Arlo squeezed Bren's hand.

"So, uh, what do you think?"

Arlo's mom bit her lip.

"A.J., Bren seems lovely, but I still think you should come home. From what Maura said, the police there haven't done anything to keep you safe."

Bren's stomach dropped at the look on her face.

"I know, but it's not just Bren. I've got other—"

"Aren't you scared, too? I mean, what's to stop that Cian boy from doing this again if he got away with it this time? I can't believe that boy's parents are lying for him. I can't see anyone from Moose Jaw doing that." She stared at the camera like she wasn't really seeing them, wringing her hands in her lap. "I thought Glenbridge was supposed to be safe."

Arlo's hand trembled in Bren's. He squeezed it but wasn't sure it helped.

"It is safe," Bren said, but at the scoff from Arlo's mom, changed course. "I mean—look, I've lived here my whole life, and I never heard of anythin' like this happenin'."

"Exactly!" Arlo's mom blurted. "If A.J.'s the problem, then we should take him away from the situation."

Bren had to remind himself he was supposed to keep from swearing.

"Katherine," Arlo's da said, his arm shifting like they were holding hands off screen, too. "A.J. isn't the problem."

"What? Of course he—I didn't mean." She took a deep breath that broke into a shudder. "I don't know how the police can let that boy wander around when you told him he was the one that did this."

Arlo's shoulders pulled in as his mom went on. He kept trying to get a word in, but he was so quiet Bren could barely hear him.

"I don't think there's a more helpless feeling than this. For something so horrible to happen, with him all away from everyone who's ever loved him."

"He isn't!"

"I'm sorry?" Arlo's mom asked, sounding like she thought she'd misheard him.

Bren hadn't realized when it'd happened, but he was squeezing Arlo's hand so hard his own had gone numb. He kissed the spot where their hands met before letting it go.

"I said, he's not away from everyone who loves him."

"Bren, that's sweet, and I'm sure you're very fond of A.J., but it's not—"

280

"It isn't just me. Everyone went out in piss-cold rain to look for him the second I told 'em Arl—A.J. was missin'."

Arlo let out a choked sob as his mom stared at them through the screen. Bren took his hand again and kissed it, not caring who saw.

"I'm really glad to hear he's got good friends, Bren. But it's not the same. I'm sorry, but you couldn't understand unless you're a parent."

"I know." Bren was working hard to keep his voice steady but could feel something crumbling at the back of his throat. "I mean, I know that I can't know. But, it isn't just friends he's got."

"What do you mean?"

"She doesn't say, but I think Mam loves him plenty." Arlo's shoulders had lifted, but he still looked like the lad Bren had met back in September. "I haven't ever seen her make perogies before, and she made a whole plate for him, that's gotta mean somethin', like."

"What do you think about this, Jonathan?" Arlo's mom asked after another shuddering breath.

Arlo's da shifted in his seat.

"I think we should hear what A.J. thinks about all this."

Shame bubbled up in Bren. He'd been pissed at Arlo's mom for talking about him like he wasn't in the room, and he'd gone and done the same thing.

"I—" Arlo paused and looked down at the hand Cian had stomped on. He wiggled the tips of his swollen fingers and stifled a hiss. When he looked back up, his eyes were shining with something other than tears. "I want to be where Bren is and . . ." He clenched his good hand into a fist. "And I don't want that piece of shit to win."

Arlo's mom gave a watery gasp, but his da was looking at the screen like he wanted to reach through it to clap Arlo on the back.

"Well, Katherine?"

Arlo's mom looked from her husband to the screen, frowning. When she spoke, Bren was sure she heard something like pride in her voice.

"Ok, we can at least talk about it."

***

When the call ended nearly an hour later, it was all Bren could do not to tackle Arlo onto the couch.

"Holy fuck, Arlo! You kicked royal fuckin' arse."

From the way he was looking at him, Bren was sure he had no idea how deadly he'd sounded.

"Whose ass did I kick?"

Bren tried to think of an answer, but his mind was too preoccupied to figure it out.

"Shut up and take the win, lad."

He put his hand on Arlo's thigh and gave it a squeeze.

"Well, thanks, I guess?" Arlo said, still looking like he thought Bren had gone round the bend.

"Seriously, Arlo, it was kinda sexy."

A.J. snorted and leaned back into the couch.

"Oh yeah, I look like I'm part dalmatian, and now I've got to text my parents like five times a day. I feel real sexy."

Bren moved to take his hand off Arlo's thigh, but stopped himself. Arlo wasn't brushing this off.

"Alright, try and think about it from my side of things, yeah?" He gave Arlo's thigh another squeeze to resist moving his hand further

282

up. "Your parents wanted you to come home, and you told them you'd rather stay here, with me."

He'd meant to say it loud and proud, but a catch in his throat made the last part come out closer to a whisper. Maybe that was the thing that made it click for Arlo, because he was looking back with a hint of pride which did nothing to tame the growing need in Bren's chest.

"All I did was tell the truth."

"Yeah? Well, all I wanna do right now is kiss you, that ok?"

Arlo leaned in, but stopped halfway there. When he spoke next, it was in the softest voice Bren had ever heard him use.

"Can we put on some music first?"

The hunger in Bren's chest stirred at the look Arlo was giving him. He'd only seen something like it once before—after he'd kissed him in the music room on the last day of term. So nervous, but steady in a way that made Bren want to laugh, cry, and kiss him all at once.

"Was already plannin' on it. Think I don't know me own man?"

Bren's body growled its disapproval when he took his hand off Arlo so he could grab a CD from his bedroom. He hadn't taken more than a step away before Arlo piped up, in a voice that made Bren's legs wobble.

"Hey, Bren, is it ok if we . . . do it in your bedroom?"

For someone who thought things to death, the lad really didn't realize how the things he said sounded sometimes.

"Do it, huh? Yeah, probably best we head there if that's what you wanna do," Bren said, giving Arlo a wink.

Bren had expected Arlo to turn red and sputter, or at least roll his eyes. Instead, he took a single, shuddering breath and rose from the couch.

"Ok."

***

The wind whistled outside Bren's window as A.J. stared at the hand trailing down his chest. Bren's fingers skimmed over the map of bruises that hadn't quite faded. The urge to apologize crashed through him like a wave on the beach. To A.J.'s surprise, it receded—back to wherever those urges came from.

"Ok, it's weird how nice that feels . . ." A.J. said above Angel's solo in "I'll Cover You."

Bren didn't say anything in reply, but kissed a bruise with a touch as soft as falling snow. It was A.J.'s instinct to say something. To pay back the feeling Bren was giving.

Instead, his hand curled into Bren's hair as a sigh escaped him.

He'd expected his thoughts to grow loud as he lay there. They had by no means vanished; dark thoughts of the world outside Bren's bedroom bubbled in the background, only overshadowed by June's looming presence.

The thoughts were no match for the warmth flooding his body, though. He had music, he had Bren, and most importantly, a house where no one was supposed to be home for hours and hours. So just this once, he closed his eyes, shut off his thoughts, and let himself be loved.

45

"Here, let me do it."

A.J. grunted but let Bren take over knotting his tie.

"Think they'll let me take this thing off early if I tell them it's against my religion or something?"

He raised his graffiti-covered cast, then let it flop down to his side. Fond as he was of the signatures, he'd trade them for the use of his dominant hand again.

"Maybe, but then you might wind up lookin' like that butler from Scary Movie."

"Nooo, my other hand isn't strong enough!" A.J. exclaimed, that particular scene having lived in his brain rent-free since he was eleven.

"Exactly," Bren said, still working at the tie.

"You saying you wouldn't love me if I had a gnarly hand?"

"I would," Bren said, planting a kiss on A.J.'s lips before taking a step back. "Long as it could still play me that song of yours."

A.J. suppressed a laugh when he looked down. Despite having two functioning hands, the knot looked like he'd done it himself in the end. He wondered if Mrs. O'Shea pre-tied Bren's for him at the start of each week.

"Looks nice and crazy, thanks."

"No one's gonna be lookin' at your tie, lad."

A.J. winced. He knew Bren hadn't meant it that way, but he'd touched on one of the things he'd been dreading most about school starting up again. Between the article in the Glenbridge Echo, "Fifth-year Glenbridge student found unconscious in wooded area, recovering in hospital", and the remnants of the attack he still wore, there wasn't going to be any hiding what had happened.

A.J. shook the thought from his head, his neck rubbing against the travesty of a knot Bren had fixed around it.

"Well, I guess we better get going."

He'd taken a half-step towards the door when Bren gave his shoulder a squeeze. A.J. tilted his head against the top of Bren's hand.

"Real proud of you, Arlo."

A.J. wondered if Bren would have felt the same way if he knew how many times he'd woken up in a flop sweat last night. A tiny part of him had expected the Guards to have found a hole in Cian's bogus alibi before he had to face school again.

"Thanks, but," A.J. let his forehead rest against Bren's shoulder. "Can we just pretend like today's normal?"

Bren's face fell, but A.J. rushed on before he could say anything.

"I just—everyone's going to be talking about it. I don't wanna have to, too. I wanna hear about how everyone's break went, and bitch about Miss Murphy and argue about whether Twomey likes blokes or not."

Bren studied A.J.'s face like he was expecting to find something written there. When A.J. stared back with a look he hoped said *I'm fine*, Bren gave a curt nod.

"Right then, let's get goin', Robolad."

***

Bren huffed as Arlo's stride took him half a step ahead. They'd been walking shoulder to shoulder the whole way to school, and it had been all Bren could do not to throw his arm around the lad's waist. Would it really be so bad if he just went ahead and did it? He didn't have time to think about it long before the yard exploded around them.

Arlo squared his shoulders and walked with his eyes fixed straight ahead, the music of the single earbud he'd kept in humming. Bren caught strains of conversations as they went. Someone was yelling about the trip they'd taken to London, another groaned about having PE as their first class. A knot in his chest loosened. This was just another start of term.

"Hey. Over there."

Bren's heart froze. He glanced to his right to see a pair of lads from sixth year looking right at Arlo.

"He's the one from the paper, right?"

"Gotta be, got that cast, hasn't he? Fuck, look at his face."

The chill in Bren's chest turned white hot. The pricks were talking about him like he was some kind of circus act, and they weren't even bothering to lower their voices.

His nails dug into his palm as he fought the impulse to tell them to shut their fucking gobs. He might have done it, too, if it weren't for the lad two steps to his right.

"You get even more ginger over break?"

Bren didn't have time to react before Mickie pounded him on the back. Arlo must have seen out of the corner of his eye, because he stopped, too.

287

Mickie stepped in front of them, looking like he'd said something gas instead of the world's lowest effort ginger joke.

"Folks didn't get you a new personality for Christmas? Shit, that was on my list."

Mickie flipped him off and pivoted to Arlo. "Feeling better? Face looks less shite than last time."

The sixth years were one thing, but he could at least shut Mickie up. He was about to do it when he realized Arlo was laughing.

"Don't worry, a couple more days and you'll be the ugliest one in the group again."

Bren laughed, and Mickie joined in a second later.

"Lucky you're with Bren there, Canada."

"Hey, watch it!" Bren hissed.

"What?" Mickie said, wrinkling his nose. "Aren't I supposed to be all supportive and shite? No one's listenin'."

Bren scanned the yard. Everyone was paying attention to their own groups, even if Bren was sure a few of them were talking about Arlo.

"Ok, fine. Thanks for bein' an ally or whatever, but keep it quiet at school, yeah?"

"Jeez, you get pissed when I'm weird about it and pissed when I'm cool." He caught Arlo's gaze and rolled his eyes. "Good luck with that one, Canada—Oi! Brick!"

A few heads turned as Mickie threw his arm in the air. They moved as a group to meet him under a scraggly old tree away from the main flow of lads.

"What class do you lot got first?"

"Maths," Bren and Arlo said in unison.

"German," Mickie added with a grunt of disdain.

288

"Right, looks like we're copying off Canada, then." He said, squaring his shoulders. "How you doing? All healed up?"

Bren wanted to slap the question out of the air. What a stupid thing to ask.

Arlo took it in stride. "I'm fine. And you saw the C+ I got last term, right? You really wanna copy that?"

Would this weird, beautiful lad ever stop surprising him?

By the time the bell was getting ready to ring, Bren didn't have to pretend he'd forgotten his worries. Arlo was mid-flow in some mad story about how his uncle had lost him ice fishing back when he was four.

"He seriously went 'round checkin' holes?" Bren asked, still trying hard to wrap his head around sitting around on a frozen lake for sport.

"Ok, phrasing, but yeah. I mean, it's funny now, but he must have been really freaked out. I was small enough I could have fit through one, probably."

Rory was laughing, but Mickie didn't look convinced.

"And you were?"

"Like, three shacks down. I guess I just wandered in and sat down? I remember them listening to really loud music. I think it was AC/DC."

"Did your uncle call the Guards?" Brick asked.

"Nah, I was only gone for like fifteen minutes. The people in the shack figured out where I belonged pretty fast. I think my uncle is still friends with them, actually."

"There's no way your country's a real place," Bren said.

"Sounds pretty Irish," Rory interjected, "except for the frozen lakes part."

"I mean it's pretty common . . . back . . . home."

The colour drained from Arlo's face as his words trailed off. Bren followed his gaze across the yard and felt his own face blanch. Cian, stupid fucking puffer jacket over his uniform, was telling a story that looked like it involved Aoife from the gestures he was making.

Every cell in Bren's body was screaming for him to tear across the yard and bash Cian's face into the pavement. It was only with intense effort that he was able to tear himself away from the happy thought to focus on the person who mattered.

Arlo's eyes were still fixed across the field. His breaths were coming in shallow bursts, and his good hand was ghost white as it clenched at the side of his trousers.

It had taken them longer than Bren, but the rest of the group had fallen silent. Rory looked like he was planning something that might have been at home in a Saw movie, and Brick was cracking his knuckles, his jaw set.

Bren took a step closer and gave Arlo's shoulder a squeeze. He didn't react—just kept staring across the yard like a statue.

"Arlo, it's o—"

Arlo ripped his shoulder out from under Bren's hand like it was made of fire. His hand shook as he fumbled for the Discman in his pocket, his breath coming faster now, but just as shallow.

"Arlo? What's wrong, are you—"

Arlo jerked away like he'd been slapped. Tears forcing their way out of eyes that refused to blink.

"B-bren, I—"

It sounded like he tried to say something after that, but it came out as a shuddering gasp.

Bren reached for him as the bell rang, but Arlo had already stumbled away through the flood of bodies. Mickie murmured something Bren didn't process. He was too busy deciding what to do.

His boyfriend had marched away like a King's Guard on speed; he was supposed to follow. But the way Arlo had looked at him, Bren had never seen him look so terrified.

What if he was the thing Arlo was running from?

46

The demon in A.J.'s chest raged louder than the music screaming in his ears as he paced the narrow aisle of the deserted greenhouse.

Move.

He needed to keep moving.

If he stopped, he was going to die.

His chest refused to slow.

Each panicked breath brought in the scent of rotting earth.

He was in the woods—lying in the mud, his body refusing to listen to him all over again.

A muffled sound.

A voice calling to him through the frenzy.

A.J. whirled at the end of his path to find Bren standing in the doorway. His mouth wasn't moving, but A.J. could still hear it: Arlo coming out of his mouth in Cian's voice.

He walked back down the aisle and turned again, leaving Bren in the doorway.

Bren, who loved him.

Bren, who would never do anything to hurt him.

"B-bren?"

A.J. stopped mid-step as the jagged edges of the world softened. He yanked out his earphones and turned back around. Bren had taken a step forward, but still looked like he was waiting to be yelled at.

"I-I'm sorry!" A.J.'s legs were still screaming at him to move, but he was able to stop them from taking over. "I didn't mean to—I—"

Bren took another step forward, arms half raised like he wasn't sure if he was allowed to go in for a hug or not. To be fair, A.J. wasn't sure if he was allowed, either.

"It's ok. Just take deep breaths, yeah? Your chest's goin' a mile a minute."

A.J. put a hand to his chest. Bren was right, his heart seemed to be stuck on hummingbird instead of human. He tried to remember how he usually breathed, but couldn't get past a one-second inhale.

"Trying—can't."

"It's ok, it's ok. Do you wanna put your music back in? We don't have to talk."

A.J.'s hands went to the wires dangling by his neck. He knew Bren was trying to help, but he didn't have a clue what he wanted.

"I don't know."

"It's ok, we can jus—"

"He said my name, Bren!"

The truth rushed over him. That was it. He'd forgotten, or maybe he'd refused to believe it until now.

"Who said your name?"

Bren looked pained as he spoke. A.J. hated that he was doing this to him. He knew he was freaking him out.

"C-Cian. He—I don't know how the fuck he knew it. But he called me A-Arlo right before h-he—"

Bren looked like he might punch a hole in the greenhouse, but when their eyes met, his face softened.

"I'm so sorry, A.J." He sounded like he was soothing a terrified animal, which A.J. supposed was close enough to the truth. "I won't use that name anymore, yeah?"

"No!" A.J. sounded like he'd been punched in the gut as he cried out. "Please don't. I like it when you call me A-Arlo! I-it's the only time in my entire life I've ever liked that fucking name."

Bren's arms moved like he wanted to go for a hug, but fell back to his sides. He took a half-step towards A.J. like he was asking for permission.

As if he were being carried by a wave, A.J. closed the distance and threw himself into Bren's arms.

"I'm so sorry, Bren. I'm so sorry."

He could feel the panic leaching out now. Leaving a trail of shame in its wake.

Why was he always so weak?

Bren's arm wrapped around his waist, his other hand finding the back of his head and pulling him close. He made a shushing noise, broken by half trembles—choppy waves that joined the ones still rolling in A.J.

"Don't got anythin' to apologize for."

A.J. buried his face in Bren's shoulder, not caring if he was getting his jumper wet.

"I love you, Bren. I'm sorry I'm so messed up."

"I love you too, A . . ." Bren's arms tensed around him. "J."

A muffled sob left him as he pulled Bren closer.

"Arlo," he said, resonant despite being muffled into Bren's shoulder.

Bren pulled A.J. closer and kissed his cheek.

"I love you, Arlo."

***

The throes of panic had long since left A.J. by the time he walked into the music room some thirty minutes later. He could have snuck out the gate and slept for the rest of the day—Bren had even said he'd tag along. But he needed to see the day through.

His legs carried him without conscious thought towards the piano at the front of the room. He lifted the fallboard and, humming to himself, plunked out the first few bars of "The Navigator" with his good hand. His left twitched in its cast, eager to give the piece the depth he thought it deserved, but the act still brought a smile to his face. It was nice to know he could still make music, even with a ruined hand.

"You alright, mate?"

A.J. looked over his shoulder. Rory was heaving his cello case against the wall.

"How the hell'd you sneak up on me with that thing?" he asked, sure that the world had glitched.

"Years of practice."

He took a step back from the cello, hands up like he was freezing it in place. When it didn't fall, he turned his attention back to A.J.

"So, you alright?"

A.J. closed the fallboard and wandered over to the seats. If it were anyone else, he might have brushed it off.

"Not really. But I feel better than I did an hour ago."

"I'm glad," he said, sliding his book bag off his shoulder, "I caught Mr. Kelleher before class. Told him you guys were here."

"Oh, thanks."

That was one less thing for him to worry about—not that he was giving the school's attendance policy much thought.

Rory flopped his composition book out and spent some time arranging it on the desk.

"It's really cool that you didn't go home."

"I definitely thought about it. Bren made it pretty tempting."

"I meant back to Canada. Glad you stuck around."

And just like that A.J. was in danger of crying for the second time that day.

"Well, I couldn't go, could I? You'd be the only one left in book club."

Rory's expression told A.J. he wasn't buying it, but it didn't feel nosy like it might have if Mickie or Brick had done it.

"Alright, I like you and everything, but I couldn't leave Bren, he's—" A.J. had never said it outside his head, so the words tasted strange as they formed on his lips. "My person."

Rory beamed like he'd just watched his kid graduate.

"Glad you stuck with him?"

A memory rattled loose at that.

It's probably going to take him a while to figure that out. Just stick with him until he does, yeah?

"Yeah, really glad."

It seemed an inadequate way to describe how he felt about Bren, but it fit in its way.

"Good, I like seeing the two of you so happy."

A.J. took his seat beside Rory, making sure to bump the chair as he passed.

"Thanks. Love you, too, man."

***

296

A.J. pulled the hem of the Harps bunnyhug over his nose and breathed in. A sigh escaped him as warmth flooded his being. Turf smoke, a hint of Lynx, and the faintest flicker of sweat—Bren in a piece of fabric. He still wasn't thrilled about having to stay at the McCarthys' again, now that the holidays were over—but at least he'd been able to take a piece of Bren's room with him.

RedBullBren69: "Alright, Robolad, I'm fucking knackered. See u down the hill. Don't forget how much arse u kicked today"

Bren had logged off about twenty minutes ago, but A.J. couldn't go yet, even if he was pretty knackered himself.

LittleMoshpitKid46: "Omg sorry! Had to wait for mom to drive me home"

"Spill, how was your first day back?"

AJWalker90: "Your parents take the car away or something?"

LittleMoshpitKid46: "Ugh, no. Forgot to plug in the fucking block heater last night. Had to take the bus, didn't want to take it back, it was a whole thing"

"But fuck the weather. How was it?"

AJWalker90: "It was ok. Basic school stuff. Bren made a Banoffee pie, but with salted chili caramel and this weird nut and crushed biscuit crust. It should not have worked as well as it did."

It took some time for Nat to reply again. He was pretty sure he knew why.

LittleMoshpitKid46: "Ok, Bren making weird pies sounds cute but what about that piece of shit? Did he actually fucking show up? I still can't believe his ass isn't behind bars yet"

A.J. sighed. It wasn't like it was unexpected. He was still surprised Bren's computer hadn't caught fire when he'd first told her Cian had pulled a functioning alibi out of his ass.

Her fury on his behalf made him feel somewhat better about the situation, but it also made the idea of telling her how he'd literally run from Cian less than appealing.

There wasn't any point in lying to Nat of all people, though.

AJWalker90: "Yeah he was there. I don't have any classes with him anymore . . ."

"I only saw him one time and I totally freaked out. Bren helped calm me down, though."

LittleMoshpitKid46: "What the fuck is wrong with that town? How is he not at LEAST expelled? Seriously!"

AJWalker90: "'As the situation remains under investigation by An Garda Síochána, the school has no grounds at this time to administer disciplinary actions. Your schedules have been modified so you have no overlap. You are expected to stay away from each other while on school grounds.'"

LittleMoshpitKid46: "What the fuck?"

AJWalker90: "That's what the principal said at that stupid meeting before term started up."

He could still picture it. He and the McCarthys, back from their holiday abroad, the literal day before term started. Mr. Dugan had rambled the speech off like he'd memorized it minutes before—which A.J. supposed was probably true—while Mr. Kelleher sat beside him looking even more tired than usual.

The McCarthys had apologized for the strain and assured Mr. Dugan that they were sure A.J. wasn't going to cause any trouble. If he'd had his say, Mrs. O'Shea would have been the one there with him. He doubted the outcome would have been any different, but he was sure she would have made Mr. Dugan nice and uncomfortable.

LittleMoshpitKid46: "Ok and why the hell isn't the investigation over yet?"

"Everyone knows that fucker did it"

AJWalker90: "'With their parents backing their alibis, there's only so much we can move on. But people talk and sometimes stories change. Until then, we're putting together the strongest case we possibly can. If anything comes back to you, no matter how small, please let us know.'"

It was easier to parrot what the Guard had muttered from across the O'Shea's kitchen table than to type it out in his own words.

LittleMoshpitKid46: "Fuck dude. Fuck that shit SO hard"

"But you're strong as hell. You got this."

AJWalker90: "Yeah, I almost died in the woods and Cian walked away without a scratch. Real strong over here."

A.J. regretted the words at once. He knew Nat was only trying to help. What the hell was wrong with him?

It was several minutes before she replied, and for once, A.J. didn't have the faintest idea what she might be doing on the other side of the screen.

LittleMoshpitKid46: "Sorry, that's not what I meant"

"But really dude, you're the bravest person I know. You moved across a fucking ocean and didn't let that homophobic fuck chase you back"

"You're kind of my hero"

A.J. could feel a lump rising in his throat. She might have been laying it on a little thick, but if there was one thing Nat didn't do, it was lie—even if it was to make someone feel better.

LittleMoshpitKid46: "Just remember. You're gonna heal up and be better than before"

"WITH your cute fucking boyfriend"

"Cian's going to be ugly and broken for the rest of his pathetic fucking life"

A.J. stared at the screen for a long time after that, his chest burning as he struggled to keep his breathing even.

Nat's words didn't change anything. He still had to go to school tomorrow, knowing Cian was there, and then the day after that, and the next one, too. But, the words stuck in his head, repeating like the chorus to a sacred song for him alone. He paused the music playing over the computer's speakers and closed his eyes. Cian was going to be there tomorrow, but so would everyone else.

47

"Come back soon, yeah? Seein' you's the best part of me day!"

The worn brass bell jingled as Miss Birdie tottered out—her weekly jam buns already swallowed up by her tent-sized handbag.

"Alright, what'll you have?" Bren asked, turning to the guy at the front of the queue.

"Two rhubarb tarts and a half dozen shortbreads."

Bren forced a smile as he reached for the first tart. If he'd had his way, he'd be cuddled up with Arlo right now. But when he'd floated the idea of calling in sick, Arlo had shot it down. Something about not being healthy to protect him twenty-four seven. Well, that and wanting to watch *Dead Poet's Society* with Rory.

He pulled his phone out of his pocket without any conscious thought and flipped it open.

Doing ok?

Yup, still over at Rory's. We might stop by later. Mickie was right, you look cute in your wee hairnet.

He knew it was stupid to be worried. Rory wouldn't let Arlo go wandering off on his own. The worst thing that could happen would be him getting bored to death from a shite movie.

The bell above the door jingled, and Bren slipped his phone back into his pocket.

"I'll be with you in a se—"

Bile rose in Bren's throat. Cian strolled towards the register like he didn't have a care in the world. Aoife clung to his arm, giggling at something he'd said like he was the funniest man on earth instead of a pile of shite in a puffer jacket.

Everything seemed to blur at the edges like an overexposed photo—everything except Cian. Bren saw him so clearly that it hurt his eyes.

He must not have seen Bren at first, because when he looked away from Aoife, he came to a stop with more distance between him and the counter than was natural.

"Hey, O'Shea. Forgot you worked here." His words came out honeyed as his lips curled up. "You alright?"

Bren ran his sandpaper tongue against the roof of his mouth.

For the first time in his life, words wouldn't come. Cian watched him for another couple of seconds, and when Bren didn't answer, he took another step towards the counter.

"She'll take a cream bun, and you can make me a black coffee. Throw an extra shot in there, too."

"Get out."

Bren was surprised to hear the sound of his own voice. He hadn't felt his jaw move.

From the look he gave Bren, Cian was either legitimately confused or doing a very good job of acting.

"Get. The fuck. Out."

Bren's voice was louder this time, but he had managed to keep it low enough that the couple in the dining area didn't look up. Cian looked Bren over again, his brow furrowed like he was trying to make sense of what was happening. Light flickered behind Cian's eyes, and his brows unknit. He looked almost sad as he shook his head.

"Fine, just give us what I ordered and we'll leave."

Aoife was still hanging on Cian's arm, but looked around like she was worried people might be listening.

"Cian, let's leave."

Cian gave no sign he'd heard her. Instead, he fished in his pocket and pulled out a crumpled tenner.

"Just give us what we ordered and we'll go."

Bren's nails were digging into his palm so hard he wouldn't be surprised if they drew blood.

"I'll get her a cream bun, but I amn't givin' you shite."

Cian rolled his eyes but broke arms with Aoife and slid the money onto the counter, keeping his eyes locked on Bren.

"You still pissed someone fucked up the little fag that hangs 'round you?"

The only thing that kept Bren from throwing himself over the counter was the thought of what it might mean for Arlo. He was sure that Cian, seeing the look in his eyes, would have taken a step back at the very least. Instead, he shoved his hands into his pockets and looked up at the ceiling, unbothered.

"Look, I know what everyone's saying. But, I'm gonna tell you what I told the Guards. I don't know who the fuck did it."

Bren could barely hear him over the rushing sound in his ears. Cian looked back from the ceiling, a wicked smile spread across his face.

"But I'll tell you this. If I knew who did do it, I'd buy them a fucking pint."

Bren leapt over the counter.

Back when he was eight, a stray dog wandered into their yard. Nan was watching him that day and had fallen asleep in her chair by the tele. The dog was some kind of scrawny mutt, with brown fur and a tongue that stuck out of the corner of his mouth.

He'd sat down in front of Bren with his tail wagging, like he was asking if Bren wanted to be mates. He'd shared half his sandwich with him, and from then on, that's what they were.

He'd always called him Lucky.

One day, Bren was walking home from school when he heard a horrible sound. He'd heard dogs bark before, even heard Lucky growl at the odd cat on their walks.

This wasn't that.

Lucky was locked in a horrific fight with another dog. His scrawny body writhing, hackles raised, spit flying as he made awful noises and tried to tear at every inch of the mottled black dog he was locked with.

No matter how Bren called him, the fight hadn't stopped . . . until the other dog had scampered away, and Lucky, seeing Bren, had trotted over with only a scrape on his nose and a limp that disappeared before the end of the day.

Bren had never understood how the fight had happened, or how Lucky had switched back to his sweet self in the blink of an eye.

As he flailed on the ground, fist coming down against Cian's face and the tile floor in equal measure, Bren understood Lucky better.

He'd taken a hit to the jaw that made him see stars when he was yanked into the air.

The world came back into focus. He could feel blood pouring down over his lips, could hear Aoife screaming, and Niamh, she was—

"Get your arse off my floor and out of my shop."

She was pulling at Cian's collar as he struggled to his feet. Whether the blood he was wiping off his chin was his own or from Bren's streaming nose, he didn't know.

"The fuck? He attacked me, you mad old bitch."

Niamh gave a snort of disgust and ripped her hand back from his collar.

"Like you weren't fucking asking for it, Cian McConnell."

From the look on Cian's face, he hadn't expected Niamh to know who he was.

"Now get the fuck out of my shop before I have Callum throw you out."

Bren looked up. It was Callum who had pulled him off of Cian. Bren gave him a look that asked to be set down, but Callum shook his head.

Aoife sobbed something as Cian rubbed his split knuckle against his nose. He held out his hand for her, but she didn't take it. He made a move like he was going to grab her by the arm, but after a look from Niamh, he stormed out the door.

"Callum, get him in the back. I think Aoife and I need to have a little chat."

Aoife, too, looked surprised Niamh knew who she was, but unlike Cian, she seemed to welcome the fact.

The ground found its way under Bren's feet again, and after wobbling in place for a second, Bren followed Callum back into the kitchen.

He was still shaking when he heard Niamh come back to the kitchen later. He kept his head hung between his knees, telling himself it was to make sure his nose didn't start bleeding again.

Why the fuck had he done that? All he wanted to do was protect Arlo, and he'd gone and made things ten times worse. The Guards would be here any minute.

"Eat."

Bren lifted his head enough to see Niamh had set down a plate of biscuits and a mug of tea on the counter next to him. Too shaky to care if this was some kind of a test, Bren wrapped his hands around the mug and took a sip. She'd even added sugar.

"I've had a talk with Erin and Cathal, and they agree that the Guards don't need to know about what just happened."

Bren started to ask who she was talking about when he remembered. The couple at the tables. Two teas, a cheese scone, and a custard tart. Every Saturday, like clockwork.

The tea burned Bren's split lip, but he took another gulp anyway.

"It doesn't matter. Cian's going to go running t—"

Niamh clapped him upside the head. It felt more like a pat than her usual swats.

"Use your head. You really think that boy wants people hearing he got his ticket punched?"

"I guess, but—"

Niamh actually patted him on the head this time.

"Trust me. Cian isn't going to say shit to anyone. Now, drink your tea."

Bren tried to say something, but stopped when he realized he had no idea what that might be.

Niamh shuffled towards the door, tucking her hair back into its net. She paused with her hand on the frame and didn't look back when she spoke.

"I'm not saying what you did was right, but Áine would have been proud."

It was impossible to miss the smile in her words . . .

48

The sound of screeching chair legs filled the room as twenty-five guys pushed back from their desks at once. Bren's eyes went to Arlo. He hadn't put his wires in yet, a good sign.

"Alright, where we headin'?"

Bren caught Conor shooting them a sideways glance but found he didn't care. People would get used to it, or they wouldn't. He couldn't control that, but he could control whether or not he spent every lunch with his boyfriend—so that's what he was going to do.

Arlo looked like he was chewing the question as Bren saddled up to him, so close their shoulders brushed. He was thinking about something, but it didn't seem to be in his usual twitchy way. If he had to put a word to it, Bren would have said it was something closer to meditation than a spiral.

"Wanna hit the canteen today? I kind of want a chicken roll."

Bren tried not to let his surprise show. They'd spent all last week shivering in the greenhouse every break. It had been a nice excuse to sit extra close on days when none of the other lads joined them, but Bren was glad of the idea of warm air with his food.

"Ah, feelin' safer now that you know yer man can throw a punch?"

Bren lifted his chin so his scab thrust out further. After he'd shown up at Rory's place with a split lip, he'd expected Arlo to worry for at least an hour. Instead, he'd kissed Bren so deeply Rory had to cough to remind them that he was there.

The spiral had tried to start up after that, but Rory had pointed out that the lack of sirens speeding towards the place meant Niamh was probably right about Cian not telling anyone.

"It doesn't hurt," he said with a look that made Bren's ears turn red.

Arlo's hand twitched like he wanted to reach out. After checking to make sure no one was paying attention, Bren let their knuckles brush. When they reached the door, Arlo pulled them off to the side.

"We can head back to the greenhouse if you want," Bren said, thinking of who was likely to be on the other side.

Arlo's chest quivered as he took in a breath. Bren knew the bruises were gone, but he couldn't help but wince at the memory.

"I just want to be warm today."

Their knuckles brushed again as Arlo pushed the door open, Bren following a step behind. The canteen was its dependable self: crowded and smelling like fried food and wet socks. Bren spotted Mickie and Brick, already at their table and was halfway to waving when his jaw clenched. Cian was sitting on the opposite side of the room. In a perfect world, the shitehawk would be eating out in the cold, but it was good to see how miserable he looked. The fact his lip looked like it was still hurting him helped too.

He was sitting next to Conor, who was turned away as he chatted with his own group. Tadhg was sitting across the table as usual, but neither of them was saying anything. In fact, Tadhg looked like he was trying to inch his way towards Conor's group.

Arlo hadn't missed Cian's presence, either. Bren's hand twitched again with the urge to reach out. It turned out to be a wasted impulse. Arlo's eyes had widened in shock, but softened into something that looked almost like pity. His lips formed words Bren couldn't make out, and he turned away like Cian was any other guy.

"Do you want anything?"

What Bren really wanted was to know what the hell Arlo had muttered, but he didn't feel like now was the time to ask.

"I'll just take a bit of your roll."

Arlo smiled as cheerfully as Bren had ever seen and headed for the queue, leaving Bren to contend with the confused pride swelling in his chest.

"You wanna tell him?"

Bren hadn't even sat down before Mickie piped up, eyes sparkling. Brick, who was already halfway through his first sandwich, grunted.

"What are you tellin' me?" Bren asked, pulling a Red Bull out of his bookbag.

"Cian got kicked off the team."

Bren's heart soared like he'd been told there'd be Christmas in January this year.

"Fuck really? How'd it happen?"

Brick shrugged and mumbled through another mouthful of sandwich.

"Not upholding the spirit of Glenbridge GAA."

Bren looked at him, but Brick went back to his sandwich like the matter was settled.

"Niamh used to babysit Coach," Rory supplied.

Christmas didn't cut it, this was like summer break with a boner for the soul.

"You're takin' the piss."

Rory shook his head.

"She's in book club with Mum. Made sure everyone was on the same page."

Mickie swallowed his mouthful of sandwich and leaned in.

"That's not even the best part. I was textin' Orlaith last night"—he shot a look around the table like he was expecting people to cheer for him and when they didn't went on—"and she said Aoife ditched him. Full on don't-ever-wanna-see-your-ugly-mug-again."

Arlo sat down before Bren had a chance to respond. He grabbed the lad's roll and tore out a chunk.

"Hey! That was like half."

Bren chewed slowly, savouring the news with every bite.

"Sorry, couldn't help meself," he said, eyes closed as he leaned back. "Wanna sit down? I'm about to make your whole feckin' week."

49

Bren glowered out at the mockingly blue sky like the day had done him a great personal wrong—which it kind of had. The sun was shining and the air was a sweet, balmy fifteen degrees—hell, he'd even seen a barn swallow outside his window that morning, like something out of Disney. And where was he? Stuck in the car on the way to suffer through community theater with Mam.

"Dunno why we couldn't get an extra ticket for A.J.," Bren grumbled, picking at the tie Mam had insisted he wear.

Mam eased the wheel to avoid the big pothole halfway down Second Street and made a clucking sound with her tongue.

"You've been carrying on like I'm dragging you off to have your teeth pulled. You'd really drag that poor boy of yours along?"

Bren sighed and let the side of his head thud against the window.

"I'd still have fun getting me teeth pulled if he was there."

"Well, I'll see if Dr. Connolly can set that up for you next weekend, but you're still stuck with me today."

"Which one of your mates ditched you anyway?" Bren asked, scooting away so he wasn't so easy to smack.

"Never mind that, just know you're making your old mam happy by steppin' up."

Bren vented some of his feelings by loosening the knot of his tie. If he was going to sit through two hours of shite, he was at least going to be comfortable while he did it.

They pulled up a block from the theater, and Bren, resigned to his fate, stooped around to open Mam's door.

"That was a fast turn-around."

Bren grunted but didn't push it further.

His heart leaped when they made it to the ticket booth to find it shuttered. Maybe he was going to have his day with Arlo after all.

"Sure you got the right day, like?"

"Yeah, we're just a little early."

He moved to stop Mam when she reached out to what he was sure was a locked door. To his surprise, it opened with a click and Mam strode inside like it was perfectly normal.

Bren looked around the room, impressed despite himself. He'd been here a handful of times over the years, always for educational rot that the teachers had said would enrich their horizons, when they weren't hissing at them to sit down and shut up mid-performance.

There were three theaters in the yoke. Two smaller ones with cramped stages and enough seating to hold about fifty people in seats that needed new stuffing about twenty years ago.

The main stage was a lot more impressive. Bren remembered the teachers using the word pro-seneium, or something like that. Over four hundred people could fit inside, spread out over the main floor, balcony, and the two layers of booths that lined the walls.

That was the stage that Mam was leading them towards. Bren wondered dully how long they'd have to wait, being as early as they were.

Rows of empty seats stood on either side of them, while the stage itself held only a sleek grand piano under warm, orangish light. It looked more like they'd gotten there early for a rehearsal than an actual show.

"You sure we're not breakin' and enterin'?"

Bren looked over his shoulder to find Mam still in the doorway, smiling back at him with tears in her eyes.

"Mam? What's goin'—"

Bren was interrupted as the sound of shoes on polished wood echoed through the otherwise silent theater. Bren turned in slow motion as his brain lurched into overdrive. His confusion was only multiplied when he found Rory standing beside the piano, dressed to the nines, and holding up that giant fucking violin of his.

Bren was about to ask him what the hell was going on when another set of footsteps came from offstage. Arlo walked on stage, dressed not in a suit and tie, but in a pair of jeans and a faded blue hoodie that Bren recognized as one of his own.

Transfixed, Bren walked toward the front row, moving by the feel of his hand against the chairbacks. He couldn't bring himself to take his eyes off Arlo.

Arlo smiled down at him from center stage, eyes screwed up against the stage light. He bowed once to the phantom audience and turned to face the piano.

A.J. had expected to feel nervous when he walked out on stage. But the moment he'd seen Bren staring back at him, mouth open in a perfect expression of cartoonish shock, everything else melted away. If being with Bren had taught him anything, it was how to worry less and smile more.

He had been plenty worried in the week leading up to this. Between waiting for Mrs. Doherty's feedback on the arrangement, swallowing his pride and asking the McCarthys to pull a couple of strings, and he and Rory practicing the piece until it lived in their

314

veins, things could have gone sideways about twenty times over. But they hadn't. He was on stage and Bren was taking his seat. What more could he ask for?

The fallboard cooled the tips of A.J.'s fingers as he lifted it back with a muffled thud. He straightened his back and poised his hands above the polished keys. The dust-swirled scent of the theater filled his lungs as he flexed the fingers on his left hand once more for good measure.

One-two-three.

One-two-three.

Rory was nearly through the intro now, low and dreamy, like the beginnings of a lullaby. A.J. had enough time for one more look at the awestruck boy in the front row, and then he started playing.

With gentle rolls and the notes tied together, the first bars of "The Navigator" rang through the expansive room. A.J.'s eyes couldn't help but flit back towards Bren as he made his way through the piece. He was still staring up at him with his mouth half open, but A.J. thought he looked more relaxed. After all, this was a song he'd heard before.

Then A.J. opened his mouth.

I spent my life drifting through static and grey,
Then you reached out your hand, said, "I know the way."
The noise left my head at the sight of your smile,
I took hold of your hand, saying, "just for a while."
Didn't know where we'd wander, with your hand held in mine,
But I followed you gladly and the world seemed to shine.
Yet I couldn't help thinking why you chose me that day.
I was meant for the background, never knew what to say.
You showed me the way.
You showed me the way.

A.J.'s voice rang out, clear and bright, though he knew he wouldn't be making his Broadway debut anytime soon. His heart lifted as he turned his head to better look at the only person whose opinion mattered.

Still I waited for silence, more static and grey,
But you held my hand tighter, and said you would stay.
So I opened my heart, let my smile start to show,
Held tight to this feeling, never thought I would know.
We've already had storm clouds, seen thunder and rain,
But if life started over, I'd choose you again.
You always moved forward, but would sometimes glance back.
I couldn't help wonder what got you off track.
You showed me the way.
You showed me the way.

This was it, then: weeks of planning and practice down to the next few seconds. He leaned into the keys, willing the feelings in his chest out through the tips of his fingers, into the notes he was struggling to keep steady.

Then you turned back to me, said "Where are we going?"
I guess I was leading, without ever knowing.
You showed me the way.
You showed me the way.
We both knew . . . the way.

A.J. wiped his tears away with his left hand, glad to give it something to do that wasn't quite so strenuous. For the first time, he didn't want to look at Bren.

Had this all been too much?

A sound broke through the whispers growing in A.J.'s head, steady and repeating. A.J. blinked away more of the wetness from his eyes as his brain tried to make sense of the sound. Clapping.

316

Someone, no, not someone. Bren was clapping. A.J. rose from the bench and forced himself to look into the crowd.

Bren, all smiles and tears, stretched to his full height as he brought his hands together like he might die if he stopped. A strange choked sound escaped A.J. as a smile broke across his face. He looked at Bren, then gave another bow to the boy who'd shown him the way.

***

Bren's hoodie flapped against A.J.'s back as they strolled together down Main Street. The day around them was as perfect as one could ask for, but A.J. was still in the proscenium. Still kissing Bren.

He would have given a great many things to keep their hands linked as they walked down the street. But they'd slipped apart in unison right before Bren had pushed the door open.

"So . . ." Bren said, walking in lazy strides next to A.J., his hands thrust in his pockets. "I showed you the way, huh?"

A.J. didn't need to look to know Bren was grinning.

"That's what the song said anyway."

"Where'd I lead you exactly?"

"Right now? A headache, I guess."

Bren swayed to the right so their shoulders bumped.

"Ah, sorry 'bout that. Want me to lead you to the chemists?"

"How about Niamh's? I'm kind of hungry."

Bren made a motion like he was going to take A.J. by the arm, but wound up scratching his side instead. They kept walking down the street, the spring breeze ruffling Bren's hair so it looked like crackling fire.

"You know, I think this means I gotta write you a song now."

"Oh yeah? What about?" A.J. said with an air of confidence that surprised him.

That was the good thing about pouring his heart out like that, A.J. was sure he was done blushing around Bren.

"Mmm, I dunno,"

Bren paused as a man stepped out of Neptune's on their right. He waited until they were well out of earshot before he continued.

"Maybe that little noise you made when I nibbled your neck, like."

A.J. was wrong. He'd never be done blushing around Bren.

"Th-that was one time! Jesus, Bren!"

"There's my lad."

A.J. was worrying how red he was likely to be when he got inside Niamh's when Bren stopped beside him. When he looked over, Bren's brow was knit in thought.

"What's up?"

"Seriously, Arlo . . . gonna remember that song for the rest of my life."

The sun on A.J.'s back felt warmer as he met Bren's eyes—hazel with flecks of blue, and shimmering with something A.J. knew Bren would deny if the lads were around.

"Well, I hope so. I plan on singing it to you again. Maybe after a year or two thou—"

Bren's lips cut him off before he could finish his sentence. Alarm bells blared. There was a couple sitting on the other side of Insomnia's window, and an old woman in carpet slippers and a shawl was pushing her groceries home in a paisley cart. Logic caught up with him as Bren broke the kiss and linked their hands. Bren wasn't blind. He had seen all that and chosen this anyway.

"Come on, Robolad, let's get you somethin' to eat."

50

The breeze from the half-open window cooled A.J.'s cheek as they pulled off the N7. Patches of industrial grey jutted out through the sea of green that had surrounded the car since they'd pulled out of the O'Sheas' driveway. He was finally seeing Dublin like the McCarthys had always wanted. He supposed it was beautiful, but all it did was remind him how different his life was about to look.

"—Glad we had a Canadian, or we'd a had raw feckin' rashers all week. Fuck Mickie for sayin' he knew how to build an effin' fire."

Though Bren was chattering away about last week's camping trip, A.J. knew him well enough to know he wasn't thinking about the woods. Or at least, that's what he hoped.

They hadn't talked about it—not really. Every time A.J. tried to bring it up, Bren would brush it off like they'd only be apart for a couple weeks, then change the subject.

"It's Terminal 1, right, love?"

It took A.J. a second to realize Mrs. O'Shea was talking to him.

"That's right. Thanks again for taking me, Mrs. O'Shea."

He knew she was rolling her eyes from the front seat, but was glad she'd stopped trying to get him to call her Maura. Relieved as he was she'd offered to drive him instead of the McCarthys, he couldn't help but wonder if she knew she was taking him in a hearse instead of her dented old Toyota.

The car eased to a stop in front of the Air Canada logo. He'd never been less happy to see a maple leaf in his life.

Mrs. O'Shea pulled the brake and stepped out of the car. Bren followed after her, grabbing A.J.'s overstuffed backpack before he could say anything.

Another hour?

"Right then," she said, pulling A.J. into a hug the second he was upright—the O'Sheas didn't linger on the hard stuff. "You call us when you get home, you hear? Don't care what time it is."

"I will."

"You see him to his gate, then, I'll park the car."

Her words were clipped in a way that put A.J. in mind of Miss Murphy when tough subjects came up.

"Right, shouldn't be too long," Bren said, wheeling one of A.J.'s suitcases up the curb. "Let's go, Robolad."

Half an hour?

"Thank you for the ride and, everything," A.J. called as Mrs. O'Shea took a step towards the car. It was possibly the most inadequate repayment he'd ever given, but it was all he could think of.

She turned back with a smile and waved her hand as if to say it was nothing.

"Safe flight!"

A.J. pulled his suitcase beside Bren, who was people-watching with an absent smile.

"Ready to go?"

No.

"Yup, gate 6. I think it's over there."

"What's the first thing you wanna do when you get home?" Bren asked as they got in line in front of the red and white logo.

Say something to him.

"Probably take a bath and sleep, I'm about to be on a plane for like eight hours."

Not that.

"Ah yeah, gonna need a proper sleep after that."

Bren heaved the suitcases onto the scale as A.J. handed his ticket over for the clerk to check.

"Gonna be good to be back home, though."

I'm not going home . . .

"Yeah, gonna be good to see everyone."

A.J. bit the inside of his cheek.

"Over here, yeah?"

A.J. double-checked his ticket before following Bren towards a pair of escalators. This was it, then. He'd told Bren he didn't want him hanging around to watch the plane take off—strange how what was romantic in the movies was awkward as hell in real life.

"This is me, I guess," A.J. said, trying hard to match Bren's smile.

Just five more minutes?

"Yeah," Bren said, staring over A.J.'s shoulder.

Please?

"So . . . can I have my backpack?"

"What? Oh!"

Bren's laugh sounded less like his usual bark as he slid the backpack off his shoulder.

"Here you go."

Their fingers brushed in the hand-off, and Bren smiled. He took a step forward and pulled A.J. into a hug. Warmth spread through him at Bren's touch, but it didn't erase the gnawing void in his stomach. This wasn't the hug of someone who didn't want to let a person go. For all A.J. knew, Bren might have been saying goodbye to Brick.

Please don't let go.

"Gonna call once you get home, yeah?" Bren asked when he broke the hug.

"Yeah, of course," A.J. said, trying to ignore the fact that he sounded like he had a cold.

"Right then, see you 'round, Robolad."

A.J. bit the inside of his cheek again as his eyes took Bren in. This could very well be the last time he saw that smile, or that weird patch of freckles on the bridge of his nose.

"See you later, Navigator."

A.J. combusted. What a moment to say that for the first time.

Bren, being Bren, chuckled back like it was a perfectly normal thing and gave him a salute. What a weird series of firsts.

Five more seconds?

The strap of A.J.'s backpack dug into his shoulder as he walked towards the escalator. He stepped to the side so a man corralling a fussy toddler could pass him, then put his foot on the moving strips of metal.

Bye, Bren . . .

"Arlo!"

A.J. was still mid turn when he was knocked back by a ginger blur. Bren's arms wrapped around his chest so hard he felt like he was back in his hospital bed. He returned the pressure, grabbing hold of Bren like if he did it hard enough, he might be able to take him back to Canada.

"W-we're gonna see each other again. Got that?"

Bren's words came out muffled, and not just because his face was buried in the crook of A.J.'s neck. A.J. tried to say something back, but his voice broke before the first syllable. He compromised by nodding into Bren's shoulder.

It was Bren who broke the hug some eons later. He looked like he'd spent the last thousand years in a pool with too much chlorine, but didn't make any moves to hide it.

"Serious, like. I'll steal a boat and drive it to fuckin' Newfoundland meself if I have to."

A.J. gave a watery chuckle and wiped his eyes on his stolen bunnyhug.

"Maybe don't say that in an airport."

"Fuck it," Bren said, sniffing, "I'm already stealin' a boat, might as well punch some Guards while I'm at it."

A.J. pulled Bren into another hug.

"I love you, Bren."

Bren's hand found the back of A.J.'s neck.

"I love you, too, Arlo."

They relaxed their grip enough to press their lips together, and A.J. was out in the rain all over again—tea and toast, his heart beating in his chest so hard it felt like he might pass out. He'd never asked Bren what it had been like for him back then, but as Bren's heart beat against his chest, A.J. thought he knew.

***

"Merci d'avoir choisi Air Canada!"

A.J. let his eyes close as he leaned back into his seat. It had been almost a year since he'd experienced the ritual of instructions, once

323

in English, then again in French. It was surprising how soothing it was, like opening the mailbox and finding a letter from an old friend.

His thumb traced along the knot at the end of his bunnyhug's drawstrings. He wondered how long the thing would keep smelling like turf and Lynx Africa—like Bren.

It was crazy how much he already missed him.

The man next to him grumbled as he adjusted the sleep mask on his forehead, clearly eager to get his seat leaned back the half an inch allowed by whoever controlled such things.

"Flight attendants, please prepare for take-off."

A.J. pulled up the window shade, ignoring the huff from his companion. He'd never liked watching the plane take off. Something about the pavement zooming by as he was squashed back into his seat by the acceleration set his teeth on edge. He was determined to keep his eyes on Ireland for as long as possible, though.

The plane shuddered, and physics did its thing. It wasn't long before Dublin looked like one of the mats he puttered toy cars along back when he was in preschool.

A.J. let his fingertips trail along the smooth plastic of his window. If he scrunched up his eyes, he thought he could make out little dots milling around down there, even though that was impossible.

He leaned closer and tried to decide which one might be Bren.

***

The raspberries turned bitter in Bren's mouth mid-chew as he let the front door clatter shut behind him. His eyes had fallen on the kitchen table, and his mind flung him back to the first night Arlo had come round for dinner. He could taste the tart Arlo had baked. Funny how he only now realized he hadn't done it to impress Mam.

His hand was already reaching for the kettle when he saw Arlo again, bustling around the kitchen like he'd been raised on the ritual. He'd never gotten around to asking Arlo how he knew the way he took his tea.

"Fuck!"

He cracked open a Red Bull from the fridge and chugged half of it, wiping his mouth with the back of his hand.

He ignored the concerned look Mam was wearing and scooted around her on the way to his room. It was the worst room in the house to be in if he was trying to avoid the ghost of the lad he'd just lost. But if everything was going to hurt, then he might as well hurt lying down.

You didn't lose him.

Bren forced himself to remember that. They were going to be together again. He'd promised. But, the soonest he could see that happening was after he'd graduated, and who knew what might happen between now and then.

Bren was mid-corpse-fall when his eye caught the flash of silver. He twisted his body like a drunken cat and landed on his pillow by cracking his spine in half.

After checking to see if he could still move his legs or not, Bren sat up and pulled the Discman onto his lap. It was the one he'd given Arlo in October. The day he'd called him his boyfriend for the first time.

Bren reached back to his pillow and grabbed the letter that had been under the Discman.

Bren,

I don't think I'm going to be able to say some of this stuff to you in person, but I still really want to say it.

Well, first of all, hi! How'd the whole airport thing go? I hope I didn't cry too much. I don't think I will. Maybe . . . Anyway, I just wanted to say thank you. Thank you so much for talking to me that first day, even if past me was 100% sure you were being a dick. I can't believe the last ten months, they feel like something out of someone else's life, and that's all because you said hi to me.

I don't know what's going to happen once I leave, but I just wanted to say, so you don't ever doubt it: I love you, Brendan Finley O'Shea. I love you in a way I've never loved anyone before, and I just wanted to say thank you for that. And for loving me back.

I hope this doesn't feel like me giving back your gift. I'm going to miss it so much, but I wanted to leave my wires with you, so you've always got a little piece of Robolad. Carry me around in your pocket sometime, ok?

Did that sound as dumb to you as it did now that I wrote it out? Well, at least I might have made you laugh. Anyway, I love you, Bren, and I'll do everything I can to find my way back to you.

I know the way, because you showed it to me.

Love, Arlo Jonathan Walker

PS: I burned you a CD so you can remember how weird and gay your boyfriend is. Hope you like it, even if Mickie's going to give you shit(e) for it all summer.

Bren popped open the CD case with a shaky hand. He had to blink his eyes a half-dozen times before they were clear enough for him to make sense of the blue bubble letters.

BREN'S BIG BISEXUAL MEGAMIX 1

Below that was a recreation of the robot doodle Bren had handed him the first day. He was holding an Irish flag in one hand and a Canadian one in the other with a speech bubble that said "Beep boop, I love my Irish boyfriend."

Bren's whole body shook as he let out a raspy chuckle. He really had fallen for the weirdest lad in the entire fucking world.

Trying hard to keep his throat from closing up any more than it already was, Bren placed the CD into the Discman like it was a holy relic and popped the wires into his ears. He lay back on the bed and conjured up Arlo as clearly as he could in his mind.

And then he pressed play.

If you loved *And Then He Pressed Play: Track One* and want to keep up-todate with what I'm writing next, scan the code below!